C000263667

Forward . . .

Extract from "Some excavations at Site Y3", in "Transactions of The Maine Archaeological Society", No. 132, vol III 2002.

". . .the origins of a well-preserved sheep skeleton excavated from pit no.15 have still not been explained to the authors' satisfaction. Carbon-dating of a bone sample suggested a date in the range AD 1400–1500, and this corresponds to the dating of material found around it. However, since this is historically unlikely, and since there was some disturbance to the pit, it is probable that the carcass was buried at a much later date, and that contamination of the sample occurred. The wolf's teeth found nearby had been pierced, which indicates an ornamental or ritual use . . .

FAMILY TREES

GWYNETH'S FAMILY.

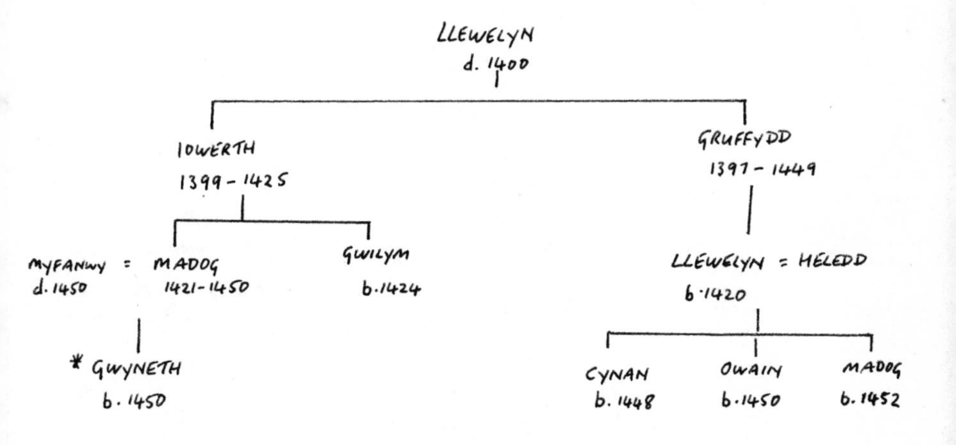

AGNES' FAMILY

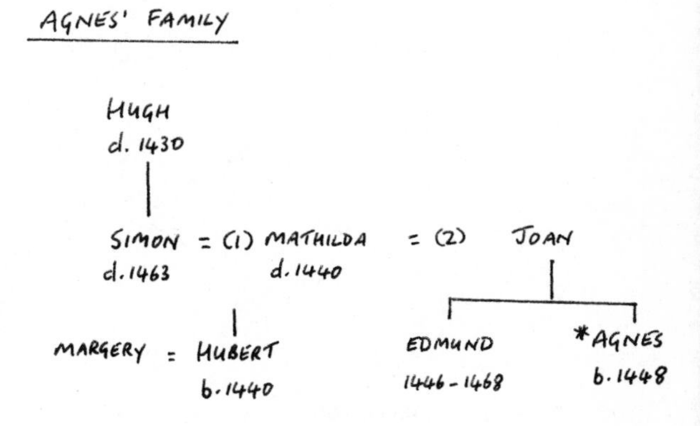

MAP OF ABERTRODDI AND SURROUNDING AREA

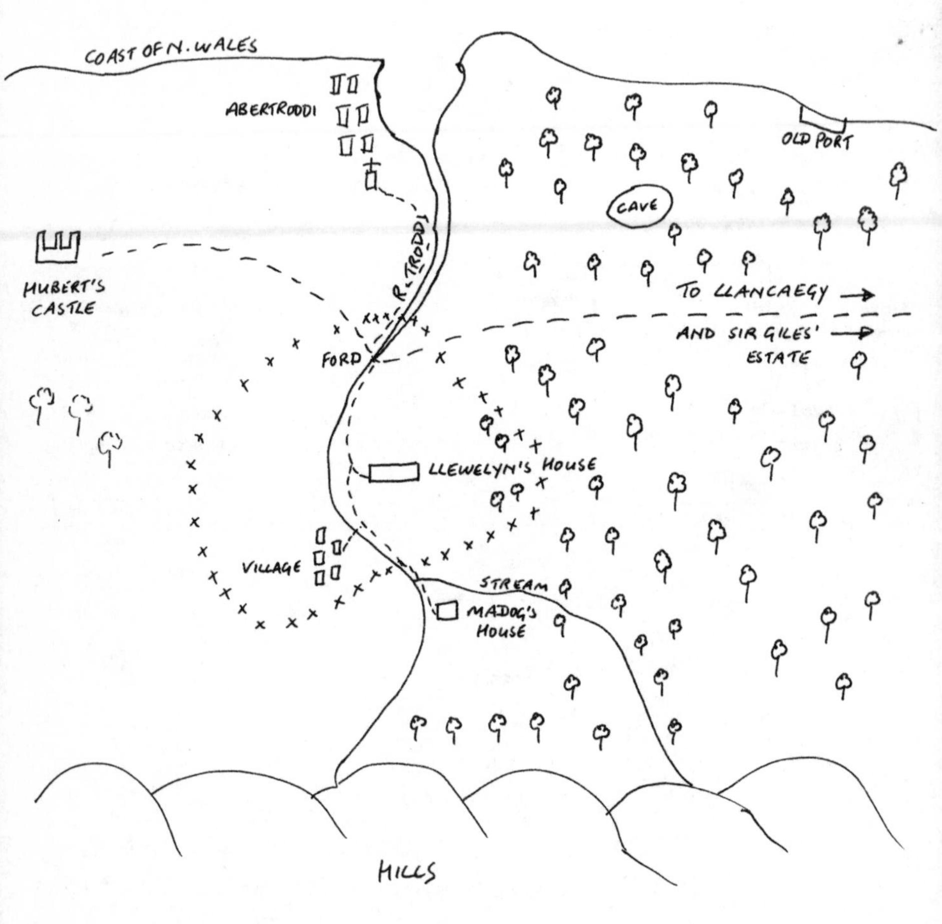

xxxx BOUNDARY OF LLEWELYN'S ESTATE

- - - TRACKS

WOODS

Chapter 1

John of Chester was not a nervous man. If he had been, he would have been singularly unsuited to his trade of leading strings of packhorses along the muddy brigand-infested bye-ways of northern England and Wales. Not for him those long pre-dawn hours spent huddling over a fire in the rain, jumping at any crackling in the trees and fingering his knife like an anxious girl. If he had to camp in the open, he burrowed inside his makeshift shelter and slept as soundly as if he were in his own bed, with his wife snoring next to him. Let his four surly men-at-arms keep watch; that was what they were paid for, and besides, no broken man who had any sense would ambush the most convenient means of getting ill-gotten goods smuggled to distant markets. So, his mind never preyed on the awful possibility of a silent arrow thumping between his shoulders as he walked along, nor on the likelihood of waking up to a cold blade at his throat. He thought of profits, and whether his lead horse was limping, and of the properly cooked food he would eat when he arrived home. Which was why he was annoyed at the unaccustomed feeling creeping up his spine as his train slid and snorted through the woods beyond Llewelyn ap Gruffydd's carefully maintained fields. There could be no danger in the October drizzle cloaking his view, or in the sighing fall of golden leaves along the track. Sir Hubert hunted outlaws as enthusiastically as he exterminated deer, and boasted in his hall that no-one had seen hide nor hair of a robber on his estates since he had come from England to knock his inheritance into shape. The locals sniggered behind their hands at his claim, yet surely no marauding band would venture so close to the centre of his outwardly cowed domain. John listened angrily. No footsteps or clinks of iron beyond those of his horses and men-at-arms and the boy, Stephen, stumbling a few yards behind him, no dark shapes flitting in and out of the innocent trees, no sudden thunder of attacking hooves. He wiped his brow. The sooner they pressed on to open ground and the next village the better. Someone might have talked unwisely about what lay beneath the innocuous loads of clean fleeces and home-grown bow staves. He turned his head without breaking stride. Stephen's face was grey and clenched with fatigue, and he gave his uncle a ghastly smile. Unwillingly, John remembered the agony of his first long trip, when he had cried every dawn with the cold, the stiffness in his legs, the filth on his clothes, and the prospect of trudging for another whole day without respite. He set his jaw. The boy had to learn, if he wanted to make anything of himself, he wouldn't gain from being coddled. Then he sighed. If some unseen enemy was about to hack them to bits, a kindness would make very little difference to Stephen's ultimate fate. He turned again. "Ride on Brock there for a while. He's got the lightest load and needs a kick up the arse. We want to make Llancaegy before dark." Too exhausted to care about showing weakness in front of the soldiers, the boy heaved himself up between the bales, pulled his cloak around him, and let his head nod with the rocking of his unwilling mount, oblivious to any strangeness in the forest.

Not so far away, it was only when Madog was lifting the fat deer on to his pony that he realised that he was being watched. He cursed under his breath, and carried on lashing hooves under the coarse belly. A good while until friendly nightfall, maybe he should leave the pony and run, hoping that the blame would fall on one of the guards from John's train he had heard grumbling along in the distance. He hadn't been careless: the pony wasn't from these parts, and he had kept his face at least partly covered with his hood. Probably only one of Sir Hubert's English huntsmen would be able to swear that it was him who had shot the deer, and they were trawling the woods way beyond the castle, making sure that their master had something to fire at when he next went hunting. Besides, although they could move almost as quietly as he did, some sound would have alerted him to their presence. He cleaned his knife in the leafy earth again, and stood, one hand on the pony's neck, concentrating on minute changes in the air, and sniffing like a dog. His scalp prickled. There was something different here. When he was small, his brothers used to try to scare him with tales of lions and tigers which had escaped from the king's menagerie in England and raced slavering to Wales, where they hunted for boys who should have been attending to their education, not sneaking off to the woods to track deer. "Another sheep has gone," Cynan would whisper in the dark, "I saw a paw-print in the mud. As big as my face."

Owain would join in. "Dafydd was cutting hazel in the far coppice. He heard a roaring in those rocks, and ran all the way back here. He fainted, and he'd wet himself."

Madog had half believed them. "Dafydd eats those mushrooms. He told me he'd seen a unicorn." His voice was reedy, and he fell to kicking them to stop them clawing at him under the covers and pretending to savage his limbs.

Now that the woods were as familiar to him as his clothes, and he was certain they weren't home to lions and tigers, the old tiny shiver of fear fluttered in his chest before his habit quelled it. He thought he could smell salt, and he sensed eyes, curious, calculating and fearless, measuring his size and the strength in his arms. He blinked once, slowly and deliberately. There it was, an unnatural shape up the trunk of an oak tree on the edge of the clearing. It would be easy now to draw his bow, and watch the strange being tumble to the ground where he could examine it. Easy and a waste. If he had a rival in the woods, he wanted to know more. He whispered in the pony's ear, and set off on a convoluted route to his father's house, a route which could be followed, but not comfortably or silently.

The gloomy day drifted towards dusk, the rain fell harder on the slated roof of Llewlyn's fine stone house, and his windows began to glow dimly. Gwyneth paused on her way back from the hen house. It had been a somewhat spurious errand anyway, to check that someone had mended the hole through which a very small fox could possibly squeeze, but she had needed an excuse to escape, if only for a short time, from the complaining men in the hall, and the bad tempered bustle in the kitchens. Of course, everyone praised God that her voyaging uncle, Gwilym, had returned safe to his cousin's house, and had found the house still standing, his cousin Llewelyn still alive, Llewelyn's sons thriving and his widowed ward still managing the household with quiet efficiency, yet after a decent interval for joy, Llewelyn had two years' worth of slights and oppression to pour out to someone who seemed to have escaped the English fist, and who, moreover, had the appetite of a horse. Gwyneth grimaced. Madog thought he was helping, slipping in with fresh venison and announcing that he would stay to eat it with them. He didn't seem to care that they would have to finish the whole animal in one sitting, and pray that none of Sir Hubert's officials decided to pay them a visit while they were at the table. Llewelyn could bleat about the law in his hall, but Sir Hubert was adamant that the woods, apart from the protected coppices, formed no part of Llewelyn's estate, since they existed exclusively for his hunting, and his summary justice was stronger than any crabbed words stored on scraps of vellum, or custom carried in the long memories of his inferiors. Gwyneth looked back at the yard and outbuildings. At least the harvest had been good, there should be no hungry children in the spring . . . a flicker of movement by one of the barns and a dog's yelp set her heart jumping. No, it was nothing, maybe one of the cats, or a pigeon, or one of the rats the cats were meant to catch. She kicked mud off her shoes, and went into the warm, and the never-ending voices.

"One way or another, we will be ruined." Llewelyn was staring impatiently at the chess board, and he moved a piece too quickly. "That English fool is getting ambitious. He'll join in, find himself on the wrong side, and end up with his head on Tower Bridge. Then they'll come after us, and all this will go." He waved at the blazing fire, his painted walls and solid furniture. "Our grandfather was lucky never to see these times." Gwilym, who had faced watery terrors Llewelyn could never dream of, smiled under his whiskers. "There are more places than Wales. I could carry you to a life of ease in the Middle Sea." He knew Llewelyn would rather cut his throat with a billhook than take to the ocean. "Anyway," he enjoyed needling his cousin, "I thought Hubert was King Henry's man, like you. Check."

The pieces jumped. "I'm no English king's man. Henry's mad, and Edward's a usurping whoremonger. God's teeth, they have ruined England and will ruin Wales, damn them both. You're a cheat, that wasn't legal move."

Gwilym smiled more openly. "And you're a traitor. Ha, I'll call on Sir Hubert tomorrow, and let him know what a viper he nurses in his unsuspecting bosom."

Llewelyn laughed back at him, "He'll have no time for a battered shipman. Tattle away to his servants, it's all you're fit for. Gwyneth, put a laxative into your uncle's drink, make his bowels as loose as his tongue." His shoulders shook under his gown, and his eyes lost their disappointed cast.

Gwyneth felt kinder towards him. "I already have. I hope you didn't drink from his cup, or you'll be as empty as Lady Margery's head before dawn."

She left them cackling like a couple of old maids by the fire, and went to the kitchens to see what they were doing with the deer.

It was hard at times not to forgive Llewelyn his incessant bitterness. In his mind, he should have been a great prince presiding over the ruins of Hubert's castle and all the countryside around, not the precarious owner of a small estate, subject to the incontinent whims of English magnates as they filtered down to those beneath them. Seventy years before, his illustrious grandfather and namesake had been killed following Glendyr, leaving a widow and two infant sons nothing but the name of a rebellious traitor. His widow, Anchoret, swallowing all kinds of pride, had given her boys, Gruffydd and Iowerth, up into service with the victorious Sir Hugh, a scion of the Beauforts, in his hastily patched up castle, and then watched with well-concealed glee as Gruffydd rebuilt part of the family fortune. Under a bland and dutiful face, he strove and schemed until the equally pragmatic Sir Hugh granted him an estate and the hand of a dispossessed heiress, whose father he had executed as an example. Pretending not to hear rumours of the illicit pale mountain gold which paid for carpenters and masons, Anchoret had lived to see the new stone house built and her grandson born, and had expired contentedly in her sleep before the news could reach her that her other, more martial son, Iowerth, had died in France. At his father's knee, Llewelyn had learned the dissimulation necessary to survive more comfortably than the barefooted descendants of princes banished to hovels in the harsh uplands, or labouring in English owned fields. He bowed his head meekly to the laws which counted his word as less than that of a serf from over the border, wrapped his tongue in public around the alien language, and hated the English with a passion so devious that Hubert, Hugh's red-faced and less wily grandson, thought that he was decent enough for a Welshman. He spent most of his time brooding over whether he had impressed enough on his sons the tricky need for keeping their ancestry alive in their hearts, their deeds outwardly blameless, and their minds on the main chance. He suspected that Cynan, the eldest, was more interested in sheep. He was unconvinced that Owain, the clever middle one, at present apprenticed to Hubert's lawyer, was to be fully trusted with his plan of ruining Hubert from within, and he feared that Madog, who called himself a horse breeder and who was scared of no-one, was born to be hung. Gwyneth, who knew she owed all her civilised comforts to Llewelyn's fierce family loyalty, was generally inclined to accept these obsessions as the price she had to pay for not being exiled to serve some cold English noblewoman, and she repaid his generosity by making sure his broodings were not needlessly interrupted by trivial household concerns, and by encouraging his sons not to argue with him. As she supervised the roasting of the great venison haunches, she decided to forestall any temper flares that night by demanding that all the men, Madog and Gwilym included, should bathe and have their hair barbered before the Mass they had ordered in two days time to give thanks for Gwilym's return. They would unite against her, and the evening would pass in happy diatribes against meddling women.

The same rain which bounced off Llewelyn's roof dribbled through a badly fitting casement in an upstairs chamber of the castle, and spattered down the uncowled chimney into a sulky fire. Lady Agnes, properly speaking the Countess of Peruzza, stabbed her needle into the tapestry and feared she was about to scream. She and her mother should never have left Venice, she should have followed her mother into that nunnery in the south of England, or, better still, they should have retired together to a Venetian convent. A lifetime of prayer and fasting would be preferable to another sodden day in this damp, draughty ruin stuck in the middle of a barbaric country with her half-brother's wife, Margery, who was quite the stupidest girl she had ever met. She wasn't sad that her husband, the aged Count of Peruzza, had died of fever, but at moments like this it was almost unbearable that the same outbreak had carried off Edmund, her beloved other brother. She imagined the expression on his face if he had been sitting here on one of these mildewed cushions being offered sour wine out of a streaky cup. He would rise elegantly to his feet, bow deeply, then hurl the cup to the floor and whip the servants until they stopped muttering in corners and started to produce seasoned logs, dry, clean linen, polished silverware, brushed floors and decent food. Hubert had an army of rent-collectors, bailiffs, controllers and lawyers, and it was beyond her how he could not translate this into a waterproof house, and why he was content with the mish-mash of buildings which had grown up haphazardly within the neglected curtain walls, not to mention Margery's sloppy housekeeping. He should put her in a convent, and knock the whole place down and start again, it wasn't as if the wreck was defensible, and it was hardly likely that the Welsh would rise up again . . .

"My, the child is so big already, and rides so high,"

Margery patted her stomach for about the fifth time that afternoon. "The seamstress assured me it was a boy, I'm so large."

"That was the great pie you ate earlier," Mona, Agnes' woman, murmured in Italian.

Margery turned querulous, and narrowed her eyes. "What's she saying?"

She disliked Mona, and trusted her even less than the native women, whom she would barely allow into her bedchamber unless her English maid was with them. Mona's father had been a captive Turk, and once, in a moment of spite, Agnes had whispered to Margery that she remained impervious to Christian teaching, and prayed to a strange God on a special carpet she kept hidden under her gown. Margery had believed her, and kept as close a watch on Mona as she could, in case she slipped out unguarded to drink the blood of Christian babies.

"She says the seamstress is right," Agnes said loudly. "She will be happy to help with your confinement, and looks forward to blessing the arrival of your lord's heir."

Margery blanched, and it was Mona's turn to pretend she wasn't laughing.

"Mona," Agnes pressed, "tell the Lady Margery what you told me earlier. The ship," she prompted. Mona took longer than necessary to bite off a thread.

"My lady," she said eventually, her English more accented than normal, "they say a great ship is tied up in Abertroddi harbour, full of jewels and spices from the Middle Sea."

Margery snorted. "That. It'll be Gwilym's. Sir Hubert says he's probably little better than a pirate. It'll more likely be full of rats and rude sailors."

This was witty for Margery, and Agnes smiled. "And is he a pirate?" Even talking about the insignificant Welsh was better than admiring Margery's pregnancy, which she treated as if it was the first since the Virgin Mary's.

"He's a . . . " Margery's lips framed the word 'bastard', then retracted. "He's illegitimate," she said, as though that explained everything. "I believe his father was killed in France in Sir Hugh's following."

She crossed herself at the name. Sir Hugh had died

before either she or Hubert were born, yet she had fallen in with Hubert's conviction that his grandfather had been the greatest man who had ever lived.

"Yes, my ladies," Mona coughed politely, "His father was called Iowerth, I believe, the brother of Gruffydd, whose son, Llewelyn, holds the Troddi valley. Iowerth had two sons, Gwilym the sailor, and Madog, who became a war captain like his father, and died in France as well. Madog's daughter keeps house for Llewelyn, whose son, Owain, is apprenticed to Master Hooper."

Agnes worked it out. "A busy family. How do you know all this?"

Mona sewed demurely on "I have a girl who is teaching me Welsh. Genealogy seems to be her favourite subject."

Margery threw up her hands. "Heaven forfend, there is no need for that. If they can't speak English like Christians, then there is no call to talk to them. Send the girl back to the kitchens, and use your time to serve your mistress."

"Yes my lady." Mona lied as easily as she learned languages. She was not going to let Agnes live in a strange household without knowing what went on among the servants.

Agnes decided to remind Margery of the duties of a benevolent lady. "Mona, was this Madog, Gwilym's brother, a war captain with my father?"

"Yes, my lady, I believe he was. A most valiant man."

Margery pursed her lips. She thought it was tactless to bring up Sir Simon, Agnes' and Hubert's father. He had lost the family estates in Normandy, although maybe it was not his fault alone that the English had been driven out by the French, and had then taken his second wife, along with Agnes and Edmund, to Venice to fritter away most of his fortune in trade, instead of coming back to England and building up a better inheritance for Hubert, his only child with his first wife. Thank God he had left the Welsh estates in the hands of his lawyers."

"And did he leave a widow and other children?" Agnes' face was pious.

"No, my lady. The girl said it was very sad. Madog's

wife, Mwfanwy, was with him in France, tending to your father's soldiers. When Madog was slain by a cruel French arrow meant for your father, Mwfanwy returned to Llewelyn's house, where she died giving birth to a girl, Gwyneth. Gwyneth married, but alas, her husband died young, and now she is protected by Llewelyn alone." "God rest their souls." Agnes was enjoying herself for the first time that day. She never had to explain anything to Mona. "I should visit this poor orphan widow, and see what she lacks. Thank God we are in a position to exercise charity, which is a blessed virtue." It never did any harm to remind Margery that in spite of the Venetian lawyers' bickering, she had left Venice with considerable funds.

Margery snorted more. "She lacks for nothing. Don't waste your generosity on her, you'll get no thanks. The Welsh are a most ungrateful people, and idle too. They would live in plenty if they worked harder and sang less, and had ears for instruction from their betters. Llewelyn is not the worst of them, and I admit Owain is a humble servant to Master Hooper, but they will never advance to our level until they abandon their vile language and immoral ways. Mona, these candles are down to nothing. Find the steward and fetch some more." Thoroughly vexed, she jabbed her needle into cloth, stood up and waddled off to the less than clean garderobe.

Chapter 2

Llewelyn's idle and ungrateful household slumped in the hall, stupefied by an excess of meat and beer and logs on the fire. The singing had died out, and most of the servants were gnawing bones in the kitchens. Gwilym was rambling his way through a fantastical story, and Gwyneth wished she had one of his magic carpets to transport her up the open stairs at the end of the hall, whisk her through the large chamber colonised by Llewelyn and Cynan, and tip her gently into her old box bed behind the partition. She wasn't sure how else she was going to get Nyrees, her aged serving woman who was already asleep on a bench, up to her mattress. Even Madog, normally alert and contained as a wildcat, had his eyes half-closed and his hands laced across his stomach, and showed no sign of leaving for his own small house further up the valley. The least obedient and probably secretly the most loved of Llewelyn's sons, from the time he could walk he had followed his own hidden paths. Two years younger than Gwyneth, she remembered how, as a tiny child, he could make himself disappear for hours, sending his mother, Heledd, and all the women into a frenzy until they discovered him sitting calmly behind a chair, or lying grinning under a rug they had picked up twenty times already. Llewelyn, mindful of the need to maintain standards, had packed Cynan off to learn manners in a large household in the Marches, and Owain off to the monks to begin the long training for a legal career, and had originally ear-marked Madog for the Church. A bishop in the family would be a huge advantage. The unlikelihood of this was clear by the time

Madog was ten and the best rider and shot in the valley. Llewelyn had then decided that it would be acceptable if he followed the relative after whom he had been named into a more regular military service. A hero's death for his son would be more bearable than having him deprived of his ears for poaching or executed as a common horse thief. He had seen the gleam in Madog's eyes when the English rode by on their carefully bred mounts. Madog, however, had his own ideas, and had run off one night to offer himself as a servant to the huntsmen on an estate twenty miles away along the coast. For six dreadful years, Llewelyn had not suffered his name to be mentioned in the house. The prodigal had missed Gwyneth's marriage and the death of her husband after less than a year, but had turned up a few months later, a lean thirteen year old with a masked expression, for his mother's funeral. Three years after that, Llewelyn learned that his son was coming back to the River Troddi. One fine summer evening, he rode upstream, past his tenants' huddle of houses on the opposite bank, and over the boundary of his estate to where a stream flowed from its own miniature wooded valley into the river. On the bright green meadow between the fork of water, men were putting up railings and building what looked like a stable block. He recognised one of them as his most skilled carpenter. His son finished hammering home a post, and touched his hat.

"Good day, father."

Llewelyn sat on his horse, marking the strong brown hand reaching up to his bridle. There were two mares swishing their tails against the midges in the pasture, and he could hear their tongues pulling at the long grass.

"What are you playing at?"

Madog's hand didn't withdraw. "I've rented the land from Sir Hubert. People will always need sound horses."

Llewelyn knew about the rental. Owain had given Master Hooper the slip, and showed him the agreement.

"Where did you get the money? And don't expect to have fodder from me."

Madog grinned, as he had done on the day he had hidden up the chimney when the fire was unlit.

"There's plenty of money in Wales if you know where to look."

Llewelyn stared at him for a long time. He was as tall as his brothers now, and twice as cunning.

"You . . . ?"

Madog put his finger to his lips. "Some things should never be talked of out loud."

Llewelyn dismounted shakily. "Those mares are in foal."

Madog took his arm. "Yes, to Hubert's prize stallion. Not that he knows. Valuable horses aren't aware that they're meant to be paid for their services, so they shouldn't be left unattended in paddocks at night."

Llewelyn's laughter set the mares pricking their ears and stamping their feet.

"We'll see what fodder we have to spare this winter," he said. "Where are you sleeping?"

Madog pointed to a rough shelter. "I'll build a house when the stables are done."

"Why didn't you visit your mother when she was ill?" Llewelyn wanted one final answer.

For the first time, Madog's eyes dropped. "I did." He leaned away, as if Llewelyn would react in the same way as when he had jumped, covered in soot, into the fireplace.

"Jesus Lord. I suppose you've been seeing your brothers as well."

Madog nodded.

"You're none of you too big that I can't take this whip to you for disobedient wretches." Llewelyn remounted his horse, "Well, come through the front door next time. You'll know Gwyneth is back, she won't let you in unless you clean your boots." He cantered off down the track, whistling one of his father's favourite tunes.

From then, it was as if the breach between them had never existed, and only the more romantically inclined kitchen girls missed the excitement of Madog's unheralded comings and goings.

"So the Jinni went through the desert to the princess's palace," Gwilym's voice rose above Cynan's snores, "and found the ungrateful camel-driver . . ."

Llewelyn's head jerked up from his chest. "I thought

he was a shoe-maker."

"What's a camel?" A boy had come through from the kitchens with more beer.

"God, the shoe-maker is already dead, and a camel is a great beast which can go for a year without drinking, gallop faster than the swiftest horse, and spit into a man's eye from a bowshot away. So the Jinni . . ."

"Are there camels in England?"

Madog opened one eye properly. "No, Rhys, only in Scotland, up in the mountains with the wild men."

"Bollocks," someone said in the shadows beyond the firelight, "the King of France has a thousand, to pull his great guns."

"Those are elephaunts."

Gwilym flexed a throat which had screamed into countless gales. "Be quiet, have you forgotten how to listen to a story? Are you going to babble all night like English ladies? Right, so the Jinni . . ."

The door opened, tallow dips flickered, and the nightwatchman's head appeared, one cheek bulging.

"My lord, a horse is coming up the track."

"Christ." Llewelyn pulled himself upright, then sank back again. "Just the one?"

"Yes." The nightwatchman started chewing discreetly.

"It must be bad news, only bad news travels at night," Nyrees moaned from her bench. Gwilym's shouting must have woken her up.

"Go to bed, old besom," Llewelyn snapped. "Rhys, into the kitchen with that dish. Cynan!" He kicked Cynan's chair.

"Heugh?" Cynan rubbed his eyes, "Is that bloody ram loose again?"

There was a moment's hush, broken only by Nyrees wheezing as she swayed up the stairs. They all knew she was right. It could be news of more fighting in England, dispossession, the death of a friend . . .

"Gwyneth . . ." Before Llewelyn could tell her to follow the old woman, dogs barked, hooves thudded in the yard, and indistinct voices rose and fell outside. The door opened again.

"My lord? A sailor for Lord Gwilym."

Llewelyn closed his eyes for a moment, and the bandy-legged figure rolled up to the table. He bowed clumsily.

"My Lord Gwilym," his voice was hoarse.

"Christ, Master Thomas, what are you doing, disturbing us at this hour of the night? You could have got yourself shot as a cattle thief."

"My Lord Gwilym," the man repeated. He looked as if he would have preferred to be on the deck of a sinking ship. "I regret . . . forgive me . . . I'm sorry . . . they've disappeared."

"What?" Gwilym's hand was on his knife.

"The two . . ." Master Thomas glanced desperately around, ". . .cargo."

Colour rose slowly in Gwilym's face. Everyone else sat up straighter. This was more entertaining than the Jinni. Gwilym's mouth started to open.

"My lord," the sailor put up his hands, "we were unloading the gun, like you ordered, and we had to find a cart to take it to the smith, and we had to pull it ourselves on account of no-one would hire us a beast, and it was dark when we returned to the ship, and when we went in with their supper, they'd . . . gone."

"Gone," Gwilym almost whispered. His knife was drawn. Words tumbled half-finished out of his mouth. "Useless drunken devils . . . cannot mind one thing . . . turn you all way . . . kill you first."

He lunged across the table, and the sailor stepped backwards.

Llewelyn grabbed his gown. "Cousin, don't stab this creature in my hall. What have you lost?"

Gwilym drove his knife through the fine cloth into wood, seized the beer jug and flung it at the sailor's head, then fell back into his chair again, his face in his hands.

"Stop that man leaving," Llewelyn's bark halted Master Thomas's reverse sidle to the door. "What did you let disappear?"

Thomas wiped beer from his tangle of hair. "My lord, I daren't say. We are sworn to secrecy."

Llewelyn looked cunning, "Well, let me guess. It can't be gold, gold doesn't need feeding, neither do silks or spices. It must be animals. My dear cousin, have you brought me back a pair of camels? Or elephaunts? Or perhaps lions, those sweetest of beasts?"

Gwilym looked out through his fingers, "I was going to tell you."

"And when would that be?" Llewelyn's tone was dangerously conversational. "When half of my sheep have been devoured, and babies snatched from their poor mothers' arms? Would you like me to ride to Sir Hubert now, and tell him that my cousin has loosed terror upon his lands? That will give him something to hunt, maybe he'll thank you, and not have us hung from the castle walls, my women delivered to his soldiery, my sons reduced to beggary . . ."

"Jesus Christ, man," Gwilym thumped the table, "they're not animals, they're . . . men."

Llewelyn changed direction without disturbing his flow. "Men? Men who need concealing? Are they spies for the King of France, or Irish rebels, or," his mind sought out devilish possibilities, "beastly Turks stained with the blood of Christian martyrs?"

"Well, you'll never know if we don't find the bastards." Gwilym was recovering. "Are you going to make speeches all night, or help me find them? They can't have gone far. If we sweep down to Abertroddi now, and spread out at daybreak . . ."

Madog stirred. He was grinning, and for a moment Gwyneth was afraid the older men would notice, and knock him down between them.

"Two strangers followed me here from the woods," he said lightly. "You could try the hay barn before we set out in the rain for Abertroddi."

Llewelyn's chair scraped the floor, and the rage only Madog could provoke shimmered through his frame. "Son of God, you led murdering Turks to my house, I've forgiven you too often . . ."

It was Gwilym's turn to prevent violence. "Llewelyn, I swear, they aren't Turks or spies or traitors. They are only . . . different."

"Lepers?" Llewelyn recoiled from his touch.

Gwilym doubled up, and tears ran into his beard.

"Cousin," he held on to the table for support, "I would ransom you for a million gold coins. Master Thomas, let's show our generous host his uninvited guests. Fetch some torches."

A rush of servants, drawn from the kitchens by the noise, scrambled to fetch the pitch-covered staves from the store behind the stairs, and plunge them into the fire, and Master Thomas smiled with relief.

"Stay here, Gwyneth," Llewelyn barked.

She ignored him, and followed the hasty crowd of men pushing out of the door and into the rainy night. The wind tore flames from the torches, and mud sucked at her shoes. The press slowed down at the barn. Gwilym handed his torch to the sailor.

"Stay behind me, Thomas. Stand back, friends, please. We don't want to startle them."

"Or set the barn on fire," Cynan growled under his breath.

An odd quiet descended. Gwilym opened the great door, and Gwyneth heard Madog's suddenly ragged breathing, and the pounding of her heart. Gwilym spoke into the darkness, and it was a language she had never heard before. A faint response came back, and Gwilym disappeared. Framed in the jumping light from his torch, the sailor's back was unmoving, yet Gwyneth found the old prayers Heledd had taught her running round her head, and her hand strayed to the tiny rowan cross at her neck.

"Come," Gwilym's voice speaking slowly in Welsh came from the door, "come, it's safe. Safe."

Llewelyn gasped, and Gwilym was there in the torch-light, standing between two tall cloaked figures. Master Thomas nodded his head as if in greeting, and the two shrouded heads nodded back. Gwyneth realised that Madog was bowing and gesturing for the ring of gaping mouths to part, so that Gwilym and his companions could pass through. In strange, solemn procession, led by the sailor's torch, Llewelyn and his household walked seven paces behind Gwilym and his secret cargo as far as the house, where Llewelyn went quickly ahead and turned, so that he could face his visitors.

"Welcome," he said, matching Gwilym's slow tones, "welcome to my house."

He ushered the trio in, and gestured to a bench. Gwyneth, pretending she had been inside all the time, nudged a gawping Rhys into stoking the fire, and relighting dips, and missed the moment when, at a sign from Gwilym, the two men pushed back their hoods. Rhys gave a high-pitched shriek and fled, Cynan's hand flew to his knife, and Gwyneth stuffed fingers to her mouth to stop her scream. Gwilym had lied, these men were surely Turks or demons from the pit. Their hair was black, blacker than night and as long as a girl's, their cheekbones were high, and their eyes the wrong shape. Worst of all, they didn't have skin on their faces, but some patterned substance, unlike anything known to humans.

Gwilym didn't appear to realise this. "Here we are at last. I can introduce you all now. You won't be able to pronounce their names, but translated into Welsh, may I present Climbs Trees," he patted the thing on his right, "and Sleeps At Noon. What's the matter, they're not ghosts."

"Their faces." Llewelyn sounded as if he was being strangled.

"Eh? Oh, that's what they do in Vinland. We're all quite used to it now." He pointed to his cousin, and his cousin's sons, "Llewelyn, Cynan, Madog." He remembered his niece, "And the Lady Gwyneth."

The men stared at each of them in turn. When their eyes reached Madog, the one on Gwilym's right raised his hand.

"Good morning. We saw you." Everyone apart from Gwilym jumped at the soft mangled Welsh.

Madog raised his hand in reply, "And I saw you."

The man imitated drawing a bow, and exchanged sounds with his companion. He spoke again.

"Good shot, God rot you. Ma-dog." He tried the name out.

"Climbs Trees," Madog smiled.

Gwilym coughed delicately, "They know some Welsh, but they mostly learned it from the sailors. Please don't be offended." He looked at Gwyneth, "Maybe you should go upstairs."

Gwyneth had no intention of leaving now she could tell they were men. "And I've never heard bad language in my life. Are they hungry?" Except for Gwilym and Madog, everyone was frozen, as though King Arthur had woken from his long sleep and decided to pay them a visit.

Sleeps At Noon seemed to recognise a word. "Hungry," he said, "hungry, yes by God."

This at least was something Gwyneth could organise. "Glynis," she saw one of the girls goggling from behind the safety of a table, "fetch what's left of the venison. Cut it properly. And some bread. Dafydd, take their cloaks and hang them up, then bring some beer. Come on, they're our guests."

Glynis squeaked, and ran to the kitchens, and Dafydd stayed rooted to the spot.

"Oh my lady, I daren't go near those oddities."

"Pah." Gwyneth went to the bench, and mimed taking off a cloak. "Aren't you hot?" she asked. Two pairs of eyes like coals bored into her.

"Bugger me." Climbs Trees stood up, and let his cloak drop to the floor. His friend followed suit.

Gwyneth tutted. "Not like that." The eyes trailed her as she picked up the heavy sailors' cloaks, and hung them on the pegs near the door.

Madog looked perfectly at ease. He fetched his bow from the corner, sat on the bench next to Climbs Trees, and launched into a proper conversation.

"Here's my bow. Do you have them like this in Vinland? I'd say you were hunters as well, from the way you move in the woods. I could have shot you, though, thank God I didn't."

It was doubtful whether they understood one word in ten, but by the time Glynis came back, the three of them were deep in a technical discussion which involved a lot of hand waving and mimicry. Llewelyn had collapsed into his chair, and Gwilym had left the bench to return to his place beside him.

"See," he was trying to explain everything at once,

"sailors know the Northmen went to Vinland way beyond the sunset in the time of our great great great grandfathers, but the course has been forgotten, and no-one has found a reason to look for it again. When I was blown to Ireland last year, coming back from the Middle Sea, I thought, why not, and carried on. It was the hardest voyage I've ever made, I could tell you stories for a fortnight, but when we landed, more dead than alive, what a country. Forests teeming with game, rivers jumping with fish, and these amiable people, though they fight their enemies without mercy . . ."

"But why did you bring them back?" Llewelyn still sounded as if a chord was round his neck.

Gwilym scratched his whiskers, "I had to. Their priests ordered them to come with us, and they'd been so hospitable, almost like Welshmen, we couldn't say no. They are the sons of their prince, you know, perfectly gentlemenly when you get to know them, and not at all violent to their friends, you needn't worry about the women's safety, and I'm sailing back with them after the winter . . ."

"That's all very well," Llewelyn watched the gentlemen neatly eating venison, and making appreciative noises to Madog, "but what are we going to do with them until then?"

Chapter 3

Agnes' announcement the following morning that she intended to ride out that very day to call on a deserving orphan widow caused more upset than she would have believed possible.

"You'd think I was planning a journey back to Venice, not a ride of under three miles," she observed to Mona, and her obstinacy mounted with the growing objections. What had begun as a passing whim to annoy Margery became a passionate desire to escape the confines of the castle, and an undertaking from which she would not be swayed.

"It's not appropriate for you to visit these people," Hubert insisted. He was conducting business with Master Hooper in the hall, and wanted to get back to discovering how he could squeeze more income from his mills. He didn't notice Owain, Master Hooper's apprentice, stiffen as he stood discreetly at a distance, holding rolls of documents.

Agnes raised her finely plucked eyebrows, "This isn't a visit of social equals." "You fool," she wanted to add. "I thought it would be to your advantage if I knew more about your neighbours. A lady can gauge the temper of a household, however mean, sometimes more easily than a man."

Hubert wasn't so slow that he didn't catch her drift, yet the novelty of being opposed meant that he could not surrender quietly. "Then there is the question of your escort. I can't spare great numbers of men to traipse around the countryside with you."

Agnes raised her eyebrows still further. Considering that most of the men in the castle hardly lifted a finger from one day to the next, this was foolish quibbling.

"A squire and a groom will do very will for Mona and me," she said firmly. "It's not as if I can be in any danger on your land."

Hubert had to retreat. "Fitzjohn will go with you, then. Now, Hooper, would a new mill solve my problem?"

Fitzjohn, a grubby and boorish youth, who spent most of his time playing dice, was summoned to the hall and ordered to see to the saddling of two suitable horses for Lady Agnes and her woman. He slouched back within ten minutes.

"M'lady," he was barely polite, "the grooms cannot find saddles for you."

Agnes had been in the company of great ladies in Venice and London, and was not going to be spoken to like a poor relation.

"I wonder at you," she said softly. "If you are here for us to teach you manners, it seems we have been wasting our time. Perhaps you would be better served if we set you to learning a trade. I hear the brewing woman needs a boy to train up." This was a cruel jibe. Fitzjohn's father may have been the bastard son of a duke, but his mother was the daughter of a brewer in Chester.

The boy reddened, and Agnes carried on, "Find the head groom, and tell him to have two horses saddled and waiting before the hour is up. Lady Margery must have at least one spare saddle, she will not mind if I borrow it." She and Mona had travelled to Wales by waggon, a tedious ordeal, and she suspected her saddles had been pilfered from the baggage. She certainly hadn't seen them since her arrival.

Fitzjohn bowed more carefully, "Forgive me, I believe they cannot find any of the Lady Margery's saddles."

Agnes shrugged, "Then what are you standing here for? Go and look. It's a sad state of affairs when a squire allows his lord's property to go missing. I marvel at my brother taking you on." She had moved to the other end of the hall from Hubert, and doubted whether he could hear her insults.

Owain's hearing, however, was particularly acute, and honed by years of trying to listen to conversations which were not meant for him. He stepped lightly to Master Hooper's shoulder, and bowed self-deprecatingly.

"Excuse me, sir, I'm sorry for interrupting." He was interrupting nothing but Hooper flapping through documents in his search for a bill. "My father had a mill built five years ago. I could send for his accounts, so we could show Sir Hubert," he bowed again, "how much a new mill would cost, and what a likely return would be."

"What?" Hooper disliked his apprentice making suggestions, it left him feeling uneasy.

Hubert, who had little stamina for business and wanted to go and admire his hawks, saw a way to bring this circling session to a close.

"Do that," he commanded, without looking at Owain, "and we can discuss this tomorrow, Master Hooper. Go through these accounts again, I have other pressing affairs."

He rose, and Owain wrote a brief note, gathered up his sober gown, and slipped unobtrusively to the stables. He had a pretty good idea where Lady Margery's saddles could be found, and he was sure that Luddy, the sharpest-eyed and smallest stable boy, knew as well.

Fortunately, Luddy was trundling a barrow towards the dung heap, and he was able to collar the boy before he could be drawn into the search.

"Luddy, my man," he said quietly in Welsh, "I need you to ride to my father's house. Give this message to him, or to Lady Gwyneth, or to anyone you can find who can read. Take my pony, and go quickly by the back way. You needn't come back so fast." He pressed the note and a coin into the boy's hand, "I'll excuse you to the groom."

He watched in satisfaction as Luddy leapt to his task, and didn't hurry to the front of the stables, where Fitzjohn was shouting at the head groom. He could hear two other stable boys laughing to themselves in the harness store.

"I've borrowed Luddy for an errand. Business," he called to the groom, and strolled back to the hall to help Master Hooper put the accounts back in order, keeping the excruciating boredom of the task from showing on his face. He must escape to London soon, to train properly at the Inns of Court. He was twenty, two years older than his younger brother Madog who was already established, and the same age as Gwyneth who was already a respectable widow. He was merely a glorified clerk for a lawyer who would probably ruin Sir Hubert without any malign help from him. If only his father could be made to understand the woolliness of Hooper's mind, he would never keep his son languishing in this ignorant household. Owain didn't over-estimate his own cleverness, yet it hadn't taken him very long to realise that he could torment Hooper by asking him seemingly innocent questions which exposed the older man's muddled thinking and inadequate grasp of the law. Some days, this was his sole amusement, apart from dreaming about how he would be taken up in London by a beautiful noblewoman with an impotent husband . . .

"Are you looking to be whipped?" With Hubert out of the way, Agnes was free to shout at Fitzjohn. "God in his heaven, I cannot believe this. A knight's castle, and not a single lady's saddle?" She gave vent to her feelings in Italian, which luckily no-one apart from Mona could understand. A lady did not normally employ such expressions.

Judging that sufficient time for Luddy had passed, Owain murmured an excuse to Hooper, and bowed his way towards her.

"My lady, sir," he knew how to strike the balance between normal politeness and obsequiousness, "pardon me, I do not mean to interfere . . . this is none of my business . . . couldn't help hearing . . . has anyone looked in the smithy?"

"The smithy?" Owain bowed again. She wasn't that beautiful, being a little short and hellish frosty, yet her anger had given a human flush to her face. A woman who could be angry could also be passionate . . . he was smooth as cream in his role.

"I have a recollection of seeing the Lady Margery's saddles there. Perhaps the smith has been asked to make some adjustments to the decoration . . ." When he had gone to have his knife repaired a few days ago, the smith had made his feelings plain.

"She won't be riding for months in her state, so I'm

not going to break my back with her fancy ideas. Ridiculous fashions." He had spat into the glowing charcoal, and applied his hammer with unusual force.

Fitzjohn scuttled off, and Agnes glared at Owain. "Why didn't you say anything before?"

Owain kept his head down. "My lady, I wasn't aware of the . . . problem."

Agnes studied him. He appeared perfectly docile, his hands were clean, his dark hair was neat, and his English, although marked by that annoying sing-song quality, was clear. Whether it was the lurking spark in his eyes, or the hint of amusement around his mouth under that strong beaked nose, she didn't trust him.

"I am to call on your father's household," she said abruptly. "Can I convey any message to him?"

"My lady is too kind. He will be honoured. If you could assure him of my good health and my wishes for his . . ."

Agnes was suddenly impatient with his elaborations. If she didn't set off soon, it would be sure to start raining.

"Yes, yes," she dismissed him with a wave. "Mona, fetch the cloaks and help me with my boots."

The horses finally arrived at the door, and the little train set off, with Fitzjohn struggling to control his mount which the head groom had hastily fed with a great quantity of oats.

It had been a difficult enough day for Gwyneth even before Luddy, pretending that he was delivering a secret message for Glendyr, galloped into the yard. Madog, seemingly happy to take responsibility for the Vinlanders, had shown them the outside privy and slept with them in the hall, and in the morning had led them on a protracted tour of the house. Nyrees, having glimpsed them from the top of the stairs, had squawked back into Gwyneth's chamber, and no-one else had done any work. Instead they stood, hands idle and eyes round, watching the two visitors as they minutely examined everything from the masonry to the pots in the kitchens. Llewelyn and Gwilym had contented themselves with shouting repeatedly that they must be concealed from the English, and Cynan had disappeared to his shepherds and farm-hands, most of whom were finding their own excuses to come to the house and join in the viewing. Gwyneth scowled down the hall at Madog. He was now showing Climbs Trees the workmanship on his knife, and Sleeps At Noon was fingering the stuff of Glynis's gown. Glynis didn't look nearly frightened enough. Gwyneth saw only trouble ahead.

"Madog," she was as polite as she could be under the circumstances, "why don't you take our guests outside? It's a fine morning, and they might like to see the yard in daylight. Glynis," her tone changed, "have you brought the butter from the dairy yet? And those cheeses won't turn by themselves."

Glynis moved reluctantly off, and Gwyneth went back up the stairs to carry on convincing Nyrees that she wasn't going to be raped and murdered.

"Look," she tried to drag the old woman to the small window glazed with real glass, "they are like innocent children."

Nyrees ventured a sideways glimpse through the tiny panes. Madog had brought his pony from the stable, and, his hand round Climbs Trees' wrist, was encouraging the Vinlander to stroke its nose. The smile which broke out on Climbs Trees' face, and his gesture to Sleeps At Noon to join him, was strangely reassurring, and Gwyneth found herself smiling as well.

"Gwilym says they have neither horses nor livestock in Vinland," she observed. "Our ways must be very peculiar to them."

"Why are they called such heathen names?" Nyrees sniffed. The English were foreign enough to her, and in a lifetime of service to Gruffydd's wife, then to Heledd and then to Gwyneth, she had never picked up a word of their harsh language.

"Gwilym says that their people sometimes name their children after what they do when they start walking, although they can change their names later if they become famous soldiers or skillful hunters." Once Llewelyn's agitation had subsided, Gwilym had been eager to demonstrate his wide knowledge of Vinland, its inhabitants and all their customs.

"Gwilym says," Nyrees sniffed again. "We should call him Doesn't Stop Talking then. Hey Steals Horses," she tapped the glass, "keep that beast from crapping on the doorstep." Her wrinkles wobbled in huge amusement, "Better get on. Keep those flighty girls busy." She waddled off, and Gwyneth tried to concentrate on the domestic round.

She was disturbed after only a brief time by howls of laughter from the yard. Unable to keep inside, she poked her head out of the door to see the Vinlanders holding on to each other and pointing, their decorated faces splitting with mirth. She followed their outstretched fingers. It was only Cynan and a shepherd, herding a group of sheep from one pen to another, helped by a scraggy dog. Madog was rubbing his forehead and looking puzzled. Climbs Trees turned to him.

"Baa," he said, and laughed even more.

"Baa, baa," Sleeps At Noon collapsed to the ground.

"Jesus," Madog saw Gwynweth, "this is going to be an interesting winter. Oh, please, Climbs Trees, no, don't . . ."

Climbs Trees was running down the yard, and throwing himself into the woolly mass, trying to seize one of these things for himself. Cynan shouted, the dog growled, the sheep scattered, and Luddy pounded up to the door and slid off the pony's heaving flanks.

"M'lady," he gasped, and thrust the note at Gwyneth, "urgent, from Master Owain."

Gwyneth scanned the familiar writing, and saw the day spiralling out of control. She yelled like one of the fishermen's women in Abertroddi.

"Madog, get those . . . madmen out of here. Lady Agnes is on her way, God help us."

Perched on her borrowed saddle, Agnes felt her spirits rise. It was probably warmer in the October sun than inside the castle, the sea twinkled over on her left, and Fitzjohn was satisfyingly cowed. True, the track was in a disgusting state of repair, and those great horrid mountains, usually hidden under a pall of cloud, loomed on the landward side, but she was free of Margery for a few hours, and had made her point. If this saddle didn't cripple her, she would join Hubert in his hunting, and she would also do something to make her chamber more habitable. Have those musty hangings taken down, cleaned and dried, and the same with the bed covers. If this widow Gwyneth was a skilled weaver, as her class of women often were, perhaps she could set her to weaving some new blankets. She didn't intend to freeze this winter. Her mind pleasantly occupied, she let her placid mare pick her way behind the rump of Fitzjohn's horse past the turning in the track which led down to Abertroddi at the mouth of the Troddi, and through the mud at the riverbank to where the water ran shallow and sparkling over a ford. Fitzjohn's horse stepped eagerly into the river, changed its mind, shied and reared. Fitzjohn kept his seat until the horse came down and added a playful buck for good measure, leaving the squire hanging round its neck from where he slid gracelessly into the water. The groom, his face straight, trotted easily by on his small pony, seized the miscreant's reins and led it, now calm, to the far bank where Fitzjohn squelchily remounted. Agnes said nothing, Mona whispered a few uncomplimentary words in Italian, and then smiled involuntarily at the groom's comment in Welsh.

"What did you say?" Fitzjohn raised his whip, as if to strike the man.

"Llewelyn's house this way," the groom waved to the right, where a narrower track branched away from the main highway and meandered off upstream.

"Idiot, I know," the squire snarled, and resumed his position at the head of the calvacade, his dignity quite shattered. Agnes hoped he would not be too rude when they arrived; he was clearly not enjoying this duty, and she had been completely unable to think of any conversational openings on the way to draw him out of his sullen shell. How she missed her late husband's lively and loquacious attendants, with their lovely manners and shiny hair, and what a shame he hadn't been completely submerged in the river. It was probably the first contact he'd had with water for months. Two men laying a hedge alongside the track were bowing as they passed, and Agnes noted that they seemed less ragged and gaunt than the creatures she had seen from the castle, and that they possessed rough, yet serviceable, footwear. There were fields on either side of the river, grazing sheep, the chop of axes from a stand of trees, and then a cluster of buildings on her left.

"Here we are, my lady," Fitzjohn recovered himself enough to mutter, and she was riding through a collection of sturdy outbuildings and barns to Llewelyn's house. She tried to hide her surprise. She had expected a larger version of the native hovels near the castle, with the same mud walls and fading thatch, or, at best, a clumsily-built imitation of Hubert's hall. This was a substantial dwelling, made with cut masonry blocks and slate. Glass winked at the windows, and smoke rose smugly from a chimney, instead of drifting in wisps through any accidental aperture. The front door was open, and a man was walking towards her.

He bowed, and took her bridle. "Lady Agnes? This is a welcome honour."

His gown was not fashionably cut, yet it was finely sewn from smooth cloth, and his hands and nails bore none of the marks or dirt of manual labour. He held himself straight, and only the greying hair above the same beaked nose as Owain's betrayed his age.

"Llewelyn ap Gruffydd?" Agnes accepted his help in dismounting. "Forgive me for calling unannounced. I wished to see your ward, since I believe I owe her some service, from her father's loyalty to mine." It would have been easier if she was calling on some peasant family with whom she could be dismissively munificent, or if she had to use the groom as an interpreter. This man wasn't her equal, but his English was just like his son's, as was the ghost of laughter in his face. He inclined his head.

"You must excuse us. You find us at our work. Please, come inside."

A boy appeared to help the groom with the horses, and they were passing over the threshold, Fitjohn's boots making a horrible noise.

"I'm sorry," Agnes was aware of how uncouth he must have appeared, "the squire had an accident at the ford."

Llewelyn didn't smile openly. "It's easily done. Come,

sir, we can find you some boots while yours dry in the kitchens. If you sit here, you can take them off. My lady, do have this chair."

Agnes sensed the squire's humiliation at being pre-empted from giving the orders, and was nastily glad. She sat on the chair by the fire and looked around. This hall was light and warm, and smelt of nothing worse than woodsmoke and wool. The wall around the fireplace was painted with a design of flowers and animals, there was a table covered with a quality cloth and strewn with papers, and at the far end, three women on stools, spinning piles of carded fleece. One of them stopped her spindle and laid it down, stood up, brushed the skirt of her gown, and walked to the fire.

"My lady." She dropped a curtsey.

Llewelyn smiled formally, "Lady Agnes, this is Gwyneth, my ward, whom you were kind enough to mention."

Agnes motioned for the woman to rise and sit on another chair, and cursed herself. It would be easier to order Margery to clean her shoes than to order this woman to weave her some winter blankets.

Chapter 4

Gwyneth was as tall as Llewelyn, and had inherited the family nose. Neither of these features was as daunting as the look of quiet authority in her eyes, and the lack of servility with which she folded her capable hands on her unshowy gown. A wisp of dark hair had escaped from her simple head-covering, and she met Agnes' scrutiny with a level gaze.

"Some refreshment, my lady?" she suggested, and stood up again to address the younger of the two spinning women. Agnes would have to ask Mona later if she had caught any of the stream of Welsh in that unraised yet carrying voice which sent the girl running to what must have been the kitchens. She noticed that Mona had already occupied the stool vacated by Gwyneth, and was trying out her latest language on the ancient body who remained. If Mona had been a man, she thought, she would undoubtedly have risen as a Venetian spy. This odd household's secrets would not be safe from her. All the same, she had to admire Llewelyn's handling of Fitzjohn, who was finding it difficult to come to terms with such confident courtesy from someone whom he had been taught not to regard as a gentleman.

"Sir," the Welshmen was saying in reasonable tones, "my cousin Gwilym has ridden down to Abertroddi to see if the smith can repair the great gun from his ship. Would you care to accompany me there, and give us the benefit of your advice?"

The squire could not see that this was ridiculous flattery, and looked to Agnes for approval. She waved him away with relief, and grasped the initiative.

"So, Gwyneth, I hear your father gave his life to save

Sir Simon, and that you were also left motherless, then sadly widowed. I am at your service." Damn them all, did that trace of mocking laughter go with the nose?

Gwyneth tried to choose her words carefully. Llewelyn and Heledd had made sure that Mwfanwy's contempt for Sir Simon had been transmitted faithfully to her daughter, along with her conviction that it was his incompetence in leading his men into an ambush which had caused Madog's death. Gwyneth had grown up sharing in the general disdain for the unworthy English in their purloined castle. It would not do, however, to be honest with this doll of a woman, who matched completely Owain's description of a haughty piece with a stick up her arse. For all she was a stranger and the widow of an unknown Venetian, she was Sir Hubert's half-sister, and had it within her power to make life a lot less pleasant for his neighbours.

"It was no more than his duty, my lady, and cheerfully done, so I have been told." She added more truthfully, "I never missed a mother's love, being brought up as a daughter by Heledd."

Her parents were myths, expanded by their deaths into an impossibly heroic warrior and the most beautiful woman in the country, who had dressed as a man to escape from France and give birth to her beloved's child in safety, before joining him as a swan seeks out its mate. They were not real like Hywel, her gawky and amiable young husband, the heir to another small estate, whom she had known since childhood, who had enjoyed music and bad company, and who had died from over-zealous experimentation with spirits and medicinal plants. She missed him not so much for himself, as for the loss of a familiar presence, and she had come away with her dowry and a yearly share of his mill's profits, to compensate for his fruitless adolescent fumblings. The only real sorrow in her life had been Heledd's death, and perhaps the marriage of her friend, Ceinwen. Even then, neither of these events had been unexpected: they were in the natural order of things, and could not be opposed.

Agnes persisted, watching Gwyneth watching the girl as she placed a tray on the table.

"I am a widow myself, I know it is not always easy to find a place in the world." In a way, this was true. She could have stayed in Venice, in the palace her husband's family were scheming to wrest from her, or risked setting up house in London, that hive of dissent and violent upheaval. It had seemed wiser at the time to travel to her unknown half-brother, to see if she could snare another husband among the English landowners far from the temptations of plot and treason. She had only been acquainted with Hubert through the dutiful letters he sent occasionally to their father, and then the polite condolence and invitation which had arrived after the count's and Edmund's deaths. Now she had taken up the invitation, she had no fear that he would throw her out, since he liked having a countess in the family, but he certainly had no-one among his acquaintance whom she could happily contemplate marrying. The aged count, hindered, it must be admitted by Mona's sleeping draughts, had been very neglectful of his marital duties, and she realised she preferred it that way. She accepted a small cake of some kind and a cup of wine, and continued.

"After all, your guardian Llewelyn has sons. When they marry . . ."

Gwyneth smiled with a self-assurance she didn't entirely feel.

"Why, then, I will have to marry again, and make my own household elsewhere."

Naturally, she had given this some thought over the five years since Heledd had died. Cynan had been betrothed to Hwyel's much younger sister almost from the moment of her birth, and although he seemed to be in no hurry to marry, the girl would surely come of age in the next two years, and Llewelyn and Gwyneth's father-in-law were both impatient to see the grandson who would inherit a considerable chunk of land. Cynan's two chubby daughters by a cheerful young woman in Abertroddi would be provided for, and were always welcome in Llewelyn's hall, but Llewelyn didn't want the complication of a brother arriving for them in Abertroddi, and the cheerful young woman turning into a litigious harridan. In the old days, such a son would be regarded as much Cynan's heir as any son born with the blessing of the Church, and torn between respect for tradition and desire to see his descendants elevated, Llewelyn raged at Cynan every time he returned from one of his visits to the little port. Cynan took no notice. He was a man, he couldn't be expected to wait forever, and children were like lambs; the more you had the better. Cynan was therefore out of Gwyneth's reckoning, and Owain might have to take orders to advance, which left Madog. Gwyneth had sometimes wondered if she should marry Madog when Cynan brought his new wife in to run the household. She wouldn't mind keeping house further up the valley, and her own income could fund improvements. On the other hand, Madog was sure to be caught one day, and she would probably be left with a brood of mouths to feed and the house burned down around her ears. Moreover, Madog was strangely more like a priest than Owain, who had far from conquered the sins of the flesh. No rumours had reached her ears of Madog flirting with serving maids in the castle, or riding to the workers' village on midsummer nights, nor that he spent more time than was necessary with the carpenter's pretty young sons. Gwyneth tried not to think of whether he had succeeded in persuading the Vinlanders to walk up the valley and hide in his house,and concentrated on the awkward guest who had caused such trouble.

"I trust the Lady Margery is well?" She made the question innocuous. Owain had often entertained them with tales of the woman's silliness.

Agnes couldn't fully disguise her expression. "As well as can be expected." It occurred to her that she was properly warm for about the first time since she had arrived in Wales, and that the wine she was drinking wasn't bad at all.

Gwyneth's next smile was less forced. "And Sir Hubert?"

Agnes let her guard slip further. "Ach, he is exercised by politics when he is not hunting."

Gwyneth felt herself relax. This woman might look like an icicle, but she was obviously very different from her sister-in-law, and most likely starved of intelligent conversation.

"These are difficult times for people of our . . . affinity," she ventured.

Agnes gave her a sharp glance. It was no secret that her family, and Hubert's mother's relations in England, were supporters of King Henry, madman or not. Hubert had avoided taking the field against the usurping Edward, he wasn't that rash, having been plagued by a recurring hunting injury, yet the estates in England had gone, which was why he had retreated to his possessions in Wales seven years previously. Henry was in the Tower, Edward ruled as King and had his spies everywhere. Was Gwyneth tempting her to some indiscretion, some tale of secret messages and intrigue, which would lead Hubert first to join his monarch in prison, and then to a traitor's death? Although he wasn't a patch on Edmund, he was still her flesh and blood, and she didn't want that for him.

Gwyneth made an impatient movement with her hands, "Llewelyn, whether he likes it or not, is one of Sir Hubert's following. You must know that privately he does not care for either side, but he would not break his word to him, or betray him."

As a matter of policy, Llewelyn had signed indentures with Sir Hubert which bound him to follow the knight in the unlikely event that he took up arms. Llewelyn had been convinced at the time that this would never happen, and it had eased Owain's introduction into the castle.

Agnes looked into her cup, "Better the devil you know?"

Gwyneth laughed quietly, "Something like that."

There was a pause, and the sense that an understanding had been reached.

Agnes gestured to the wall, "That painting is very fine. It looks almost new. Who did you find to do such work here?" There was nothing like it in the castle.

Gwyneth wished the colour hadn't rushed to her face. "To tell the truth, it was first done when Heledd was alive. It had faded, so it was me who repainted it."

The week, well before her marriage, when the travelling painter and his assistant wife had stayed to ply their trade, had been one of the happiest of her life. Seeing her interest, Heledd hadn't stopped her from sitting with the woman as she mixed colours and filled in the designs drawn by the craftsman, nor from making her own experiments with the left-over paints. Once she was widowed, and had her own money, she regularly ordered pigments and brushes from Chester John, and practised on her bedchamber wall as a distraction from the endless chores. Still, Lady Agnes would probably consider this an unsuitable occupation for a gentlewoman, and would revert to her frozen courtesy. Agnes didn't. She stood up and peered more closely at the brushwork, and sat down again.

"I will be truthful back, and say that it is not as good as the work of some of the Venetian ladies. Mind you, it is far better than any I have seen outside London." She realised that Gwyneth was staring at her, "What?"

"Are there lady artists in Venice?" Gwyneth had suddenly seen the depths of her ignorance of the world outside these valleys.

"It is far from unknown. Of course, they are not as famous as the men, even though some paint most of their masters' or husbands' pictures." She shrugged, "That is the way all over, as far as I can see."

"Isn't it so." Gwyneth hesitated, "Please, I have never travelled. What is Venice like? And London?"

To her credit, Agnes didn't boast. She described something of the palaces and churches and gardens, the great houses and people from all over the world, but didn't forget the noise and filth and beggars, and the horrors of their crossing to England. The sun passed its lower midday zenith, the men returned, and it was time to ride back to the castle. Agnes suffered a twinge of regret. It was unlikely that she would call again. This woman didn't need her charity, and they couldn't be friends. However, she had made the break from the castle, so the next time she wanted to ride out would be easier, and Fitzjohn's temper had greatly improved. His horse had calmed down, his boots were dry, and he had put the Welshmen right on their gun.

"It is a noble piece, my lady, but that smith will never be able to repair it.It needs new bolts casting, and I think they agreed with me." He hesitated, not sure if this was appropriate conversation for a lady.

Agnes smiled at him as they jogged down the track. "If you have an interest in ordnance, you should cultivate it. Too few Englishmen are skilled in these matters. Now, in Burgundy . . ."

From a workshop, Cynan watched them go and sighed with relief, his hands automatically twisting and weaving the split hazel rods. His father would probably be angry again if he found his heir making a hurdle like a common labourer, instead of behaving like a gentleman and attending to their aristocratic guest, yet he didn't care. The job needed doing now, and it was quicker to do it himself in this spare hour than to chivvy one of his men. His clever brothers thought he was simple, and that didn't bother him either. Life was simple, that was the best way. You learned how to look after the land and your stock, and they looked after you. In the miserable years he had spent away from home training for his station, he had come to the conclusion that he didn't want his life to depend on the favour of those above him, on the machinations of lawyers, or on how prettily he bowed and spoke. Yes, he could play the landlord, and he would be a fool not to enjoy the luxury of their hall, but somehow the hankering for lost glory which haunted his family had passed him by, and he didn't share his father's passion for revenge and advancement. He knew he could survive if he lost everything, and had to eke out a living as a humble shepherd, unlike Owain, who, for all his quick mind and ambition, would be helpless if he had to fend for himself without influence. Madog could probably survive anywhere, yet even he enjoyed the family name and sense of natural superiority, although God alone knew what really went on in that boy's head. Cynan hoped he was keeping those damned foreigners of Gwilym's out of mischief, they were another disruption he could do without, and there would be hell to pay if that prim little miss caught sight of them and fell from her horse in fright. He grunted, finished off his handiwork, and went off in search of some dinner.

Madog was leading the Vinlanders through the woods in the little valley beyond his stables. They made no more noise than he did, even though they had never been in this place before, and they were easy to be with. Unlike other people, even his brothers, after the sheep episode they didn't demand attention, and moved behind him as if they had walked this trail together many times. The only man with whom he could compare these visitors from an ocean away was the ancient huntsman from whom he'd learned his skills, a man who had spent so long in the forest that he was more like one of the wolves he shadowed than his fellow humans. At about the time that Madog's mother had died, the estate along the coast had been troubled by poachers more wily than the peasants who still sometimes blundered into the trees with their bows, and got caught through leaving trails of blood and heavy footprints. Instead of rousing out all his men and patrolling the woods day and night, the old bastard had sent Madog off alone to find them.

"If you get rid of them, I'll teach you more," he had said, his eyes cunning with challenge. "If you fail, don't come back."

Stung by the harsh unfairness of his task, Madog had silently vowed to come back anyway, and smother the cantankerous senile fool in his sleep. For a day he had stalked backwards and forwards to no avail and shivered when night fell, getting hungrier by the hour as his bread ran out, until on the second morning he found himself sitting on a rock by a stream, about to succumb to the temptation of lighting a fire to cook the pigeon he was going to shoot. He bent to splash his face in the water, and saw the charred bone caught against a tree root. A bone which had been cooked outside, gnawed and then thrown into a stream to be hidden. Well before midday, he had found the empty campsite upstream, concealed in a sheltering jumble of rocks on the bare hillside, beyond the edge of the forest and outside his current master's jurisdiction. He didn't think of going back for help. He filled his leather flask from the stream, enlarged a hollow under a rock, crawled beneath it and waited. They came, not that evening, but the evening after, three Welshmen with ponies, ready to slip down to the woods before dawn, hunt, and fade away back to the hills before they were noticed. Madog knew all this. He knew everything. He was no longer hungry or asleep: he had melted through the earth and become the buzzard watching them from the sky, the blades of grass beneath their feet, the cool air brushing their faces. He knew to let them hobble their ponies, light a small fire, eat their supper and settle down, with one man keeping watch. He also knew that the guard couldn't see him as he slid from under the rock, strung his bow and shot him in the arm. He shot the other two in the leg where they lay, before their companion's shocked cry could fully awaken them. He drew his bow again, the arrow pointing straight at the guard's throat.

"I'm not going to kill you, and I'll leave you your ponies. Hunt in other woods while I'm here."

He left them, and wasn't afraid that they would shoot him in the back as he disappeared down to the treeline.

When he limped into his master's stableyard, the revelation had passed, his head ached and his legs were trembling. The old man was sitting at the doorway of his little bothy, mending a quiver.

"Come in," he said, pulling aside the hide he used as a door.

Madog, who slept with the other hunt servants and stableboys in the hayloft, had never been invited in before. Through his shaking, he managed to be taken aback that the hut was clean and tidy, and not the musty animal's lair he had imagined. He collapsed on to a stool, and tore into the loaf he was handed.

"Don't eat too quickly," the old man said. "You found them?"

Madog nodded, his mouth too full for speech.

"Did you kill them?"

Madog shook his head. The old man smiled.

"Look at me."

Madog looked into his eyes, and in their depths saw the buzzard he had become, circling the dark hills.

The old man nodded in his turn. "Yes. That might never happen again, but you will always carry it with you."

Madog blinked, and worried that he might faint. The old man didn't seem to believe that he needed any further explanation, and started rummaging in a wooden box.

"You know not to kill unless you have to. You can have this now." He handed Madog a grey object on a leather string. "Put it round your neck, boy. The priests don't approve, but the old ways can protect you as well. It's from a wolf your great-grandfather shot."

Madog's fingers nearly failed to grip the worn tooth. "My great-grandfather? Llewelyn?"

The old man wasn't going to give much away. "I hunted with Gruffydd when I was young. I'm going to send you somewhere else now."

Madog put his head between his knees. He was so tired, his bones were screaming. His tormentor cackled. "Don't be soft, boy. You've plenty left in you. Anyway, you can take a pony. Behind Raven's Mountain there's a stream which goes over a rock face as flat as an old pancake. There's a pool in some thorn trees. Sit and have a look at it for a while. You'll thank me."

Madog took his time. As soon as he was back in the woods, he found a comfortable glade and slept for hours. Then he lit a fire and cooked a pigeon, and slept again before riding up into the high hills. After hours of sliding up and down barren slopes, he found the pool and sat religiously next to it, half-believing in some magic which would send up a beautiful faerie woman from its clear bottom. It took a long time for him to realise that the sparkles in the water could not be explained by the sunlight alone, and when he did, he laughed for the first time since he had been sent after the poachers.

"Does my father know about this?" he asked the huntsman on his second, more happy, return.

"No. Gruffydd never told him." The old man threw a handful of sticks on his fire, and the flames softened the deep lines on his face.

"Why not?" Madog may have fallen out with his father, but he still believed that he was the noblest man in Wales.

"Llewelyn didn't need it."

An obscure fear made Madog crouch closer to the fire. "Will I?"

The old man spat. "I'm not a fucking prophet, boy.

But you'll do to keep the family secret, it shouldn't die with me. I know you'll be careful. The smith in Abertroddi can be trusted. Now piss off, I'm tired."

The family secret. Madog wondered in the months that followed, and looked differently at the huntsman. Take away twenty years and a hard life from his face, and maybe he did resemble . . . it would be unusual if his great-grandfather had not had more than one woman. Yet why had he not used the gold himself? The old man died suddenly, like a light going out, leaving Madog's questions unanswered. Still, he hugged the secret to his bosom along with the wolf's tooth, and it had brought him here, to his own house and his congenial trade, and his new friends. The soft clop of ponies' hooves on the forest floor brought him to a silent halt. He turned, the Vinlanders vanished into the bushes by the path, and three mounted figures came at him through the trees.

Chapter 5

"Jesus, it's only Madog." The leading rider reined in his mount. "What are you doing, creeping around here? Do you want to be taken for a poacher?" He looked pointedly at the unstrung bow in Madog's hand.

Madog smiled amiably at Hubert's English huntsman. "Who would be so foolish as to interfere with my lord's game? No, my brother keeps coming to me with tales of wolf tracks by his sheepfolds, so I am taking a little walk to put his mind at rest."

The huntsman hawked in derision. "You Welsh frighten yourselves with fairy tales. There's not been a wolf near here for years."

One of his companions patted his pony's neck. Madog had sold it to him, and it was a lovely natured surefooted beast. "I saw one up in the hills this summer, but they'll not come this close this time of year. Only if it's a hard winter, and then we'll see to them. How did that mare do?" When he had bought the pony, Madog had been troubled by a sick mare.

Madog's smile deepened, "She recovered. She'll breed for a while yet. Your pony looks well."

"He's worth his weight in gold . . ."

The lead huntsman cut in, "We've no time to sit here gossiping. Keep out of these woods a week today, Welshman. Sir Hubert's having a big hunt, and won't take kindly to uninvited guests. Sir Giles is coming. Tell your peasants to keep their pigs clear."

He kicked his pony and trotted off, his companion sketching Madog a not unfriendly wave. Madog looked thoughtfully after them. Sir Giles was his erstwhile master, and a man who took his hunting seriously.

Gwyneth was moderately satisfied with the family's performance at the mass in the little church in Abertroddi the next day. Even Cynan was tidy and clean, having been persuaded not to examine his sheep's feet in his laundered shirt and brushed outer clothes, and Madog had obeyed his father's express instructions to leave the Vinlanders at his stables. The whole valley knew of their existence by now, but this was meant to be a solemn occasion, not a fair with squealing children and gawping adults, and if Gwilym's rough sailors could turn up patched and shaved, then the family shouldn't let them down. After the service, Gwyneth waited in the porch for Llewelyn to finish talking to the priest, and watched his three sons standing together in the drifting autumn rain. Owain had been given leave from the castle to attend, and was talking quickly, while the other two were trying not to laugh too loudly within the church's boundary. For a brief second, Cynan put his hand on Owain's shoulder, and Madog ruffled his hair, and Gwyneth felt the old sense of exclusion from their private male world. Then Madog's quick eyes were distracted by someone on the main street below the churchyard, and he stiffened. He patted Owain's arm, lifted his hat to him, and was gone. Owain saw Gwyneth, and came back into the porch, sprinkling raindrops like pearls from his cloak.

"You got my message yesterday, dearest cousin?"

Gwyneth smiled at him. He had always been the easiest to talk to. "I did. Thank you for the warning. I think we managed to look respectable and gainfully employed, and not as if we were harbouring outlandish foreigners."

Owain laughed quietly. "I didn't know about them until now. Maybe I shouldn't have sent Luddy after all, and have let our chilly Contessa come across them. She needs something new to shock her, now that she has got used to Lady Margery. Did she offer to take you into her service, or to grant you a few pennies a year for your father's trouble?"

Gwyneth didn't know what made her defend the small woman who certainly wouldn't be giving her a second thought. "She can't help who she is. She was quite polite. I learned a great deal about Venice and London, and how wet it is on a ship."

Owain's face changed. "I hope we never have to find that out for ourselves." He brushed water from his hat and looked more soberly into Gwyneth's eyes. "I haven't told father yet. I think Bartlett is up to something. He doesn't know I know, but he sent his man off with letters to Bristol this morning. I don't like it, he is walking around like a cat in the dairy."

Gwyneth shrugged, "Maybe it's just business. Or maybe he is writing off for a wife." She thought that would make Owain smile, but it didn't.

"I think they are letters for France. He is meddling, and will drag Sir Hubert into his schemes."

It annoyed him that he couldn't work Bartlett out. Everyone assumed that this older man, who had lived in the castle in some undefined capacity since before Hubert had arrived, was a natural son of old Sir Hugh's. He appeared to have a source of income, judging from the number of books that appeared for him in traders' packs, and he dressed as a man of learning. He spent most of his time in the chambers he had appropriated in one of the older towers, and Owain longed for the day when he could safely sneak into them, and see if they were really full of alchemist's equipment, horoscopes and magical instruments. Bartlett rarely left the castle, however, and practically never acknowledged Owain's presence. As far as Owain could tell, Hubert didn't consult him on day to day business matters, yet he generally treated Bartlett with a kind of deference far removed from his usual brusqueness, which made Owain wonder if Bartlett had some hold on him, some knowledge of the family history which Hubert wanted to keep hidden.

Gwyneth dismissed his fears. "You don't have enough to keep you busy in that castle. Some of Margery's stupidity may have rubbed off on Hubert, but I can't imagine that he would join anything risky unless he was sure he would be on the winning side. He's out of sight here, and does what he pleases. Why should he jeopardise all that?" She left unsaid what she guessed Owain dreaded. Men could be induced to follow hopeless causes by the promise of wealth and power, and supporting a move in Henry's name would bring rich rewards in the unlikely event that it succeeded. It would be certain to fail, however, and their peaceful existence would go up in flames. She shook her head.

"Maybe it's treason just talking like this. Llewelyn's coming, let's go home and eat."

If men like Bartlett had to find their own supper, she thought, they wouldn't have time for their clever machinations.

Behind the Abertroddi smithy was a yard enclosed by outbuildings, used by the smith to store broken implements and the necessaries of his trade. The darkest and dirtiest building was the charcoal shed, whose very air was thick with grime, and it would take an extremely sharp eye to notice that the heaps of fuel were piled, not against the back wall, but against a hurdle partition, blackened by years of use. An agile man who knew where he was going could easily slip between the partition and the rear wall, and find the waist high boarded gap in the wattle and daub rear of the shed. If he knew where to press the boards, he would find that they swung easily open, and if he crouched down and wriggled through, he would find himself in an unexpectedly neat small room, furnished with a table, benches, and a couple of chests, and warmed in winter by a charcoal brazier. He would have to be trusted by the smith to know all this, and also to know that if he stood on the chest in the corner and pulled at a peg protruding from the rough ceiling boards, a trap door would open and he could poke his head through into an upstairs room of the building next door, which was conveniently an alehouse. Madog, naturally, was familiar with the room, and a few minutes after he had left the churchyard was sitting at the table with another man, trying to make sense of his mutilated English.

"Twa ponies. They're guid wee beasties," the man said. In the light of a handful of dips, Madog could see the rope burns and cuts on his hands.

"Where are they from?" Madog asked.

The other man grinned, revealing broken teeth, and

tapped his nose. "No' frae near here, sonny."

"And where's Alexander?" Madog tried again.

The man coughed with laughing. "I'll no' be telling you that, bonny laddie. Now, are ye in or no'? Ye'll be missing yerself a bargain."

Madog thought. If he went ahead with his tempting plan, it would be horribly risky. The first rule he had learned was not to make a mess in his own front yard, and the consequences if he was caught were too awful to contemplate. On the other hand, it would be such an entertaining coup to pull off, and his scalp prickled with excitement. There must be a way he could do this. He felt in his pouch. The bag was heavy, and dared him to make the next move.

"Can Alexander stay in these waters for the next six days?"

The Scottish sailor opposite him puffed his cheeks. "Aye well, it's a wee while longer than he was planning. The weather's no' improving, and he'll no' want to risk storms."

Madog made up his mind, and pulled out the bag. "It'll be worth his while. Give him this, and tell him to be at the old port six nights from now. How will the tide be then?"

The sailor calculated. "It'll be fair enough just after dark. Ye'll have some merchandise for loading, then?"

Madog showed his teeth, "I hope so, and better beasts than ponies. If I don't turn up, he can keep the bag till next time. If I do, he can return it, and we'll settle a price at the port." He wasn't afraid of being cheated. Alexander and he had done business often enough to know that the other wasn't to be crossed.

The sailor took the bag and spat on his palm, "Shake on it, wee manny. Six nights from now, the old port, just after dark."

They shook hands, and the sailor stood on the chest, tugged the peg and pulled himself effortlessly out of the room.

A little later, the smith crawled into the room, and looked at Madog as he idly scratched the table top with his fingernail.

"Do I want to know about this?" His eyeballs and teeth were white in his streaked face.

Madog glanced up, "No." He changed the subject, "I think I might need another batch preparing." Even in this room, it was wise not to speak too openly.

The smith drew himself to his feet, and put his massive hands on his hips. "John of Chester won't be back till spring."

Madog rubbed out the marks he had made on the table. "I know. Call it insurance. I can hide it when it's done."

"It's up to you." The smith picked up the flagon of beer on the table, and drained it in one go, "Bring me the stuff when you're ready. The harbour-master will think I'm casting for that bloody gun if he notices anything. How're your heathens today?"

They chatted in the manner of old friends until Madog left by the way the sailor had gone, and rode off to his father's house for another excessive dinner.

In the days before the hunt, the inhabitants of the Troddi valley followed their usual routines, harsher for some and more lax for others. Llewelyn's tenants and workers rose groaning with the chillier dawns to beat winter to mending fences, gathering firewood, spreading muck and all the tasks that had to be done to survive short days and cold nights. Gwilym's sailors sewed canvas and repaired ropes, while Gwilym argued with Llewelyn over how much return he could expect from his investment in the voyage. Cynan picked out animals for slaughter, and Gwyneth supervised the smoking, the salting, the making of blood puddings and the storing of apples and beans. Ragged Abertroddi children pulled seaweed from the shore for their bread, and their fishermen fathers worried at the mean price paid by the castle for their dried catch. Madog and his man, Ellis, thatched a new stable, and taught Climbs Trees and Sleeps At Noon how to feed and water the horses. They seemed to like staying at Madog's house, and he saw no reason to send them back to the cramped and uncomfortable ship. If strangers called, they dissolved into the background, and otherwise they spent the days mastering Madog's bows and fishing in the river, absorbing this new world with their calm curiousity. Over in the castle, Owain fretted about his life slipping away in pages of dreary documents, and Agnes found her saddles. They had been dumped in a damp, little-used storeroom, and after shouting at the nearest servants, she was filled with pleasure that she could now hunt with Sir Giles in a style which befitted her position. Hubert was anxious to impress this more powerful neighbour whose estates marched along the coast, and although Agnes found him crude and arrogant, she planned to derive some entertainment from his company. He was a widower, and she was looking forward to his attempts at gallantry, and discussing them later with Mona. Unknown to all of them locked behind hills and forests, Bartlett's man boarded a ship in Bristol, and in London the streets rang with armed men and bells.

On the day before the hunt, Madog finished his thatching and rode his favourite white-nosed horse down to Llewelyn's house, leading an anonymous pony. He found Gwyneth counting crocks of honey, and took her outside to her herb garden for a talk. The late afternoon sunshine turned the dying grasses into gold and the last flowers into defiant embers. Gwyneth's shadow was the same length as Madog's as she argued with him, and finally gave way, stamping back to the house to cuff Glynis round the ear for hanging about the stables to see if the Vinlanders would follow Madog down. The next morning, she was indisposed, and kept to her chamber, with Nyrees barring the door as fierce as any guard dog, letting the household muddle through without its mistress and her aide. In the castle, the chaos was worse. Squires rushed around on garbled errands, horses whinnied and nipped at their grooms, hounds bayed, pans flew at servants' heads in the kitchens, and Margery stayed in her bed with a fit of the vapours. Luddy was beside himself with excitement. That odd woman of the remote Lady Agnes had heard him singing with the potboy and two grooms one evening, and word had somehow filtered up to the great lords that this quaint music would be suitable rustic entertainment for the hunt when they stopped for refreshments. As a result, Luddy and the gleeful potboy were bouncing together on one patient pony in an advance party of servants and laden animals, sent ahead to set up awnings and rugs in a clearing, where the ladies could rest if it all became too much. The Lady Margery never rode out in the chase, and Hubert's English huntsmen were willing to take Lady Agnes' decision to attend as a mark of their sophistication and the superior quality of their hunt. After all, had she not hunted with the King of Venice, whom a well-travelled serjeant at arms insisted was called The Dog, and who used tame tigers to outstrip his prey? She would see what a fine pack of hounds could do, and what wonderful country this was, not like Venice which, according to this same serjeant, was all swamp and water and fit for nothing but fishing.

Led by a taciturn huntsman, the advance party clattered towards the ford, and Luddy saw a familiar horse with a white blaze on its nose splashing through the water towards them. Its rider was muffled up against the early morning mist, but there was no mistaking the feathered hat pulled down over his brow, or the lack of spurs on his boots. Only one man of substance in the area never wore spurs.

"It's Madog," Luddy informed the potboy, who rarely escaped from the kitchens, and who did not have such elevated connections.

Madog lifted his hand in greeting to the huntsman, and moved smartly out of the way of the oncoming calvacade. Before he headed down the track towards Abertroddi, he added to the sum of Luddy's happiness and pride by waving again and calling out to him.

"Luddy, are you turning hunter for the day?" His voice was hoarse through the layers of cloth over his mouth.

Luddy's chest swelled. "I'm to sing for the ladies, sir," he squeaked.

"Well, good luck to you. I'm off by boat to Holy Island. I mustn't miss the tide." With that, he squeezed his horse with his naked boots and cantered off, clods of mud flying in his wake.

Considerably later, the main body left the castle in a babble of noise and colour enough to frighten any deer for miles around. Agnes wasn't bothered. She had her own comfortable saddle back, and had persuaded the grooms to give her a decent mount, not a mimsy mare. The sun had conquered the earlier mist, and she was convinced that, given an open stretch of country, she could outride Giles on his great prancing horse more suited to the lists than to jumping ditches. She was aware that her elaborate headdress was perhaps a trifle extravagant, yet it was far more fashionable than any that Margery possessed, and there was no rain to spoil the expensive gauze which floated from its crown. Mona had contented herself with observing that it would save her from a cracked skull when she fell off, and wore a sensible arrangement of plain cloth. They rode across the ford and up the Troddi valley, past Llewelyn's house and way on upwards to where the trees and fields petered out into open moorland, with Giles instructing Agnes on the deficiences of Welsh agriculture, and the merits of English estate management.

"They are not an enterprising and organised people like us," he concluded, perspiring under his heavy velvet hat, "no wonder we brought them easily into our realm." He spoke as if he was the king himself, not an obscure provincial knight.

Fitzjohn, riding to one side, unexpectedly came to the Welsh's defence. "They invented the longbow," he muttered, "and some have adapted to gunnery."

Giles ignored him, and Agnes turned to give the youth a brief smile. He had made some effort with his appearance, and seemed to have had his hair cut, and to have shaved, judging by the nicks on his chin. He blushed furiously at Agnes' attention, and she laughed to herself. There were many things a youth would do for a hopeless love, all of them to her advantage . . . the hounds gave tongue in the woods, a deer burst from the treeline over on their left, and she was off, galloping over the tussocky grass with the wind in her face and Giles thundering and swearing behind her.

After two more deer had been chased into the ground,

Agnes was secretly relieved to be led by a satisfied huntsman downwards to a pleasant clearing in the woods. She was afraid that her headdress needed some running repairs, and she was out of practice for riding so hard. They were in a side valley from the Troddi, with a stream bubbling nearby, awnings hanging from the trees, a pile of rug-covered cushions for her and Mona to sit on, a fire with a makeshift spit turning above it, and servants holding wine. She left Giles' groom to tie their mounts to a sapling at the edge of the clearing, and walked stiffly to a seat. Mona sat gingerly next to her.

"I thought this was going to be a gentle morning's hunt, not a horse race," she said in Italian. "You don't have to work so hard to impress Sir Giles, he already thinks you are a spirited piece of flesh."

Agnes twisted her mouth, "Sweet Jesus, I'd forgotten how courtly English men are. Shall we pack for a move along the coast?"

Mona picked a twig from the top of her boot, "His house has a better roof than your brother's."

Agnes took a cup of wine off the anxiously hovering Fitzjohn, "It's decided then. Call on the lawyers to haggle over a settlement. Thank you Fitzjohn," she added in English, "and would you be so kind as to fetch us some meat?"

As she ate, she became aware that four figures were shuffling into line in front of her, their eyes fixed to the ground. Two scruffy small boys, red to the ears and with tide marks around their necks, and two grooms, one of them so old and bow-legged she was surprised he could stand upright. The ancient coughed, checked his three companions were in place, tapped his thigh and opened his mouth. Agnes forgot to chew. She had never heard music like this, not in the choirs of great churches in Venice, or in the cultured houses of her husband and his friends, or in the entertainments lovingly arranged by Edmund. Harmonies natural as the running water and complex as the veins on a leaf filled the clearing, and she felt a shift in her chest, as if a door had opened into a strange and beautiful garden she desperately wanted to enter. The song ended, and the four bowed raggedly,then looked at her in apprehension. She put her cup down, and clapped her hands.

"Oh, please sing another. Mona, ask them to sing again."

Mona addressed the old man in Welsh, and his little band bowed again. He said something, and Mona translated.

"I think that was a hymn to the Virgin Mary, and now they're going to sing about St David."

This time they sang unselfconsciously, their heads high and their eyes direct, and Agnes didn't notice the sun going behind a cloud or the whisper of movement at the edge of the glade. She was afraid she was going to cry over Edmund again, no, she was light as a swallow skimming the fields at dusk, and life was too precious to waste in considering spending it with oafs like Giles. When the singers made their final bow, she nudged Mona.

"I'm not carrying any money. Tell them they will be well rewarded when we return home."

There was another conversation, and Mona smiled at Agnes. "He says they sing only for love, and to ease your ladyship's sorrow for her husband and her old home. I think."

Agnes bowed back at the four, and contemplated the small boys. They could be cleaned up, and although they were Welsh and must be base-born, they were young enough to be taught politeness, and surely Hubert would not begrudge her two tiny servants. To have such music in her chamber whenever she wanted . . .

A frightened cry broke into her musing.

"Sir Giles, sir, your horse, it's broken free."

She snapped her head round to the sapling. Two bridles flapped folornly in the rising breeze, and two expensive animals had disappeared.

Chapter 6

Agnes wondered how men managed warfare, when two missing horses caused such uproar. Figures crashed calling through the trees, Hubert blustered, and Giles kicked his groom mercilessly, until Fitzjohn, who was every minute turning out smarter than Agnes had given him credit for, shouted above the hubbub that the bridles had been cut, and so the horses hadn't slipped free by themselves. There was a dreadful pause. Hubert turned grey with shock, and then purple with rage. His honoured guest's horse, not to mention one of his own prime beasts, had been stolen from under his nose. The running and barging and counter orders stopped.

"Whip in those bloody hounds," Hubert roared. "We'll track the bloody bastard down. I swear, Sir Giles," he gripped the other man's shoulders, "he will be hanging from my walls by nightfall."

Sir Giles snarled, and seized Fitzjohn's mount. "He'd better be. Where's your best tracker?"

The best tracker was Clegge, the taciturn huntsman, and he had Luddy by the ear. He wasn't reluctant to say the name which was hovering in most of the servants' minds.

"What did that son of a whore Madog say to you this morning? Hey? Are you in on this, you scrawny Welsh shit?" He shook the boy, and slapped his face. Tears in his eyes, Luddy's rudimentary English deserted him, and Clegge reached for his whip.

"Sirs, that young devil Madog was around this morning," he said to the knights. "I'll get the truth from this whoreson brat." He lifted his arm and swung.

Agnes was not particularly soft-hearted, but in her

mind, this unlikely canary was already one of her servants, and no-one was going to beat him senseless without her permission. She swept out from under the awning, pulling Mona with her. In lighter moments, Agnes' mother, who had once attended the queen, performed imitations of this superior lady to amuse her children, and Agnes remembered every one of her proud mannerisms.

"Stand back," she said to Clegge. "Does this creature even speak English? How can he tell you the truth when you are hitting him? Mona, question the boy."

Her acting was formidable, and no-one told her to withdraw from this men's business. The first blow had knocked Luddy to the ground, but now he stood up, his teeth gritted in his determination not to cry out. He was Glendyr's man, he had been captured by the enemy, and he would reveal nothing, not even if they tortured him to death. His mother would weep, his sisters would wail, and his name would live forever as a byword for heroic self-sacrifice.

"Boy," the odd woman was talking to him in halting Welsh, "tell me what Madog said."

He squinted at her. What had Madog said? He was going to Holy Island by boat . . . Luddy was a bright boy, whose mind had not yet been dulled by years of back-breaking work, and who would have gone far if he had been of gentle birth. He knew at once that telling the truth, rather than courting a heroic death, was what he was meant to do.

"I'm trying to tell you all," he said clearly in Welsh. "Madog said he was going to Holy Island by boat, and wanted to catch the tide. So he can't have stolen your horses, you sons of bitches."

The Welsh servants hid their grins, and Mona translated, leaving out his final observation.

"There you are," Agnes said. "Shouldn't you start tracking the real thief while the trail is warm?"

Hubert regained some control. "You, Stamford," he pointed at the huntsman who had bought his pony from Madog, "go to Madog's stables and search them, and if you find nothing, ride to Abertroddi, speak with my harbourmaster, and see if Madog comes ashore. Fitzjohn, stay here with the ladies and the hall servants. Clegge, let the hounds smell those bridles, and find us a trail. Come on, they can't have gone far."

The clearing began to empty, and the first drops of rain started to fall.

Madog stood under the overhanging bank of the stream with his prizes. God, it had been so easy. Giles' great horse could have been a handful, yet a few whispers in its ear, and it had come away as sweetly as his old mare, with the other horse following like a foal. He stopped praising himself. Clegge might prove more skilful than he thought, he was already tired, and there was still danger ahead. He leant his head on the charger's nose, and let his hearing travel to the noises upstream. The hounds had sniffed their way to the water, and Clegge had urged them through to cast on the opposite side. This was where it could all go wrong. If they came too far downstream, he would surely be spotted. The hounds gave tongue, and he could hear the vengeful search party moving away through the woods. He let himself relax a fraction. They had found the false trail he had laid at dawn. It was an old trick, to wipe the bridles with the same pungent bundle he had used in the morning, and it seemed to have worked for him again. Carefully, he led the horses on. Soon he would have to leave the stream as it turned to flow into the Troddi, climb out of the little valley, and work his way towards the shore. He knew the exact place where he wanted to cross the main track, and if he could do that without being seen, then all he had to do was reach the hidden cave only a mile from the old port. And if it came to the worst, he could always abandon the horses and run. Even the weather was on his side, with the rain becoming heavier, and the wind rising. He ignored the chill of the water licking his thighs and stepped patiently onwards, the sound of his pursuers fading by the minute.

Stamford trotted through the trees towards Madog's house. A low branch swiped at his face, and he ducked automatically. Would it be quicker to go back to the stream, and follow its course to the stables? No, this was a more direct way, even though it wasn't so easy on horseback. He supposed he should feel more outraged than he did over the terrible crime that had been committed, yet he was a phlegmatic man, and although he would obey his orders, he didn't share in his master's fury. He knew he wouldn't find anything in Madog's stables. He had heard the rumours about the Welshman, and preferred not to know where his pony had originally come from, but only an idiot would be so reckless, and Madog certainly wasn't a fool. He had the better part of the deal anyway. He could ride down to Abertroddi, and sit in the alehouse out of the rain until Madog returned from his sea trip, no doubt puking from the waves which must be building up marvellously in this wind. He hummed to himself, and wondered which of the alehouse girls would be around this afternoon. He was duty bound to call in at the stables, although if he didn't linger, he should have enough time, and he could set a boy to watch out for Madog. What was a disaster for Sir Hubert was turning out to be an unexpected holiday for him, and he rode faster as the trees thinned out, and Madog's tidy homestead came into view.

Hubert cursed the rain streaming down his face, the uneven ground, and his whole pack of useless grooms and huntsmen, not to mention that milksop Fitzjohn who should have kept his loud mouth shut. He had a good mind to thrash the lot of them, and turn them out to starve, for not having the wit to notice that someone was stealing horses right before their eyes. Sir Giles, whose hat was ruined, would hold him in contempt, he would be the laughing stock of Wales, and where the hell was this trail leading? He looked up. They were coming out of the trees, and ahead lay the vastness of the hills, invisible behind the low cloud dripping over their flanks, and capable of hiding an army, let alone two horses and an unknown number of thieves. Clegge jogged back to speak to him.

"Sir, shall we carry on? It looks like the trail goes up there." He pointed to a cleft in the hills.

Hubert resisted lashing out at the man with his whip. "Of course. They can't be that far ahead. What?"

The man hesitated. "It may be servants' talk, sir, but the grooms are saying . . ."

"What?" Hubert repeated, and flicked his whip.

Clegge took the hint. "They are saying that this could only be the work of one man. Alexander, the Scotch pirate. He is famous, sir, he stole the Scottish king's horse from a dock once. He has been known to come to Wales."

A bitter humour made Hubert smile. That made it better then. What was good enough for the King of Scotland would surely be good enough for Sir Giles.

"He won't be familiar with these hills, will he, Clegge," he said. "When we catch him, you can ride to the Scottish court for our reward. Keep moving."

In the clearing, Agnes was becoming steadily colder and angrier. The fire was hissing in the rain, the servants were hoarding the rest of the wine for when Sir Hubert returned, and her precious saddle, which had survived a journey across Europe, had been stolen in her brother's back yard. She made up her mind. Unrest or not, she would travel to London before the winter set in, and find a husband with a warm house. Christ, she would rather be in the Tower, or maintained as a fat merchant's mistress, than put up with this misery. The final insult came when one of the ropes holding up her awning snapped in the wind, and the monstrous quantity of water which had already gathered in the fabric splashed down the back of her neck. Her furious cries goaded Fitzjohn into action.

"My lady," he threw his own cloak around her, "if you would ride your woman's mare, and she doesn't mind managing on one of the baggage animals, I will lead you back to the castle."

A vision of a roaring fire and ordered domesticity floated in front of Agnes' eyes.

"You'll do no such thing," she said through chattering teeth. "You'll take me to Llewelyn's house, before I perish from the ague."

Gwyneth, recovered enough to pore over the household accounts, was in her room when the flimsy door from Llewelyn's chamber swung open, and Glynis flew inside.

"Oh my lady," she was overcome with yet another novelty, "that Lady Agnes is here as wet as a drowned kitten, and the English lord is saying to Dafydd that we have to take her in, and we'll hang if she so much as sneezes, and they're dripping all over the floor I just cleaned."

For a second, a sick fear ran through Gwyneth's heart. Was this anything to do with Madog's charade this morning? She looked round the chamber. There was nothing to give her away, and she stood up like the innocent widow she was.

"Well, we don't want to hang, do we? Nyrees, go to the kitchen and heat some wine with your warming herbs. Glynis, come with me, and try to act like a lady's maid for once. Shut the door behind you, to keep in the heat."

They processed through the masculine disorder of Llewelyn's chamber to the top of the stairs, and Gwyneth glanced down. She fought a terrible urge to laugh. Three disreputable figures stood in the hall, dripping, as Glynis had said, all over the floor. She recognised the English squire, even though he had what looked like a rug draped over his shoulders and his hair was plastered to his head, and that peculiar woman with the clever eyes, who was the only one sensibly dressed. The Lady Agnes was a mess. Swamped by a too large cloak and topped by a ridiculous headdress which was bending in the middle and swathed with shreds of gauze and dead leaves, her white face was a study in wretchedness. An unforeseen wave of pity rocked Gwyneth, and she went quickly down the stairs. Llewelyn appeared from the storeroom, where he had probably been hiding the furs he and Gwilym were concealing from Sir Hubert's harbour-master. He bowed.

"Lady Agnes. Fitzjohn, my dear sir, you are always damp when you call."

To her surprise, the English squire smiled. "This time it wasn't my fault. Sir, forgive us, we have had a mishap while hunting. If I could beg hospitality from you for the Lady Agnes while I ride to the castle for her waggon, I would be most grateful."

"But of course. Surely, you must rest here and dry out

before you venture off again. Rhys, Rhys, where is that boy . . ." He knew the skinny Rhys was struggling with an enormous bear skin.

Fitzjohn was being noble. "Do not trouble yourself. If you could stable Lady Agnes' woman's mare, I will be off directly."

"My dear Fitzjohn, at least sit while we find you a cloak. Rhys . . ."

Agnes wanted to shout and stamp her feet, as she had done when she was a child. What about me, I'm going to die on this very spot if you don't stop talking, and help me. She was saved from this further indignity by Gwyneth, who came swiftly to her side, a look that maybe went beyond polite concern on her face.

"My lady, please, let the girl take your cloak, and your woman's too. If you would honour me, come up to my chamber, it is warm and more private. Sir," she turned briefly to Fitzjohn, "do not fear for your lady's health. We will give her the best care we can."

Fitzjohn inclined his head, Agnes was relieved of the sodden cloak, and all she had to do was climb the staircase running diagonally up the end wall of the hall. It was almost too much. Her legs were stiff, her wet clothes clung to her, and only Mona's hand at her back prevented her from stumbling and probably flying to her death on the flagstones below. She was led through a door at the top of the stairs, and into a cold room, gloomy in the afternoon rain, and smelling suspiciously of male feet and unwashed linen. There was a fireplace, but it was unlit, and her spirits sank further than they had when she was crossing the Channel with no escape from the tossing hell of the ship. She would have sunk to her knees and wept, if Gwyneth had not crossed the room and opened another door in a wooden partition.

"In here," she said.

Now Agnes nearly wept with relief. Warm air hit her face, the soft light of a few tapers welcomed her, and she was sitting on a chair while Mona unfastened her stupid headdress with chilly fingers.

"You can't stay in that gown," Mona muttered, peeling away Agnes' own fur-trimmed cloak which had born the brunt of the waterfall, "perhaps . . . ?" She looked at Gwyneth, who was lifting a chest lid.

"Towels," Gwyneth said, giving her the expensive cloths, which Gwilym had donated to her marriage box, as if they were everyday objects. It would never do for these two ladies to know that they normally used old shirts and whatever rags came to hand. Hell, she only had two decent winter gowns, and she was wearing one of them. The other would be far too big for Agnes, and would most likely be donated to a castle servant if she let it out of her sight. She looked again at the small figure. Her hair, unloosed from its pins, was already frizzing up into honey-coloured curls, and her neck was pale as a dove's breast. She stopped herself from staring, and remembered. The blue gown Heledd had had made for her one winter before she had grown so tall. It had been her favourite, and so far she had resisted cutting it up, or handing it over to some deserving family. Her heart was beating faster. She went back into the chest.

"There's this," she said, holding it up. "It's very old, I'm afraid, but still in one piece. It's not what you are used to . . ."

"God in heaven," Agnes spoke for the first time, "I would wear Fitzjohn's rug if it was dry. Please, hand it over, or I swear I'll steal your bedding. I am a woman brought low by rain, and have lost my scruples."

"She's not lying," her serving woman said. "She came away from an inn in France wearing the bed curtains."

Agnes laughed, and Gwyneth suddenly sensed that a fog of impersonal courtesy had been blown away, and that they were letting her a few steps in to a more friendly place.

For the life of her, Agnes couldn't tell why it was important to put this efficient woman at ease. Perhaps it was only overwhelming pleasure at being out of that foul weather, and in a room which was recognisably civilised. There was no fire, but blessed heat radiated from a cunning brazier filled with glowing charcoal, there was a rug at her feet, and the plastered walls were a riot of colour, far removed from the restrained design in the hall. She smiled again.

"This is Mona, who pretends to be my servant. Really, she is a favourite wife of the terrible Sultan of Turkey, snatched from his harem, and when she is rescued, she will have me tied in a sack, and thrown into the Bosphorus."

"And it won't be a day too soon," Mona said. "Come, take off that gown which you paid far too much for, and put on this. It is more your colour anyway."

Gwyneth averted her head while they started the operation, and was horrified to find her nails digging into her palm. She attempted to make her voice light.

"The woman who pretends to be my servant was meant to be warming some wine. I'll go and see where she is."

"No, please, Mistress Gwyneth, I'll go, and may I take this cloak and gown to dry with the others? There, it fits perfectly." Mona sounded satisfied, and Gwyneth could look again. Agnes had a towel over her hair, and her cheeks were beginning to turn pink.

"Mona, how about you? Don't you need something dry?" Gwyneth hoped she wasn't speaking out of turn. She needed some distraction.

Mona held the cloak,gown, and Agnes' boots at an arm's length. "I didn't try to drown myself, and my cloak is more suited to your unreliable climate. No, thank you, I shall do very well. The kitchens are at the other end of the hall?"

Gwyneth nodded, and Mona went out, leaving her alone with Agnes.

"Are you warm enough, my lady?" Gwyneth felt she had to say something. "Shall I fetch you a shawl?"

Agnes stretched her hands closer to the brazier. "I'm in heaven. I envy you this room, it is the most comfortable I have been in since I came to Wales."

Gwyneth couldn't stop her eyebrows rising. "But my lady, surely, in the castle . . ."

Agnes snorted, "Listen, in the castle my chamber is damp as a cellar, and the hangings have been up since Agincourt. No-one brings me dry logs, and it smells of mice. The cats are as idle as the servants."

She spoke carelessly, but Gwyneth stiffened. Perhaps, holding those delicate fingers to the blaze, she had no comprehension of how hard it was to keep rooms warm and dry. How you had to rise from the shelter of your bed in freezing winter dawns, and force yourself to light fires, sweep out mud, air bedding and wash linen, which ended up hanging in the kitchens because of the rain, and came back smoky and covered with smuts, so you might as well not have bothered. Then Agnes redeemed herself.

"I know. It would take a thousand servants to make that place habitable. And I have been spoiled by living too long in places where it doesn't rain all the time."

Gwyneth wanted to keep busy. She tipped some more charcoal into the brazier, and threw in a few sprigs of dried herbs for their scent. Where were Nyrees and Mona? Making the wine?

Agnes wriggled her toes luxuriously on the rug. Her hostess had lost that look of mockery, yet her face was still guarded. In some ways, she was like Mona: calm, practical and not inclined to fuss unnecessarily. She was being so serious, though, maybe she never laughed freely, or made up ridiculous stories to counteract the harshness of the world. She looked so pleasant when she smiled. Agnes didn't think.

"I haven't explained why we turned up uninvited," she plunged in. "Some bold thief stole Sir Giles' horse and mine while we were resting. My saddle, which I had especially made from the finest leather, is gone, and my brother and Sir Giles are even now tracking this blackguard to hang him this very night. I do not mind so much for the horses," she prattled on, "but I will happily see him hang for the saddle, and for rendering me soaked to the skin." She still wasn't thinking. "There was some talk of your kinsman, Madog, but of course he has gone to some island, so . . ." She saw Gwyneth's face. ". . . So that is naturally a foul slander, and perhaps it was some broken man, or outlaw from another place. I'm sorry," she adjusted her towel nervously in the tense silence, "I have insulted you and your house. How can I ask you to forgive me?"

She had seen the rage in Gwyneth's eyes, and was unaccountably scared.

Gwyneth forced a smile to her lips, and extended her hand. "It was no insult. Madog would be flattered to be suspected of such a wicked crime." She tried to pick a way out of this peril. "Madog likes to think he is a law unto himself, yet he is Sir Hubert's tenant, and not entirely careless of his duty. And, yes, he has gone to Holy Island. There is a hermit there, a most pious man, and it is our family's custom to take over food and blankets for him before the winter. Please, believe me, there is nothing to forgive."

She was so angry with Madog, she thought she would burst. He had drawn her into his play-acting without telling her why, and now she had compounded her guilt by lying to Agnes, who was not only a great lady, but also human, and amusing, and so beautiful she would make a stone ache. Lord help me, she thought, I almost want to see him caught and hanged, I am falling into a pit and there is no way out.

Chapter 7

Madog judged himself far from being caught and hung. There had been one bad moment when he was within yards of the main track, and two woodworkers, bundles of hazel rods on their shoulders, had appeared, walking along the track away from the ford. He guessed that they were delivering the rods to the old pigman whose isolated hovel lay further on in the direction of Llancaegy, and fortunately, they were too wrapped up against the weather and bowed down with their burdens to look away from the few muddy yards directly ahead of them. He had waited until they had plodded out of sight round the next bend, ghosted across the track in an instant, and reached the cave without seeing another soul. He had known about the cave in a bramble-covered inland cliff since he was a boy. It was small, but dry, its entrance was not easy to find, and it had come in very useful over the past two years. He kept a small store of fodder hanging in nets from the roof, and various comforts in a wooden chest tucked away on a ledge. The horses didn't seem to mind their new stable, especially after he had removed their saddles, rubbed them down, covered them in rough blankets and given them a feed, and although he couldn't risk a fire, he was warm enough in the spare dry hose he kept for such occasions, and a similar blanket. He had lit a couple of dips to give at least the illusion of warmth, and stretched out on a pile of straw to rest before nightfall and the final part of his little scheme. For several moments, he contemplated what he should do if Alexander failed to turn up at the old port. This eerie collection of broken down jetties clung to the coast eastwards of Abertroddi, which lay on the west bank of the Troddi estuary, and was said to be haunted by the ghosts of the men who had used it long ages ago, even before the days of the kings, when there were no Christians in Wales, and savage priests made human sacrifices in the woods. On winter nights in the alehouse, there was sure to be someone who knew someone else who had strayed down there after sundown in search of a runaway animal, and had heard hideous scream and moans in the dark, and had never been right in his wits since. It was true, however, that half the town suspected the other half of using the crumbling wharfs for business which needed to be kept from the eye of Sir Hubert's harbour-master, and so there was no harm in retelling stories which might keep busybodies away. Alexander had come into the old port before, and Madog had no fear than he would run aground or miss his bearings, yet sailing was an unpredictable business. The wind could be wrong, or he could have been delayed elsewhere, or blown half way to Ireland . . . Madog stopped worrying. If Alexander wasn't there, he would take the horses to a man he knew in Llancaegy. He could ride one of them, and would arrive well before dawn, and the animals would be over the hills by the time Hubert thought to start looking elsewhere. He smiled, and shut his eyes for a while.

Carrying a lighted dip, Cynan clomped up the stairs to the chamber he shared with his father. The day was fading, he was wet and had enough to worry about without being distracted by the wild rumours and gossip spreading down the valley. Sir Hubert's best horses had been stolen in the woods by a band of Scotch pirates, Hubert had sent men to fire Madog's stables, and Lady Agnes had been attacked by the thieves and was now dying in Gwyneth's chamber, which was inconsiderate, even for her. His most reliable shepherd had urged him to send to Abertroddi for the priest to give the unfortunate lady the last rites, while others had suggested that they should knock together a litter, and have her conveyed immediately to the castle, so that no-one could accuse Llewelyn's household of hastening her end.

Llewelyn was thumping around in the storeroom with Rhys, and wouldn't answer his shouted questions, so he was going to change his wet clothes, and try to extract some sense from Gwyneth, who could usually be depended upon not to exaggerate. The sound of female laughter coming through the partition suggested that no-one was dying at the moment. He stripped off his wet hose, and sat on his bed, rubbing his legs with a shirt from the floor. He was sure he'd left some hose hanging near the fireplace last week, they should be dry by now. He stood up, and lifted the taper. Light footsteps sounded on the staircase.

"Rhys," he said as the door opened, "what in God's name . . . Christ."

It was an unknown woman, balancing a tray of steaming cups on one arm as she closed the door. She gave a small cry, and the tray dipped alarmingly to one side. Cynan leapt across the room to steady the tray, then remembered his semi-nakedness, and tried to pull his top garments down with the hand holding the taper. Tallow dripped on his leg.

"Christ," he said with more force, and jumped a pace backwards.

The woman managed to save the tray.

"Forgive me, I didn't realise you were here."

She spoke in English, and her voice was unlike any Cynan had heard. Low and musical, it reminded him of wood pigeons or the murmur of the Troddi in summer. He held the taper upright, and picked up the shirt to hide his legs.

"No, no, it's me who's at fault, I am so sorry . . ." He had a horrible feeling that he was blushing like a boy. For the first time in his adult life, he wished he was a courtly gentleman, who would know the clever and right words for such circumstances.

"I am Cynan, this is my chamber," he said. He realised that this was inadequate, and almost rude. "I mean, I didn't expect . . . I was changing . . ." In the light of the taper, the woman looked like a dusky princess, escaped from one of Gwilym's stories.

"Sir." The woman made a half-curtsey. "I am Lady

Agnes serving woman. I must . . ." She pointed her chin towards the door in the partition.

"Of course." Cynan thought better of helping her with the second door. Lady Agnes might not be dying, but the sight of a crude half-clad Welshman would not be conducive to her health. He waited until the woman had passed through, then sat on his bed again, his head in his hands. Owain would laugh for a week if he heard about this.

Mona kept her face composed. She probably wouldn't entertain Lady Agnes with the meeting. She had heard from the castle servants that Llewelyn's heir, although highly regarded as an honest man, was a simple farmer compared with his brothers. She had known who he was at once, and cursed herself for not knocking on the chamber door. He would think she was little better than a shameless kitchen girl. He was broader than Owain and without that air of slippery cleverness, and, in spite of his confusion, Mona had come away with the impression of a steadiness she wasn't used to seeing in men, as well as of a fine pair of legs. From an early age, when her mother had managed to place her in the count's household, she had learned what selfish brutes men could be, and she was thankful that with maturity and her position at Lady Agnes' side, she did not have to use them to advance. Some were attractive, and pleasure was not to be denied, yet she knew that they were inherently unreliable, and it was best not to believe their promises. Well, this sturdy fellow was betrothed to one girl, and had another woman in Abertroddi to keep him warm until his marriage, so she should forget what she had seen, and tend to Lady Agnes, who seemed to be on the road to recovery, judging from the flush on her face.

Up in the hills, tempers were not improving. The trail had ended in a stretch of upland bog, and, cast the hounds as he might, Clegge knew in his bones that they would not pick it up again. If the day had been clear, they would surely have caught sight of two large horses being led into the bare wilderness, and the most clever thief could not command wind and rain to hide him. He suspected that they had been fooled, and was wrestling with his conscience. His duty was to tell Sir Hubert that they had been duped into rushing in the wrong direction, and that they should return to the clearing and start again, working through the woods to the main track. If the thief had used the highway, and even if he was now well on his way to Llancaegy, they would have more chance of tracing him there than they did in this godless wasteland. He gnawed his lip. Sir Hubert was not a bad master as masters went. His rages were not premeditated, and he was not needlessly cruel, yet it was unlikely that even his indulged huntsmen would escape his violence if he was told the truth, and Clegge saw no virtue in pain. He didn't want to be limping and aching for a week. He would make another cast, and perhaps the hounds would pick up the scent of a hare to occupy them until night fell in earnest, when hunger and defeat would prompt Sir Hubert to abandon the chase.

In the Abertroddi alehouse, Stamford stretched his legs to the fire with the easy conscience of a man who had performed all that was asked of him and more. At Madog's stables, he had found only Ellis, Madog's man, who professed to speak no English, sitting under the overhanging thatch mending harness. He had recognised Stamford, and with gestures and smiles had offered him beer and a free run to look around the establishment. Madog's old mare snickered contentedly in her sweet-smelling stall, a few ponies stood huddled against the rain in the paddocks, and his small house was empty. The fire was banked up, and there were no horses hiding on the sleeping platform at one end of the room or in the shadows underneath. If Stamford had been in less of a hurry, he might have wondered at the sailors' greasy cloaks hanging on a peg, but the road to Abertroddi was calling him, and he waved cheerily to Ellis before hurrying off. There were more encouraging signs at the port. Madog's horse was tied up at the smithy, and Sir Hubert's harbour-master broke off from tallying figures to take a turn with him and make enquiries. The harbour-master was a conscientious man, who did his best to balance between the letter of the law, which demanded Sir

Hubert's share of all the trade conducted through the harbour, and his burgeoning sympathy for the poor souls who had to risk their lives in such an unforgiving element to scrape a living. Although he did not take bribes as such, small gifts and the locals' polite tolerance meant that he raised enough income to satisfy Sir Hubert without having to poke his nose into every single bale, sack and barrel which passed from ship to shore and back again. His diligent enquiries bore fruit. The smith confirmed that Madog had left his horse early in the morning, and several people had seen the young man jump into a fishing vessel which had put out to sea, and not yet returned. One of these witnesses was the English master of a cog tied up to the pier, and thus an impeccable source. Having been assured by the harbour-master that Madog would be sent to him when he reappeared, Stamford was free to escape from the rain and enjoy the delights of Abertroddi's only place of entertainment. He called for more beer, and gave a winning smile to the girl who served him.

His lightness of mind was shared by the servants left in the clearing, who were making the most of their unaccustomed leisure. With the restraining presence of Fitzjohn and the ladies removed, they had fastened an awning more securely, coaxed another fire into life beneath it, and wrapped themselves in rugs to doze, throw dice and tell stories. Sir Hubert had said nothing to indicate that they should search the woods on their own account, so they let Luddy have a cup of wine to make up for that bastard Clegge's heavy-handedness, and waited patiently and virtuously for someone to come and tell them what they should do next.

"No, it's surely impossible." Gwyneth, her anger abating in this unexpected conversation, felt confident enough to contradict Lady Agnes.

Agnes was animated, and waved her small hands. "Think of ships, and all that can be carried in them. Men, horses, guns and trading goods. Yet the wind blows on their sails, and moves them forward in spite of their weight."

"It's not the same thing at all." Gwyneth took another fragrant mouthful. Nyrees had excelled herself with her long brewing in the kitchen, and Agnes was clearly feeling the benefit.

"Why not? You say the air won't support a man's body, yet if you throw a gun into the sea, it will sink. It doesn't on a ship, even though water will not support the weight of iron."

Gwyneth wasn't sure about this argument. "But no man has ever been able to fly, although some have tried." She was aware how lame this sounded.

"Aha," Agnes settled back, looking smug, "there must have been a time before men discovered how to build ships when they couldn't cross the seas. Now they can, and the same will happen with air."

Mona picked more debris from the gauze of Agnes' folorn headdress. "You must remember, though, that humans can swim. That proves that water will support a man's body, and air doesn't, whichever way you look at it."

Agnes threw up her hands. "Bah, you're both dull. Think of it another way. If you let a stream run over the grinding stone of a mill, the stone will not turn. If you use a mill-wheel, however, and all those clever cogs and machines, a little stream can turn the most enormous stone. In the same way, a machine could be used to blow people through the air."

"I see now," Gwyneth was grave. "I will go and ask the men to build you a mill-wheel attached to a boat with a sail. That way, you can fly to the castle, and prove us both wrong, then Sir Hubert can use the device to fly over all of Wales and find his thieves. If they build two, Cynan can use one to look for his sheep when they are in the hills."

Agnes laughed. "And what would Owain use it for?"

"That is best left unsaid. Spying on beautiful maidens would come into it. I think, for his own sake, he should be prevented from sharing in your invention."

"And I thought he was such a polite young man." Agnes didn't want to think about returning to the castle, especially in the wagon. It would be far more pleasant to stay here until the morning when the rain might have stopped, and the thief hung, if he had been caught. The room was so warm, that boxed bed looked as if it were the least draughty place on earth, and she wouldn't mind sharing it with Gwyneth, who was not so solemn after all. Her thoughts wandered unbidden, then she gave a little jerk when she realised where they were going. That was impossible, and not at all what she had intended. She wasn't an ignorant girl; she had lived in Venice where such matters were discussed by quite respectable women when they were closeted together with no men to eavesdrop, and she wasn't inexperienced. Her husband's attractive niece, who had stayed for a week on her journey between two convents, had seen to that. Agnes couldn't deny that she had enjoyed those langorous afternoons while the count took his rest, and her servants were banished on meaningless errands, yet she had not thought to repeat that lazy pleasure with anyone else. She couldn't consider a servant, she hadn't met anyone of her own rank so enticing, and, close as she was to Mona, she couldn't order her priceless companion to do something she had never shown any inclination of wanting. Gwyneth, on the other hand, had a firm mouth, and hands which she could easily imagine sliding round her waist and . . . Good Lord, the woman was Welsh and little more than a farmer's widow. She would put the whole ridiculous idea out of her head, it must have come from this peculiar brew she had drunk so much of. The faint rumble of wheels came through the walls, and, her heart sinking, she realised that Fitzjohn had returned, and she would have to leave.

The coming of night saw far more activity in the valley than was usual for dark autumnal hours. Fitzjohn sat beside the driver of the swaying waggon as it lumbered along to the castle, and congratulated himself. He had roused up the unwilling servants, and made them sweep out its damp interior, beat cushions and rugs, and light lanterns until it glowed like a fat lamp, and Lady Agnes had been so gracious that she hadn't once tapped on the canvas to complain about the risk of fire. Her normally sharp eyes had a hazy cast, and Fitzjohn put this down to the rigours of the day, and the indignity of having to wear a borrowed gown which even he could recognise had never been fashionable. She was far above him, yet loyal squires could follow their mistresses when they married old men, and, his mind strayed to the realms of the improbable, his father's illegitimacy did not necessarily have to be a permanent state. There was more than one great man whose ancestry had been tweaked to show hidden marriages coming to light, and dates of confinement to have been wrong, and his blood was as noble as that of any of the fools who squabbled around the crown like crows on a stricken lamb. He gave the driver an encouraging thump on the back and offered him a drink from his flask, as pleased as Stamford that he had avoided an arduous chase after thieves in the rain.

The end of the chase was, as Clegge had predicted, a foul-tempered retreat to the clearing. Forewarned by the noise, the servants jumped up from their lounging by the fire and stood, their faces attentive, with the remaining wine. It didn't save them from sundry kicks and blows, but, unlike their fellows, they were dry and rested, and they hadn't sent Sir Giles off on a false trail, so their silence on the straggling ride back to the castle was happier than Clegge's dread apprehension or Sir Hubert's lip-chewing mortification. Sir Giles was no longer even acknowledging him, he would have to hang someone as the thief, any peasant unwise enough to venture out tonight and cross his path would have to do. Lost in his torment, he knew nothing of the exhausted rider setting out on a fresh horse from Llancaegy.

Madog too, absorbed in his own cunning, was ignorant. He scouted round outside the cave, found nothing threatening, and led the horses out. The saddles, which alone would have been worth his trouble, lay bundled on the charger's back, and he followed the trail to the old port with barely a stumble. The air grew saltier, the sound of waves joined the spattering of rain through the trees, and he tied the horses to a branch before leaving the trail and crouching behind a ruined wall at the edge of the forest. The hairs on his neck stayed down, and he was certain he hadn't been betrayed. An inky swell slapped against the jetties, and, yes, he could make out the darker bulge of a squat ship moored to one of the piers, a dim light swinging at its masthead. He stood up and hooted like an owl. An answering hoot came from the pier, a shielded lantern flashed three times, and he walked without hurrying on to the finger tickling the sea. A torch flared, a figure came towards him, and he was smiling into Alexander's black-bearded face.

"You'll be wanting your wee poke back," the pirate said, the gold winking in his ear.

Madog clapped his shoulder, "And more. See what I found in the woods."

He drew Alexander back into the trees, and the pirate whistled.

"You'll no' take a straight swap for the ponies, then," he said. "How dangerous are they?"

"Very." Madog untied the halters. "I'll not deceive you, if I were you I'd sail to Scotland tomorrow to sell them. I'll take the ponies and a reasonable price for them, because of the risk."

"I've a feeling your idea of a reasonable price is no' mine. Hurry up, the tide is falling."

They haggled without rancour through the business of coaxing the ponies out of the ship and the horses on board, and Madog had hardly put the two clinking bags in his pouch before sailors were untying ropes and the ship was lurching away from the pier.

"God keep you, Madog," Alexander's voice came from the stern, "I'll be back after the winter if we're spared."

Madog waved his hand in farewell, and let a wave of triumph overcome his fatigue. He was the best horse thief in Wales, and it was short work to lead the ponies up the trail and settle them in the cave, then run back to the old port and leap into the fishing boat which had silently appeared at the end of the pier.

"Christ, Madog, you're cutting it fine," its master said. "We were nearly aground, you devil."

Madog could not stop laughing as he tipped a stream of coins into the fisherman's hand.

"You should have more faith, my son. How could you

founder, when I have been with a man of God all day?"

The fisherman crossed himself. "Lord protect us from your blasphemy. I pray for your mother's soul. I suppose you want us to come into Abertroddi with plenty of noise?"

Most of Abertroddi, including the harbour-master, heard the hearty singing in praise of St David moving along the harbour front. A torch in his hand, he put his head out of his door, and saw Madog, sea-water dripping from his cloak, leading three fishermen in exuberant song. Out of deference to this piety, he waited until they paused for breath before accosting the Welshman.

"Madog, Sir Hubert's man, Stamford, is in the alehouse. You are to report to him."

Madog bowed, and resumed his song, stopping only at the alehouse door where he waited, as if reluctant to defile his zeal with its profanity. The harbour-master saw two of the fishermen enter, and come out after a long interval with Stamford slumping between them. Madog cupped the huntsman's head with his hands, spoke at it for a while, then let the fishermen drag him back inside. The harbour-master considered. It might show Stamford in a worse light if he himself rode to the castle to tell Sir Hubert of Madog's return, yet the message had to be taken. He sucked his teeth. Perhaps a bucket of water over Stamford's head, and he would ride with him to make sure he arrived safely, and that Sir Hubert was given all the details. Stamford would thank him in the end for bringing him back to his duty, and it never did any harm to have people obliged to him. He strode to the alehouse, thinking of buckets.

Still singing inside, Madog retrieved his horse from the smithy, and set off on the final stage of his long day's journey. Not all his senses were dimmed by jubiliation, however, and he was no more than mildly startled when a tall shape appeared at his bridle by the ford.

"Climbs Trees," he said softly.

"Madog," the Vinlander replied equally quietly, and vaulted neatly up behind Madog. Madog thought he saw him smiling before he jumped, and that if his Welsh was better, he would have been quite voluble. As it was, he put his hands on Madog's shoulders, and spoke into his ear.

"Lady Gwyneth. You see. Must."

Madog's heart tightened, and a nagging anxiety slid like a cloud over his exhilaration.

Chapter 8

Gwyneth waited in her chamber, her hands trembling with rage. The sight of Climbs Trees and Sleeps At Noon gliding into the hall at suppertime had only increased her fury. If they were looking for food, it meant that Madog had not returned from his crimes, and even now, pitiless men might be hunting him down like a hare. She had pulled Climbs Trees to one side, and forgotten her residual fear of his outlandish face and expressionless eyes.

"Find Madog," she had said." Bring him here." She kept her voice quiet, and pointed to the floor in front of her. "Madog, here," she repeated.

Climbs Trees stared at her. She thought she saw contempt in his gaze, but she refused to drop her eyes, and the markings on his cheekbones twitched.

"Good," he said. "Yes, Lady Gwyneth." He almost bowed, before joining his companion, who had Glynis' silly head hovering at his shoulder.

"I'm going to put that girl in a convent," Gwyneth thought, and frowned at Cynan who was wiping his nose morosely on his sleeve.

LLewelyn took his place. "Madog has been on Holy Island all day," he said, "so if anyone says otherwise, they will find themselves without a roof this winter. And how was Lady Agnes, Gwyneth?"

Gwyneth answered politely, and wondered why Cynan looked as if his best rams had been eaten by wolves. Now he and Llewelyn were still sitting downstairs by the fire, Nyrees was already asleep on her mattress, and she was straining her ears for the sound of Madog's horse.

When the tap came on the small concealed door in the gable wall of her room, she didn't know if her sudden tears came from relief or anger. The hanging moved, and there was Madog, smelling of fish and horses and sweat. How like him to use the almost forgotten side entrance to the house, and come up the narrow staircase built into the thickness of the stone, rather than go through the hall and face his father and brother.

"Cousin," he began, throwing off his hood, his face weary and exultant.

Gwyneth threw a cup at him.

"You bastard idiot. What have you done? What have you made me do? I'll turn you over to Sir Hubert, and damn my own neck. You'll ruin us all, and what will it do to Llewelyn when you are hung, you fool. Do you think you are so clever and Hubert is so stupid? Jesus Christ, if your mother was alive . . ." She was trying to whisper. Nyrees snored on.

Madog took a step backwards, then two forwards, and put the cup down.

"Cousin, it was only horses. Everything went easily. Sir Hubert will never be able to prove anything, and even he cannot hang me without evidence. It is the law."

"The law. He is the law in these days, he can do as he pleases. And it is never only horses. Hubert will never forget the insult, he will hang some innocent man to please Sir Giles, and you will have blood on your hands. Lady Agnes as well, what will she think of our rough country, and if she should take a fever . . ." She stopped.

Madog raised his eyebrow. "It is not like you to be so kind to an Englishwoman." He paused, and his eyes, which always knew too much, narrowed. "Have a care, Gwyneth. She is not . . ."

"How dare you. Who are you to tell me to have a care? You foul-minded . . ."

Nyrees stirred and groaned. "Children," she said as she had done when they were tiny and fighting over a cake, "I'm fetching a stick now." Her snores resumed.

Madog smiled nastily. "You're only angry because you enjoyed it this morning. But don't fret, I'll respect your delicate conscience from now on. Shall I give your share of the profits to the poor?" He clinked the bags in his pouch.

Gwyneth wiped her cheeks. "What profits?"

Madog's smile became more superior. "My dear cousin, I'm not going to keep merchandise like that in my stables."

Gwyneth turned her back on him. "Get out. I swore to Lady Agnes that you couldn't possibly be the thief, and now you have made me a liar to her. Keep your money, I'm sick of your games."

She heard him sigh, and his voice changed. "Oh Gwyneth, please, don't take it so hard. Forgive me, I was tempted and I fell. I'll not risk it again. You know how much I owe you."

He might have been pretending to give way, but Gwyneth had to accept his olive branch. The world was too uncertain to allow a permanent rift between them. She faced him again.

"If you clear your name with Hubert, I'll take what I'm owed. It'll come in useful when I have to flee,and set myself up as a seamstress in a place where no-one knows my infamous connections."

"There'll be no need for that. A few more days like today, and you'll be able to buy out Hubert, and offer Lady Agnes your charity. Alright," he stopped Gwyneth's hand as it reached for something heavier to throw, "I'll present myself at the castle tomorrow, and throw myself on his lordship's mercy."

Gwyneth brushed him away. "The rumour is that Scotch marauders were the culprits. Perhaps that might help you."

Madog grinned normally. "And that's closer to the truth than you might think. Pleasant dreams, and I'll have my spare clothes back, if you please."

Gwyneth gave him the bundle from under the bed, and shoved him through the door. She hated it when he was right. Once or twice when they were children, she had worn his clothes so that they could play tricks on poor old Dafydd, and it was the truth that she had enjoyed her early morning ride to Abertroddi, and sneaking onto her uncle's ship. It was far easier to stride around in Madog's clothes than in the gown into which she changed in Gwilym's cabin, and she found herself wondering if her mother had felt the same secret pleasure on her journey back from France, in spite of her grief and the growing child within her. Riding unseen back to the house on a pony from the smithy had been far more tedious, and she had had an anxious wait in an abandoned charcoal-burners' shelter until Ellis appeared to take the pony from her, and she could dodge the servants to creep through the side entrance up to her chamber. Nyrees thought that she had been on some assignation with Ceinwen, and she didn't disabuse her, although all that had finished with Ceinwen's marriage. She snuffed out the tapers, shut herself away in her bed, and tried not to think of light hair and cool grey eyes.

Madog didn't need to present himself at the castle the next day. The horseman from Llancaegy pounded on Sir Hubert's gatehouse door while the knight was stoking his vile humour with cup after cup of wine, and, late though it was, demanded to be taken in to him.The news he brought drove all thoughts of vengeful hangings and beatings from Hubert's head, and shortly after dawn, Fitzjohn was being admitted into Llewelyn's house.

"Llewelyn, sir," he rushed forward and grabbed the older man's hand, "thank the Lord that we see this day. King Henry is restored, and the usurper York has fled. A messenger came last night from London with the news. Now our dark times are ended," he finished dramatically.

"Good God," Llewelyn said, and detached himself from the squire. "Are you sure?"

"It isn't a trick," Fitzjohn was earnest, "Sir Hubert knows the man who came. He's a faithful servant to the Beauforts, and wouldn't bring false news." He remembered his duty. "Sir Hubert is holding a thanksgiving mass tomorrow at noon, and he asks you and your household to come, and to dine with him afterwards." He was learning tact, and didn't repeat Hubert's exact words, which were, "We'll make a great show to impress the Welsh clods. After all, we may not have to live among them for much longer."

Of course, Lady Margery couldn't travel in her condition, and winter was fast approaching, but Sir Hubert was already thinking ahead to the spring. When his son was born, and the days began to lengthen, he would travel to England and those lost estates. With justice returned, York's supporters would be stripped of their possessions, and he would need to be at hand to be rewarded for his fidelity. He had already dropped several loud hints that it must have been fleeing Yorkists who had stolen the horses, and sent Fitzjohn off to broadcast the good tidings. Sir Giles, mollified by the thought that his host might be on the verge of a great fortune, graciously consented to stay for the mass. The countess was becoming an even more attractive prospect, and although her woman claimed that she was too exhausted by the previous day's events to receive him, he knew that he would have time enough to press his suit. It was suitably womanly of her to be weakened by the shock, she wasn't so strong after all, and a vinous feast the next day could only work to his advantage. Rubbing his hands, he went off with Hubert to fly the hawks, attended by a relieved Clegge, who had forgiven Stamford for being sick on his boots in the night, and excused him from supervising throwing bloody meat and intestines to the hounds.

"We're in clover, mate," he had said, tearing into a lump of fatty pork he had filched from the kitchens. "Back to proper hunting in England, and maybe with King Henry's court, God bless him. Sure you don't want some of this?"

Stamford had turned greener, and fled from the room, and Clegge had laughed his rare laugh.

The harbour-master, too, looked out at the port and saw, not the small wharf and squalid fisher cottages, but the bustling quays and mighty commercial buildings of London. He was experienced and trustworthy, and itched to inspect and tally complex cargoes, with different goods all taxed at different rates. Silks, spices, armour, guns, fine wines and spirits, handled by cultured merchants, not fish and wool and pig-iron, presented by gaunt-faced men who stared at him as if he was snatching food from their children's mouths. He would be there at the mass tomorrow, Sir Hubert would take him to one side, and he would tell him of the recommendations he was making to the King's officials in London port. A man who could persuade that rogue Gwilym to declare all his cargo would go far under the rightful king, and soon the miserable poverty of this place would be nothing but a memory to remind him to be grateful and charitable.

Very few of the Welsh were counting fortunes to be made. They would still have masters who taxed them, and whether Henry was king or not would make no difference to the chances of a mild winter, a good harvest next year, and plentiful fish in the sea. When Fitzjohn left, Llewelyn, whose status brought more complex concerns, sent messages to Gwilym and Madog requiring them to attend him that evening, then rode off to call on Gwyneth's father-in-law. Madog, shadowed by his Vinlanders, arrived in the late afternoon, having retrieved the two ponies from the cave and installed them in his stables. He found Cynan at a sheep pen, tally sticks in his hand. He didn't look too pleased to see Madog's guests.

"Don't be afraid," Madog said, "they're used to sheep now, they won't chase them into the river."

Cynan grunted, and watched as Climbs Trees leaned over the railings to scrutinise the animals, while Sleeps At Noon sidled off towards the house.

"So, what do you think?" Madog asked. "Are we rejoicing? Does father think Sir Hubert will rise to high office and take us with him?"

Cynan's blunt hand played with the sticks. "I doubt it. If you haven't addled his senses with worry over your thieving, he'll think what I think."

"Which is?" Madog didn't realise he sounded condescending.

"York may have fled for the moment, but he'll be back. He has been king, he has tasted power, and for all his faults, he is a strong man who knows how to govern. King Henry is more godly, yet he is simple, and would be confused by these sticks. Your friend here," he gestured to Climbs Trees, "would have more notion of what it is to be king. Henry's queen, though, will fight for him as she always has." He clenched the sticks together. "What I believe is, Sir Hubert will be foolish and show his hand. He will call out his following to support the king, there will be fighting, and whoever wins, I will most likely end up with my head stove in by an English axe." He dropped the sticks, and let them lie on the ground. His mouth twisted at Madog's expression. "I'm not a complete half-wit. Any peasant with ears in the valley could tell you the same thing."

Madog took his arm, "No, I haven't heard such a good explanation from anyone. But there's no reason why you should fight, you are . . ."

Cynan pulled his arm away. "There's every reason. I'm father's heir. His indentures bind him and his son to taking up arms with Sir Hubert. Owain can't be called on to fight, and you'll find an excuse to avoid it, so it'll be me. I have used a sword before, you know, I can hold it the right way round."

Only one of the many horses Madog had handled had ever kicked him, and he felt the same shocked hurt.

"What's made you think I have such a low opinion of you? And why do you say I'll find an excuse not to fight? I'm not a coward."

Cynan spat. "No, but you're a thief, and you don't care what damage you do. You think Sir Hubert's fair game. In any case, he would be crazy to let you near him. Father says he hates him and wants him ruined, but he would never shoot him in the back in the field."

Madog raised his fist, "You stupid sheep-molestor . . ."

Then he was lying in the mud, his head ringing. He felt his mouth, and saw blood on his fingers.

"Christ, I didn't see that coming." His voice sounded strange through his burst lip, and Cynan's boots were coming closer. He tensed himself for the kick he was due. A hand came down instead.

"Ah hell, I suppose I'd better let you get up and hit me back," Cynan said.

Madog pulled himself upright. "I'll forego that pleasure. You're quicker than I thought."

"And I still hit harder."

Madog checked that he hadn't lost any teeth. "You're

not in a very good mood today."

"I wanted to hit someone, and you were in the right place." He was the eldest, and had made his point.

Madog, spitting out blood, accepted his defeat. "I've never shot at a man to kill him, I wouldn't do that to Sir Hubert. Besides, he's more fun alive."

Cynan, who had never aimed his bow at another human, looked at his hands.

"I thought you killed some poachers years ago." He didn't want Madog's experience, although maybe he should. Only monks and clerks were squeamish.

Madog finished wiping his mouth. "I don't know where you heard that. I didn't kill them, I just winged them." He wondered if Cynan still wanted to hit someone. He shifted slightly to one side, and noticed that Climbs Trees was observing them with a total lack of concern. He tried to pick his words.

"Cynan, I'm not saying you couldn't fight if you had to. You've had more proper training than I have, and you're as strong as the next man. Think it over, though. You've got children, you're going to be married, you run the estate. I have no responsibilities. If it comes to it, let me go in your place. I promise I'll try to behave."

Cynan picked up his tally sticks. "Do you think I'm the coward?"

Madog lost patience. "Jesus Christ man, I'm offering you my support.What will happen to your girls if Henry's cause is lost, this estate goes, and you are dead in some ditch? At least if you're alive you'll be able to protect them, even if you have to live as a shepherd in the hills." He regretted his last words, but Cynan smiled.

"I should hit you more often, it makes you more likeable. This is all guesswork. Sir Hubert may not go to war, King Henry might hold on to the throne, and we might be standing here in ten years' time having the same argument. Do you think Climbs Trees would like to learn how to milk a cow?"

Madog recognised that this was Cynan being generous. "He might."

They walked off, and a stranger wouldn't have known that they had been fighting.

Gwyneth knew them better, however, and saw that Cynan was happier, and Madog more subdued. She got him on his own, as the family were gathering for supper.

"What happened to your face?"

"Cynan hit me." His lip was swelling, and his tongue was thick.

"Someone had to." She relented, "I'll ask Nyrees for one of her potions. You have to look presentable tomorrow. Why did he hit you? The . . . merchandise?"

He rolled his eyes. "That, and politics. He's not as dull as he makes out."

"At last you've realised. Tell everyone you got hit by the sail yesterday. It'll make your story more likely."

"There's my father and Owain to come yet. I'll be carried into Sir Hubert's dinner on a litter."

The dinner. Gwyneth had been telling herself all day that she was as empty-headed as Glynis. Momentous events had occurred in England, the household could be on the brink of advancement or ruin, and her only thought was that she would look like a peasant compared with the ladies in the castle. There was nothing she could do to make her other gown smarter or turn it into silk. Lady Agnes would be elegant and patronising, and it would be as if she hadn't sat covered in towels in her room, laughing like a friend . . . Gwilym was tapping her on the shoulder. His face was slightly red.

"I'm not saying you don't always look as you should, but would you like to have this for tomorrow? That castle will be draughty as hell."

She unwrapped the creased linen, and pulled out the finest woollen shawl she had ever seen. It slipped through her fingers in an indigo stream, softer than the down in a prince's pillow.

Gwilym cut off her thanks. "If you make sure Cynan is wearing a clean shirt tomorrow, it'll be worth it. The sooner that boy gets married the better, he gets all of the pleasure and none of the nagging with his piece in Abertroddi."

Llewelyn was of the same opinion. The pessimistic voices round the table rose and fell, and Cynan grew morose again as his future was decided.

"Angharad is growing fast," Llewelyn said. "There's no sense in you coming with me if Hubert calls in those indentures, which I wish I'd never signed. Madog will do just as well. Then at least when we are killed and Hubert is attainted, you can move to Glyn's estate. You'll be able to watch out for Owain and Gwyneth."

Gwilym, who could sail out of trouble any time he pleased, laughed. "Christ, you'd all better cheer up for tomorrow. We're meant to be overjoyed at the restoration of the king, and the return of Christian justice. Owain will be Lord Chancellor, and Madog will be Master of the King's Horse."

"Yes, and every animal will have its proper owner shouting for compensation," Cynan said.

"Don't be rude about your brother who's going to die for you," Llewelyn said. "He went to Holy Island, which by rights you should have done, and got hurt for his trouble."

Cynan opened his mouth, and Madog kicked him under the table. "I don't intend to die," he said. "I'll be on a very fast horse."

"Suppose we'd better find some armour for you. More expense." Llewelyn started on another source of annoyance.

Gwyneth retreated upstairs. Tomorrow looked set to be an ordeal, and she would be surprised if they survived it without anyone else getting thumped.

Chapter 9

Owain waited nervously in the castle chapel for his family to arrive. His father and Gwyneth could generally be trusted to behave, but his brothers and Gwilym were another matter. He wouldn't put it past Cynan to appear smelling of sheep dung, or Madog and Gwilym to exchange loud remarks in Welsh about the state of the chapel and of Lady Margery, who was sitting on one of the few chairs looking like the mythical sea-beast Gwilym talked about. She had never been a small woman, and now she dwarfed Lady Agnes who sat next to her, sneezing with the dust which rose into the air when anybody moved. The chapel was hardly ever used, and a day of haphazard sweeping had made very little impression on years of neglect. Someone had taken a brush to the pillars and walls, and now flakes of paint hovered in the damp air and settled like snow on shoulders and hats. Two of Hubert's dogs were prowling around, their tails wagging at the scent of rats, ignoring Hubert's sporadic shouts and whistles, while a clutch of bristling cats spied on them from a windowsill, and the crowd of milling servants and attendants aimed surreptitious kicks at their flanks. Behind Agnes' chair, Luddy and the potboy stood in a startled daze, their eyes fixed desperately on Mona. Luddy had feared the worst when a groom had dragged him from the morning mucking out, and dumped him on his knees in the stable yard. He was going to be tortured again because of the day before yesterday, and this time they might use branding irons or spikes or hang him up by his thumbs until he was crippled like his uncle who had once stolen a calf, and whose twisted body was only kept from starvation by his mother's generosity . . . He had looked up, and seen the foreign woman crooking a finger at him.

"Come with me," she had said, and had led him at a brisk pace to a back scullery. Morgan, the potboy, was already there, looking with suspicion at a tub of hot water in the middle of the room.

"Right," she had said." Take your clothes off and get in."

Luddy's mouth had fallen open, and his feet had frozen to the floor. This was the meaning of the warnings his father had whispered to him before he had been sent to the castle, and now he was going to be interfered with in a way his father had not exactly specified. Morgan was obviously thinking the same thing, and made a bolt for the door. The woman said something that sounded like swearing in a foreign language, and blocked his way.

"You have to wash." She made scrubbing gestures with her hands, "No-one's going to touch you."

She went out, and when she came back, carrying a pile of clothes and accompanied by a Welsh maid with an armful of shoes, the water had turned grey, and quite a lot of it was on the floor. She had smiled, and Luddy had suddenly stopped being scared.

"Good. Now try these on for size."

The Welsh maid had explained while they experimented with garments that were far superior to anything either of them had ever owned.

"Lady Agnes wants you for her servants, God help her. Just try to keep clean, be quiet, do everything Mistress Mona here tells you, and watch what Sir Hubert's pages do. They can be little shites, and they'll tease you, but don't let them provoke you. If you're caught fighting them, you'll be lucky to get your old places back. That's better, I suppose, you're both a bit more presentable. Though I'll have to comb your hair."

That was torture enough for them, until, tired of their squealing, Mona pulled some scissors from her belt. Shorn like lambs, they followed her and the maid into the previously forbidden hall, up staircases and along a passage to the incontrovertible proof of their elevation, an odd little corner furnished with a chest and a mattress covered with blankets.

The maid looked at them more kindly. "Keep the spare clothes in the chest, and you can take the mattress down to the hall at night if it's too cold for you here. But you must bring it back in the morning, and be ready for when Mistress Mona wants you. Be good, now."

They nodded dumbly, and Luddy pinched his arm through his smooth sleeve to check he was awake. He wrapped himself in an old horse rug in the hay at night, and Morgan curled up in the ashes of the fire, which accounted for the singe marks on his legs, and the peculiar texture of his hair, even after the scissors. Neither of them had ever needed a chest before, or the comb Mistress Mona was giving them, or the lessons which swiftly followed. How to bow, how to hold a cup, how to stand like a statue and not pick your nose. It was all too much to remember, and, standing in the chapel, Luddy almost wished he was back in the stables. But then Owain caught his eye and winked at him, and he felt a rush of excitement. Who knew where this could lead? He might be taught how to fight with a sword and play the viol and even to read, and he might never have to shovel dung again, or be shouted at by that bastard Clegge. He lifted his chin, and ignored the nudges and sniggers of Sir Hubert's spotty knobbly kneed pages.

Agnes, delighted with her new servants, let Margery's chattter flow in through one ear and out of the other, and thought about better clothes for them. The hand-me-downs they were wearing were clean, but they were not particularly well-fitting or colours she would have chosen, and it was too late in the year to send off for some quality cloth. Perhaps that sailor Gwilym would have a suitable bale in his cargo; she would have to ask Gwyneth. Her heart bumped. Gwyneth might not come, and she would have to endure a horrible dinner, with Sir Giles leering at her on one side, and Margery eating everything in sight on the other. There was more movement behind her, and she sneezed again. Owain sighed with relief. His family had come in, and they all looked sober, from Llewelyn leading the way in a fur-trimmed gown, through Gwilym with his beard brushed and

Gwyneth on his arm, to Cynan and Madog, both uncommonly smart and relaxed with each other. Owain peered more closely. Madog had been hit in the mouth recently, judging from his swollen lip, and, his eyes down and his expression pious, he was giving no sign that he could hear the murmurs which followed him down the chapel. Cynan, on the other hand, was gazing anxiously around, until he saw what he wanted and gave a little bow and a self-conscious grin. Curious, Owain strained to see who he was greeting, and turned his surprised squeak into a manly cough when he saw Agnes' woman incline her head. You old goat, he thought, save some women for the rest of us, and he began to squeeze through the knots of people to reach his brothers and interrogate them. He missed the moment when Agnes turned and saw Gwyneth, and he didn't notice that Gwyneth was still red when he reached her.

"What happened to Madog's face?" he asked her under his breath.

"Cynan hit him", she said, fussing with her shawl in a way that was quite unlike her, "but don't say anything because they've made up, and no-one else needs to know."

"Cynan is a man of secrets," Owain said. He expected her to rise to the bait, but her face was blank.

"I daresay," she said, and moved aside to let him pass.

Frowning slightly, he went to Madog's shoulder. "What's this I hear . . ."

A quavering sentence in Latin interrupted him. The priest had appeared, and the mass had started.

Sir Hubert would have done better to have summoned the fiery little priest up from Abertroddi, rather than to have trusted his own confessor to take the mass. The castle priest was an old man whose services were rarely called upon except to hear Sir Hubert's perfunctory confessions, and to soothe Lady Margery in times of crisis. He spent most of his days supposedly saying prayers for Sir Hugh's soul, and hours of sleeping in a kneeling position in a corner of the chapel had not honed his preaching skills. He gabbled his way, with only a few misplaced bells, through a service ingrained in his memory, and then began to address his flock. After a few sentences, it was clear to everyone who understood English that he had not grasped the significance of the occasion, and that he was lost in an obscure homily on the permitted degrees of marriage. Sir Hubert, his wife, and Sir Giles, who had the advantage of being seated, gave up and shut their eyes, Agnes recited in her head all the poetry she knew, and everyone else shuffled, coughed, and began whispering to their neighbours or drifting to the door with the thought of dinner gaining ground in their minds. Emboldened by the fact that the dogs had settled, jaws lolling, at Hubert's feet, two of the cats crept down from the windowsill and stalked across the front of the altar to search for crumbs. The dogs' ears pricked up, their eyes opened, and four dense bundles of fur, claws, teeth and muscle hurled themselves spitting and howling into the body of the church. The priest stepped backwards, tripped on his robes and fell, a woman screamed and the wave of disrespectful laughter started to rise.

"God save King Henry." The huge cry that could only have come from a sailor's lungs boomed to the roof and dislodged another century's worth of dust. Sensing that an end was near, the congregation took up the cry, and Sir Hubert was able to lead his wife and guest out of the chapel with a semblance of dignity.

Her face aching, Gwyneth walked behind Llewelyn to the hall. Even he had had to hold on to Gwilym for support once Hubert had exited, and a stray tear still glistened on his cheek. She had no great hopes of the dinner; Owain was never very complimentary about Hubert's table, but her family's mood had lifted, and they were ready to stay for as long as politeness demanded. Hubert's steward, however, viewed their entrance with despair. He knew intellectually that he was meant to have an iron grasp of the niceties of social rank, and he could manage well enough with the type of visitor whom Hubert usually received, yet his mind had gone blank when he was told that Llewelyn and his household were to be invited. On the one hand, Llewelyn was a landowner, and so should be placed somewhere close to his host.

On the other hand, he was Welsh, and should be a long way down the table, among those who were lucky enough to eat in the hall. His compromise had involved moving the salt cellar, and intending Llewelyn to sit in line with it, with his family ranked below him, so that he would neither be insulted nor given ideas above his station. His plan was already unravelling, since Lady Agnes had made the astonishing statement that she wanted "Mistress" Gwyneth to sit next to her, so that they could converse, and it was out of the question for the girl to sit above her guardian, and equally out of the question for Llewelyn to sit next to Bartlett or Sir Giles. Hadn't anyone whispered into Lady Agnes' ear that etiquette made her request impossible? It made you think that she had learned nothing while she had been in Wales. By the time everyone had sat down, he might as well not have bothered with his laborious diagrams, and anyone who knew anything would have been shocked. Llewelyn, with his sons by him, was only one place away from Bartlett, and only his piratical cousin, who had plonked himself next to that slimy harbour-master was anywhere near his proper seat. Sir Giles looked put out, Sir Hubert looked somewhat wild, and the steward mentally threw up his hands and signalled for the wine to start flowing. Heavy drinking might obliterate the nobility's sense that all was not quite as it should be.

Torn between embarrassment and amusement, and aware of Luddy's anxious breathing down her neck, Gwyneth was able to study Bartlett as she sat. He had looked through her once with his supercilious eyes, and then resumed his low-pitched conversation with Sir Giles. Gwyneth couldn't tell what he was saying, but he was oozing self-satisfaction, as if he had single-handedly put Henry back on the throne. His ink-stained fingers played with his cup and he smiled, and for a moment, a shiver of fear ran down her back.

"Have you brought your flying machine?" Agnes asked. "I think it'll come in useful very soon."

"How do you think we came here?" Gwyneth answered, and felt herself shivering again, this time from the delight in the grey eyes which rested openly on her face. She tried to keep thinking of normal things through the blur which followed. A succession of ambitious dishes which all tasted of fat, the rising tide of voices as the drink came faster, Agnes making her laugh with her imitation of the priest. Beans, she would think of beans, and whether they had enough. She wanted to be at home, not in this inadequately cleaned hall among people with whom she didn't belong, and she wanted the dinner to go on all night, so she could stay next to Agnes. There was a crash and dangerous laughter at the end of the hall, where someone had tripped up a laden servant. Agnes turned.

"I think we should go to my room." She cursed herself. That had sounded almost desperate, and Gwyneth was blushing. It was hardly possible that she could see the images in her mind Agnes was doing her best to ignore.

"I mean," she summoned Mona with a wave, "it's becoming slightly too noisy for me in here. Besides, you can tell me if my walls are in a fit state to be painted like yours." She thought that was inspired, they could talk about plaster, Mona would be there with her little pages, and she would not be tempted to do anything unladylike.

"You fool," Gwyneth told herself, "how could you even entertain the thought that Lady Agnes meant anything different?"

Luddy and Morgan fell over themselves to open doors and light the way through gloomy passages, and she was in a large room, hung with fading tapestries and scarcely warmed by a smouldering fire. She saw Luddy view the contents of the log basket with contempt, and whisper something to Mona.

"The kitchen?" she murmured back. "That's interesting. Show me." She raised her voice, "We're off to steal some dry wood. Is that all right?"

Agnes nodded. The three went out. Carrying a taper, Agnes moved to a wall, and lifted a hanging.

"You see? Is it too damp? Come and touch." Her voice was higher than usual.

Gwyneth put her palm to the clammy surface. "I'm

afraid so. If you took the tapestry down, and maybe had a brazier in here, but it's winter, and perhaps you'll have to wait . . ." Her heart sounded like the hooves of Madog's horse.

"Jesus Christ," Agnes said. She was so close, Gwyneth could feel her breathing and the warmth of her hand holding the fabric, and see the flecks in her eyes. Agnes put the taper down, and the hanging flopped back into place.

"Gwyneth."

Small hands were on Gwyneth's shoulders, her head bent down, and the shock of pleasure ran through her breasts and between her legs. Narrow hips moulded into hers, soft skin melted beneath her lips, and clever fingers were moving like flames under her shawl.

"Ah Christ," Agnes said again, "you are like a queen." Her mouth came back to Gwyneth's. There was a bang at the door.

"Lady Agnes? Forgive me, Mistress Gwyneth's family are leaving." Fitzjohn only had to put his head round, and he would see them.

"Stay." Agnes kept her hands where they were.

"How can I? You know I can't." Gwyneth shut her eyes, and made herself step away. "Thank you, sir. I'm coming." She readjusted the shawl, and walked out, hardly seeing Mona and the boys returning in triumph with their loads of wood, or Sir Giles weaving unsteadily behind them.

"What shall I do?" Agnes leant back on her pillows, her eyes almost accusing Mona.

Mona sighed. The day had already been far too long, and she could have done without having to persuade Sir Giles that her mistress really didn't want to entertain him in private. Thank goodness Fitzjohn had been there to guide him back to the hall, and was still lying across the foot of Luddy and Morgan's mattress, apparently awake and the least drunk male in the castle. If Sir Giles managed to slip past this self-appointed guardian, Mona would be tempted to stab him with her scissors out of sheer spite, rather than to protect a woman who did nothing but present her with problems.

"It's not my place to advise you, my lady . . ." The pillow thumping on her head cut her off.

"Yes it is. Do you want me to write and ask my mother? I'll shrivel up and die before her reply comes back, and it'll only tell me to say a thousand Hail Marys and abstain from carnal thoughts."

"That might be a good idea." She let Agnes hit her again. Although they had never spoken openly about it, she was perfectly aware that Agnes and her husband's niece had not spent those afternoons embroidering cushions. If that was where Agnes' tastes lay, she shouldn't be surprised if she had been captivated by this widow, whose charms revealed themselves slowly, like a view opening up when the clouds lifted. She frowned. She liked what she had seen of Gwyneth, and she didn't strike her either as a giddy girl or a deceitful manipulator. Who knew, though, what resentments these defeated people still nursed under their polite faces, and what secret ill-will they bore towards their English lords. She had to keep Agnes from scandal and disgrace, and put aside the ignoble thought that a connection between her mistress and Gwyneth might lead to more meetings with Cynan.

"My lady, I can't stop you being close with her, if that is what you really want and she is willing, and you know I'll do whatever you ask to help you. Only . . ." She didn't know how blunt to be.

"Only what?" For a moment, Mona saw Agnes' resemblance to Hubert.

"Only, can you trust her? She is Welsh, you are an English noblewoman, she might have other motives."

"I don't believe that. If she wanted to use me, she would have jumped at the chance to stay today. And friendship between women isn't a sin, even if they are of different rank."

Mona could see that she was set on her course, and wanted confirmation, not advice, let alone a theological discussion. She used the argument she'd been avoiding.

"Perhaps she didn't stay because she's not really interested in you. I have to tell you what the gossip is . . ."

With their sore heads and resumed misgivings about the future, the men of Llewelyn's household didn't see much wrong with Gwyneth over the next few days. If they noticed, they put her sharper than usual tongue and early bedtimes down to indigestion, and to the general worry which pervaded the valley. Cynan was immersed in his own gloom, and Madog, who might have sensed the truth, spent his time in his own establishment with his guests. With no-one to confide in, Gwyneth wrestled with her thoughts in silence. It was a drunken kiss from someone who was used to having her every whim indulged, and was far removed from the affection she had known with women before. She should ignore it, Agnes was just bored and looking for diversion, and she wasn't a servant to be bullied into pleasing her. Both of them could find more suitable objects for their desire, and avoid an entanglement which would only bring hideous complications. She wouldn't waste any more hours reliving the feel of that body in her arms, or imagining that Agnes wanted her as an equal, but would direct her mind, like the men, to the likely consequences of the events far away in England. Although she didn't usually let Llewelyn's habit of imagining the worst affect her, she made herself take his warnings more seriously. Of course life was precarious, even for a moderately comfortable widow like herself. Bad harvests affected everyone, you could become ill, and the spectre of lawlessness and chaos had always hovered at the edge of her life. She had never properly imagined, however, what it would be like not to have Llewelyn or his descendants as lords of the Troddi valley, and not to wake up every day to the same solid walls and familiar hills. All these had continued while individual souls like Heledd and Hwyel had come and gone, and the thought of strangers sitting in the hall, while she wandered, empty and dispossessed like a wild animal, was too terrifying to bear. This was her place in the world, and her heart would break if she had to leave it, even if she ended up shut in the safety of a convent, or lodged in a corner of her father-in-law's household, making herself useful by helping Angharad with Cynan's children and sewing their shirts. It would be easier to abandon respectability, and become a brewer in some distant town, and she began thinking of the practicality of journeys, and how best to carry money. A week after Hubert's dinner, she was counting coins for the seventh time, when Rhys tapped on her door.

"Lady Gwyneth, the Englishwoman is coming up the track. She's not smiling."

The neat silver piles toppled, and when she stood up, her legs trembled like the bare branches outside in the chill November wind.

Chapter 10

Rhys was right. Agnes, looking as if she had eaten a clump of rhubarb, swept into the hall with Mona and Fitzjohn in her wake." Mistress Gwyneth," she said formally, "I would consider it a kindness if you would show me your herb garden. Fitzjohn, please see to the horses. Mona, come with us." After a delay while Gwyneth fetched a cloak, she swept out again, and Fitzjohn found himself rolling his eyes at Rhys. He wasn't sure what was happening to him these days. Before Lady Agnes had come along, he had been in a fog, avoiding anything that smacked of effort. He was a younger son, his inheritance was minimal, and he was stuck among these shifty natives whose ways were incomprehensible to him, so he might as well drift along as easily as possible. A tiny voice of common sense told him that he didn't have a chance with Lady Agnes, yet his fascination with her opened doors he had never known existed. There was more to the world than the ramshackle household of a provincial knight, and he didn't have to settle for the blinkered life of his fellows. To his surprise, he was discovering that he enjoyed instructing those two awe-struck boys Lady Agnes had taken on, that Mona made him laugh, and that learning a few words of Welsh wasn't as hard as he had imagined. Perhaps Lady Agnes would travel abroad again, he would go with her and would end up as a famous commander, with the latest ordnance in his hands. He beckoned to Rhys to follow him, and started telling him the horses' names.

The atmosphere was less amiable in the herb garden. It wasn't raining, but it was cold, and Gwyneth could tell that there was no real enthusiasm behind Agnes' frigid questions about which herbs did well in this soil and climate. It wasn't hard to see that Agnes was very angry, and, accustomed to dealing with irrational rages, Gwyneth waited to see if she would come to the point.

"There is something else I must mention," Agnes said, when they had exhausted the beneficial properties of feverfew.

"Yes, my lady?" Gwyneth could play at being humble, even though her own temper was beginning to bubble.

"I believe, from talking to Master Hooper, that this household has been allowed to fall behind in its duties."

Mona hung back, and pretended to be interested in the dead leaves.

"Forgive me," Gwyneth said, "I'm not sure what you mean." She wanted to slap that prim little face.

"Honey. I believe that this estate owes my brother a third of its honey every year, and I can find no record that this has ever been done. My brother is over-generous to you."

Gwyneth clenched a fist under her cloak. Thank heaven she had listened to Llewelyn and Owain's many discussions about the legal history of Llewelyn's possessions.

"My lady, I think you'll find that that particular obligation ceased when Grufydd was granted these lands in his own right. It only applied when the estate was a tenancy of Sir Hugh's." She decided to rub salt in the wound. "You may want to study our documents to clear the matter up in your own mind. Of course, if the castle is short of honey, we would be more than happy to help you out." Chew on that, you little madam, she thought spitefully.

Agnes flushed. "You peasant's leavings. I can break you. I can have you turned out and forced to whore in the streets, while your men go barefoot in the snow."

"And I'm sure the thought brings you great happiness, my lady."

Agnes turned on her, and Gwyneth saw the tears of fury and something else in her eyes.

"Why is she better than me? Are you so low that you prefer a farmer's wife? Is it because I am English? Do you think you can play with me and then throw me away?"

Gwyneth leant backwards. "What? Who? It wasn't me who . . ."

Agnes stamped her foot. "Be quiet. That woman you visit, did you think I wouldn't find out? How stupid do you think I am?"

Gwyneth had never known anything like this burst of joy. "Oh Lady Agnes, she's married and pregnant. Yes she was my friend, but I don't visit her for that any more."

They were staring at each other, and the ground was spinning under Gwyneth's feet.

"How can I be sure?" Agnes' voice was quite different.

Gwyneth started to smile, "You'll have to trust me."

"It's hard."

"It's hard for me. There's so much separating us."

"Not so much that we cannot cross."

Gwyneth knew she was blushing, and kicked at a tuft of grass. "So. Will you ask me to come to the castle to look at your wall again?"

Agnes was pinker. "I think I feel a chill or a fever coming on. It would probably be very bad for my health to ride back to the castle today. Maybe I'll be forced to spend the night here."

Gwyneth's body felt as if she had jumped into her brazier. "Are you sure?"

Agnes touched her arm. "Do you want to wait any longer? Do you want me to explode right here like one of Fitzjohn's guns?"

Mona heard the laughter and smiled grimly. At least she had her decent cloak if she was banished to a hayloft for the night.

It wasn't hard to arrange. Fitzjohn was sent back to the castle with instructions to return the next day, and Nyrees gave Gwyneth one sharp look then pronounced that the Englishwoman needed peace and quiet, and she and that strange woman of hers would sleep with Glynis, who needed an eye keeping on her anyway. Going through the pretence of installing Agnes in the box bed and fetching potions from the kitchens, Mona could see that her mistress and Gwyneth, for all their outward propriety, were moving together in some separate world, and that nothing, short of an armed attack on the house, would stop them. Although Gwyneth didn't linger in the hall that evening, it was still an age for both of them before she closed the door firmly behind her, and stood by the bed.

"Now I'm really in pain," Agnes said, her legs moving under the covers.

"We can't have that," Gwyneth's voice was thick. "Shall I ask Nyrees for some more medicine?"

The sheet slid down from Agnes' shoulders. "No. Only your hand will do."

Gwyneth shut them in, before her groans could be heard downstairs.

"You've done this before," Agnes said, unable to stop her circling and stroking, even though a cockerel was already crowing down in the yard.

Gwyneth smiled. This was as far removed from her fun with Ceinwen as the sea was from a fish-pond.

"The winter nights are long here. There's only so much sewing one can do. And so have you. Otherwise you wouldn't have known to . . ."

Agnes giggled. "My husband's niece. She was a good teacher. Although this is better, you're ten times more beautiful and not a nun, which probably makes it not even a minor sin."

"A nun?" Gwyneth raised herself on one elbow, "Have you no shame at all?"

"Not after tonight. Can you paint portraits?"

Gwyneth stopped kissing her. "Why? Do you want me to paint one now?"

"Certainly not." Agnes hips stirred, and the inexhaustible desire welled up in Gwyneth's belly. "Only I can't keep coming here and falling ill. If you came to the castle to paint my portrait, though, it could take a long time and lots of visits. Then there's the herb garden to advise me on, Welsh remedies to teach me, the list is endless . . . don't stop."

"I'm not going to. I'm trying to distract you from thinking up any more work for me."

Alexander knew that he was not a good Christian, but then very few of the Black Douglases, to whom he belonged, could be counted as such. At the age when high-born children were still being cuddled by their nurses, his widower father had taken him to sea, figuring that it was never too early for him to start learning his trade. Somehow he had survived the first few months of terror, damp and perpetual motion, and before he reached his teens he could steer and reef, was almost impervious to pain, and thought no more about swinging through the rigging in a gale than most landsmen did about climbing stairs. The sea was his ally and his adversary, a force which could never be mastered, but which sometimes allowed itself to be used, and other times brushed puny sailors aside, like a man swatting a fly. Alexander had absorbed its capricious cruelty, and, having an intimate acquaintance with death, he had no great respect for the lives of those on shore who set themselves up against him.Yet he had a moral code of sorts, and kept within its limits, just as the sea never trespassed inland to swallow up farmers ploughing their fields or minding their beasts on the hills. He had never forgotten his first proper sea-battle, when his father had sunk an English ship full of soldiers, and had launched a couple of boats to row towards the foundering vessel. He had seen his father's men pluck the English sailors from the sea, and heard them shout to the enemy captain to jump to safety from the wreckage, while all the time beating desperate soldiers from their gunwales.

"There's nay luck in killing sailors," his father had explained. "The sea takes enough of us, and it could be our turn tomorrow. Anyway," he had smiled, "with nay sailors there'd be nay trade, and where would that leave us?"

It was from long habit, therefore, that Alexander picked up the Welsh fishermen clinging to a rock amidst the splintered planks of their boat. He had sailed with the horses to a small lawless port in England, turned in a handsome profit, and then set off for home. Although he knew that the wind was about to change from the prevailing friendly south-westerlies, even he was caught out by the ferocity of the unprecedented east wind which blew him back under bare poles towards the coast of North Wales. Luckily, the wind died and veered round to the south before it sent him all the way to Abertroddi, yet he was still anxious to leave these waters, and a part of him cursed the fishermen for their stupidity in letting themselves be caught out when they should have known better. He would never have rowed to their harbour with these grateful wretches either, if he hadn't recognised their home port and remembered the willing woman who ran the alehouse. Temptation had won. He had money in his pocket, his ship had survived the blow unscathed, he was full of life and deserved a reward for his kindness. Two hours at the most, then he would be back on board and slipping over the horizon before dusk. His rowers, mollified by the beer donated by the fishermen, hunkered down on the quayside and watched him roll to the alehouse with only a few ribald and envious comments, happily ignorant that the primitive village belonged to Sir Giles, and that sharp, hungry eyes were watching their captain's progress.

Later, Alexander made himself grateful that his most pressing business had been concluded, and he was lying back drinking beer and eating a pie when the armed men burst through the door and started hitting him. Silence had always been his preferred policy, and he kept his mouth shut through the blows, the screamed swear words, and the dreadful moment when they tied a rope round his wrists, and dragged him down the stairs, out of the door and along the track leading to God knew where. Through the blood running into his eyes, he was also grateful to note that his men were rowing like hell out of the harbour, and that no-one seemed to be following them. It was all he had to be grateful for during the rest of the day and the night which followed. He was kicked and pulled for several uncomfortable miles to the gatehouse of a small yet impressively thick-walled castle, with a fine collection of banners flying from the battlements. Any lingering hopes he had that this was some minor quarrel he had forgotten about vanished when he was jostled into a hall and flung down on the flagstones at the feet of a corpulent gentleman wearing an expensive gown and a look of skewed satisfaction.

"My fishermen say you are Scotch? Are you Alexander the pirate?" A spray of spittle accompanied the question.

Alexander said nothing, and let his body soak up the shocks from the man's whip.

"I think you are." The man was panting. "I think you stole my horse. We will give you a taste of our hospitality here, and then send you on to enjoy Sir Hubert's before you are hung. Strip him."

Gwyneth was leaving the castle well after dark as the rider clattered up to the hall. She was wishing she could stay, and spend all night behind the curtains, thinking of new ways to please Agnes and laughing in their passion, but the decencies had to be observed. Poor Mona, who had spent most of the day teaching Luddy and Morgan their ABC's in a chilly corner, had looked at the end of her patience, and Gwyneth knew that Agnes was stretching Fitzjohn's goodwill by requiring him to escort her home in the dank night. Still, she was throbbing pleasantly from Agnes lips, and she could return in a few days time when absence had made them both hungrier . . .

"Hey Fitzjohn," the rider blocked their way, "good news. We've caught your horse thief."

A great spasm of fear made her sway in the saddle.

"Oh yes?" Fitzjohn recognised Sir Giles's squire brimming with importance, and he affected boredom.

"Yes. A piratical Scotchman with a big black beard and probably not much skin left by now. We're sending him over here to Sir Hubert tomorrow as a present, and you can have the honour of hanging him, if he's still alive. He'll have told us how he did it by then."

"What joy," Fitzjohn murmured. "Come, Mistress Gwyneth, the fate of some unlucky sailor needn't concern you. Our thief indeed," he snorted as they moved out of earshot, "they've most likely picked up some stranger who was silly enough to come into their port, and pinned it on him. How's your uncle these days? How long does he plan to stay here?"

Gwyneth tried to hide her dry mouth. "For the winter, I think. Have you been on board his ship yet? He likes entertaining visitors, but don't believe half his stories. I was a grown woman before I realised that he didn't have a mermaid wife in his cabin."

She had made him laugh, and worked hard to keep him amused until they could see the lights of Llewelyn's house, and he was persuaded that she would now be safe, and he could rush home to insult Sir Giles's messenger. As soon as he was trotting off down the track, she kicked her fat pony. Time was running out, and Cynan jumped up from the fire at her crashing entrance, so different from her usual unobtrusive movements.

"What?" He was gripping the poker like a sword. Llewelyn was staying at Glyn's estate for a few nights, and Cynan thought it would just be his luck for a disaster to happen while he was meant to be in charge.

Gwyneth forgot that he wasn't normally privy to her secrets. "We must find Madog. Now. Get your horse."

"Alexander won't talk." Madog's face was stubborn under the livid mark on his cheekbone. Gwyneth hadn't bothered to try to hold Cynan back from lunging at his brother again.

"How can you be so sure?" Cynan looked bitterly at him. "Who knows what they are doing to him. Would you be strong enough to keep quiet if they had caught you? And he doesn't owe you anything."

Madog kept quiet. It would be useless to attempt to explain, even to this new Cynan, what kind of man Alexander was, the depths of his stubborness, and the nature of his odd bond with Gwilym, who years ago had first captured his ship and then conveyed him in some style to a neutral port. Alexander had returned the compliment within a twelvemonth, and regarded Gwilym's family as almost equal to his own clan.

The fire showed unaccustomed lines of authority round Cynan's mouth. "You're the best shot in Wales. If he hasn't talked yet, your only hope is to lie in wait and shoot him while they're bringing him to Hubert. Then he can't betray you." He smiled, not very pleasantly. "I'll do it myself if you won't. I'll not see them hang you and break father's heart."

There was a faint rasping from the corner, where Climbs Trees was sharpening a knife. Gwyneth had no idea if he and Sleeps At Noon grasped what was going on, but she could have sworn that he had laughed when Cynan had swung at Madog. She remembered the fright of seeing them for the first time, and Gwilym saying how they fought their enemies without mercy. Her mind was suddenly very clear.

"All right, you two." She could have been Heledd, breaking up an argument over a game of checkers. "No-one's going to shoot Alexander unless they absolutely have to. Madog, can you make Climbs Trees and Sleeps At Noon understand you?"

The harbour-master sat at an upstairs window, feeling strangely disgruntled. The activity on Gwilym's ship had started shortly after dawn, when a cart carrying the great gun had rumbled down from the smithy. With a huge amount of swearing and shouting and sailors pulling ropes, the gun had been heaved on board, closely followed by Cynan and Madog, who had leapt on to the deck and stood next to Gwilym as the vessel was warped out into the bay. Now they were testing the gun, and if the harbour-master squinted, he could see the two young men laughing and clapping their hands to their ears as the boom echoed back from the hills, making his windows rattle and distracting him from his ledgers.

"Noisy bastards," he said to his frightened dog, and refused to admit to himself that he wanted to be out there on the choppy water, putting a match to the fiery powder, instead of adding up figures like a thrifty housewife.He inked in a wrong total, and ruined his quill in crossing it out with unnecessary force. God, he wasn't sure if he could stand another winter in this place.

Tied to a broken down nag, Alexander wasn't sure if he could stand another hour. He was used to blows from falling spars and loose ropes, and to being cold, so Sir Giles' whip and a night in a vile stone cell with water running down the walls would not normally have broken his spirit. Someone's enthusiastic kicking, however, had landed several times on the ribs he had cracked in the summer, and he was frightened. He had been frightened at his involuntary scream when he tried to pull on the clothes they had thrown in for him in the morning, at his groans when he was manhandled on to this rotten horse, and he was still frightened at the likelihood of more of the same treatment when they reached their destination. His breath whistled through his nostrils as he kept his lips shut to stop the squeals of a wounded animal and pleas for mercy pouring out. He was going to end his life choking and pissing at the end of a rope, not fighting like a man or sinking at last into the sea's embrace as it reclaimed its own, and all because he had followed his prick. Worse still, he would be among strangers, with no-one who knew him to play a lament, or hold his eyes as he travelled on his final journey, and if the priests were right, this agony was merely a foretaste of his eternal lot. He lifted his chin. Rot the lot of them. He was a Douglas and would spit in their fat English faces, and know that the black hearts of his clan would remember this insult down to the last generation. When they heard the news, the old women in the hills would cast their spells over their bubbling pots and the young men would hone their blades, and Sir Giles' and Hubert's families would be cursed with still-born babies, blighted fortunes and unexplained stabbings in dark alleyways. His horse stumbled, and in his cold sweat, he didn't hear the beginnings of an inexplicable noise coming from the hillside above them. The captain of the heavily armed party heard it, and at first thought it was someone chopping at a tree or banging in a post in the woods which lay about a mile ahead of them, marking the border of Sir Hubert's lands. Then he realised that the sound was behind them. He looked round, and saw nothing but the track winding across the open ground. The low pounding stopped, and he shrugged and glanced at his grey-faced prisoner. He could see that the Scotchman was in no shape to make a bid for freedom, and he was looking forward to the reward Sir Hubert would lavish on them for bringing him in, and being generous enough to let him be hung where he had committed his crimes. The sound started up in front of them again, and one of the horses whinnied. It wasn't the chop of an axe or the bang of a hammer, but more an irregular drumming, and it was getting louder, building up into a pattern and now it was on both sides of them, weaving faster like the heartbeat of a man running from danger . . . His men were lifting their heads, and the youngest foot soldier was staring about him, his eyes wide. The drumming stopped once more. Jesus Christ, he couldn't see a fucking thing. The hillside was bare apart from a few rocks and scattered trees, maybe he should send a couple of the older horsemen out to investigate.

"Hob, Francis . . ."

The young soldier whimpered, and grabbed at his sword. The drumming was close, and now someone was singing, except that it wasn't a song, it was the howling of a vengeful ghost, the horses were dancing and shying, and Hob had an arrow in his throat, and the foot soldiers were running, and a dark shape was coming at him. He screamed at what he saw until a knife silenced him. Alexander screamed as well. He had died in the saddle, and his pain had followed him into hell, where two of the devil's helpers had seized his bridle and were pulling his horse towards the woods. He heard his high-pitched wailing, and blacked out before he could see the human figure waiting for him in the trees.

Chapter 11

Madog sat in his peaceful house, watching Climbs Trees and Sleeps At Noon eat their way tidily through a mountain of bread and a pot of stew. He still felt a bit sick. Not as sick as Gwyneth, who, green-faced and wobbling, had thrown his clothes at him in her room a while earlier, but sick enough to find that bread had stuck in his throat, and that all he could swallow was beer. The two Vinlanders had washed the ash from their faces and chests, burned their makeshift drums out in the yard, and put their clothes back on, yet he could never see them as completely amiable and perhaps slightly child-like again. Tucked behind the trees, he hadn't had a clear view of the fight, but he had heard the terrible noises, and seen the black dots scatter and fall. Then there had been Alexander, looking as if he had shouted himself to death, his face covered in bruises and cuts. When they had finally got him to the hut in the hills, and seen what lay under the shirt sticking to his skin, Madog had panicked, and forced down his throat far too much of the precious poppy juice Gwilym had given him. He hadn't been able to bear Alexander's cries once he had recovered consciousness, or the tortured look in his eyes. If the men who were already combing the woods and shoreline made it up to the hills and found him soon, they could hang him and he wouldn't know anything about it. Madog sighed. He was used to being master in his world. There wasn't a horse he couldn't handle nor a wild animal he couldn't track, he was sitting on a fortune which could buy half the forests in Wales if he wanted, and he had secretly relished showing off his skills to his guests. Now these strangers to Christian mercy had demonstrated that they could vanish on a bare hill-side and kill easily with unfamiliar weapons. He didn't think they had fully understood his instructions to scare off the armed guard, not slaughter most of them. His family were no more dependable either. Cynan was changing from a simple-minded sheep lover into an authority almost as shrewd and bad-tempered as their father, and he could no longer imagine marrying Gwyneth, whom he had always assumed would be a cheerful and long-suffering companion. He sighed again, and Climbs Trees looked up at him and smiled.

"You not soldier," he said.

Madog wondered if this was an insult. "No," he agreed. There was no point in arguing, having seen what their idea of a soldier was.

Climbs Trees nodded. "No. You different. You . . ." he consulted with Sleeps At Noon, and said a word in his own language.

"What?" Madog thought he would do their dirty work for them. "Coward? Like a woman?"

Climbs Trees' eyes went to amused slits. "No, like . . . doctor priest."

"Oh." Madog wasn't sure what he meant.

Climbs Trees carried on smiling, "Gwyneth good man."

"Woman," Madog corrected automatically.

Sleeps At Noon gave what sounded like a slightly vulgar laugh. "Dress like man, live like man." He saw Madog's confused frown, and made a placating gesture, "Good, bugger it."

Climbs Trees reached out and briefly touched Madog's hand. He was no longer smiling. "Madog, this small country." He cupped his palms, "Small trees, small hills, small people." He looked directly into Madog's eyes, and Madog felt his heart contract. "Our country big." Climbs Trees arms spread out, "You big man." His hand went to Madog's neck, and before Madog fully realised what he was doing, he had pulled out the ancient wolf's tooth from where it had hung since he had been given it.

"See," Climbs Trees said, and pulled something out of his own shirt.

Madog started. The dips gave him enough light to see

the tooth in Climbs Trees' hand, so like his own that they might have come from the same animal. He had a blinding vision of a world held together by spiralling threads.

"How?" His voice was hoarse.

"We are brothers," Climbs Trees was entirely calm. "We have found you."

An owl hooted loudly from the track where Ellis was keeping watch, and the two Vinlanders moved like linked shadows.

Cursing monotonously under his breath, Fitzjohn rode slowly up the track, accompanied by Stamford and a bunch of the least active castle men-at-arms who, lacking mounts, were finding the walk in the dark hard going. It was typical that the message had come from Gwilym only this morning, saying that the gun was ready, and that he would be welcome to come aboard in three days time when they gave it a proper firing at sea, after a preliminary trial that day. He had been so pleased, he hadn't really taken any notice of Sir Giles' squire, or registered his growing unease as the day wore on with no sign of his Scotch pirate. Then when the white-faced messenger from Llancaegy thundered into the castle with a garbled tale of a massacre by a horde of demons, and of survivors so frightened they could barely speak beyond calling for their mothers, the chaos had been too great for him to sneer at the unfortunate young man. After a sensible captain had suggested that the demons might be the pirate's crew, Clegge and the most experienced soldiers had been detailed to search the shoreline for a sighting of their ship, while Fitzjohn had been given the unenviable task of looking through Welsh houses and barns in case anyone had given shelter to these devils. At least Sir Hubert, showing a hitherto concealed intelligent restraint, had squashed the squire's hysterical demand that he should torch every building belonging to a Welshman.

"I'm not making my tenants homeless for a crime which wasn't even committed on my land," he had said, with an emphasis on the "my". His expression had been suitably grim, yet Fitzjohn wondered at the hint of humour in his eyes when he turned from the squire. Of course, no-one in the castle would say it out loud, but if letting a thief steal your guest's horse was careless and bad-mannered, losing the suspect when you had him under armed guard was even more reprehensible. Even so, Fitzjohn had not enjoyed disturbing the sullen peasantry and poking through smelly outhouses, and he had dreaded facing Llewelyn with the news that he was ordered to search his property. His invitation to the ship would be revoked, and he would be seen as an overbearing Englishman, which, for some reason, disturbed him. It was a stroke of luck, therefore, that Llewelyn had not been at home, and it had been his eldest son, a cloak thrown over his shirt, who had listened to his stumbling explanation when the nightwatchman let them in.

"Heavens above," he had said, his face sombre, "we don't want to be murdered in our beds by any Scotch pirates. We'd all better look."

Servants had been called, squeaking maids roused from their slumbers, and a blushing Fitzjohn had declined Mistress Gwyneth's offer to look under her bed. They had found nothing, and at Fitzjohn's attempt to say good night in Welsh, Llewelyn's son had suddenly smiled.

"Don't forget my brother's house up the valley. If we've been woken up, I think he should be made to suffer too. And tell him that he still owes me for that hay."

So now Fitzjohn was hammering wearily at yet another door, with his men supposedly fanned out in case anyone made a break for the trees, although he suspected that they would bolt if so much as a cat leapt out at them. It felt more remote up here, the Troddi sounded louder, and when an owl shrieked in the woods, one of the men-at-arms jumped and dropped his rusty halberd. Fitzjohn swore at him, and was lifting his fist to the door when it opened.

"Go away," the shadowy figure inside said. "If you're riding out to fight for King Henry tonight, I'm not interested."

Fitzjohn wondered if this was a joke, and stuck out his bottom lip. He wasn't going to have his useless search party laughing at him behind his back.

"I'm coming in," he said. "We're looking for the Scotch pirate. Stamford, take the men and search the stables. Properly."

He barged through the door, and heard it shut behind him. The single dip burning above the fireplace flickered. A little voice told him that he was now trapped, and he held on to his sword hilt as he turned to face the figure. He had seen Madog at the Mass in the castle, but never so close, and he was alone with the subject of all those rumours. Madog could shoot down a bird from a mile away, he could tame the wildest horse without a whip or spurs, he had killed thirty men when he was a boy, he was a magician from the old tales who could turn himself into a hawk or a salmon, he was a thief. Fitzjohn saw a man not much older than himself, skinnier than his eldest brother and stronger than Owain, whom Fitzjohn was coming to realise was sharp-tongued and amusing under his clerkly exterior. He was still dressed in spite of the late hour, and had a knife at his belt. Fitzjohn made himself meet the dark eyes, hooded in the dim light, and not flinch at their bored contempt.

"Look then," Madog said abruptly, and sat down on a bench by the fire.

Fitzjohn looked. The house was small and hardly better than a peasant's hut, with its rough cut timbers and floor of hard packed earth. It was clean, though, with tools and harnesses ranged neatly on the wall by the door, and the floor had been swept. Without asking permission, Fitzjohn took the dip and inspected the barrels and sacks standing in order under the sleeping platform. Beans, beer, flour, oats, onions hanging in nets, some cheeses on a shelf, nothing out of the ordinary. Gritting his teeth and ignoring the householder, Fitzjohn climbed the ladder to the platform. Madog didn't even have a bed, only a pile of mattresses and blankets with a couple of chests for storage, and there was no-one crouching under the covers or clinging to the roof beams. He came back down the ladder, and his nose twitched. There was a faint scent he couldn't identify, hovering above the smells of the banked-up fire, the tallow dip, recent cooking, leather and sweat. It was sharp, almost like the musk of a dog-fox . . .

"Found anything?" the voice from the fireplace startled him.

"You know I haven't," he said, and gripped his sword again.

Madog's teeth showed, and then his voice changed. "Are you Fitzjohn?"

"Yes, what of it?" He was fed up with this charade. If the Scotch pirate was going to jump out of some hidden cupboard and stab him, he wished he would get it over and done with.

Madog's tone was more polite. "You're kind enough to ride my relative, Gwyneth, home from the castle. I hear you don't bully Luddy and his friend, and you've dared to be alone in here. If I were Sir Hubert, I'd be grateful for such a squire."

Fitzjohn let his bad temper with the day overcome his prudence. "And if I were Sir Hubert, I'd have you watched day and night. You're up to something, for all you're sitting there like one of the Wise Virgins."

Madog laughed. "But you're not Sir Hubert. Would you like some beer?"

Fitzjohn shook his head and put down the dip. "No. I'd only drink with you if you were safely in a cell. I'll join my men, they won't have found anything either."

He stamped out, the laughter following him to the stables and his unhappy band of warriors.

Up in the hills, Alexander didn't know if he was dead or alive. He was sailing his ship on an ocean so smooth and clear that when he looked over the rail, he could see the mermaids combing their hair on the sandy seabed, and the shoals of golden fishes darting around them. The rail of his ship was solid gold as well, and the mast and spars, and his sails were the finest spun silk. That was all as it should be, and he smiled as the ship left the water and began to float up a wide silver highway into the sky. His father was waving at him, and grinning as he had never done in life, and he had a beautiful woman on his arm. Then the ship hit a rock, a foul wind from nowhere blew it back, and the sea had become grey and stormy. Painted demons leered and reached for him, he tried to shout, he fell and was carried away on a horse with white wings which spoke to him in a strange language. The limping man in whose hut he lay heard the rattling breaths, and thought about digging a grave in the morning. He should have shot Madog in the back when he'd had the chance, and saved the world and himself a lifetime of trouble.

"I expect you've heard the news," Agnes said when Gwyneth visited her two days later, and they had recovered enough to talk.

"About the wild pirate and the devils?" Gwyneth tried to keep her voice light. "Of course. We had Fitzjohn searching our kitchens for them in the dead of night." She didn't want to talk about this, or to be reminded that the deaths of Sir Giles' men were at least partly on her conscience. She wanted to feel that small body arching beneath her one more time, before they had to call Mona.

"No!" Agnes had pulled away from her, "That's terrible. I didn't realise . . ."

Gwyneth reached for her, "What do you expect? We're Welsh, and anyway . . ." Christ, it had been on the tip of her tongue to say that Madog wasn't blameless. How long could she keep these secrets, when she ached to share everything, not just rushed pleasure with this gift of a woman?

"Anyway what?" Agnes' eyes were narrowed. Gwyneth wondered briefly why she, and not Hubert, seemed to have inherited Sir Hugh's brains.

"Anyway nothing."

It wasn't enough. Agnes sat up, and started feeling for her clothes.

"Gwyneth, I'm not stupid." She spoke crisply. "Mona's Welsh is getting quite good, and she tells me everything. I know the gossip about Madog and those foreign sailors from the ship he has staying with him. And I tell you," her words became less crisp, "I don't care. I don't care if they're Turks, like people say they are, or Spanish Moors or two-headed man-apes from Muscovy. I probably don't care now if Madog did steal those horses, I don't want to know, I don't want to know about the pirate and it's too bad if you're insulted by my suggesting that you know about them. All I care about," she was almost angry now, "is not upsetting this. We've only got a short time, and it'll be even shorter if Madog causes trouble between our families." She paused. "Maybe I am stupid. I trust you, and believed you when you defended Madog and said that you didn't see your friend any more. Perhaps you were lying, and all the time you're laughing at this ridiculous Englishwoman . . ." She looked round, and saw that Gwyneth wasn't laughing. "Oh."

Gwyneth was shocked. She hadn't cried like this since the day they had buried Heledd.

"I can't tell you about Madog, and I didn't lie about Ceinwen, and why have we only got a short time?" She couldn't believe that Agnes' words could hurt so much.

Agnes' face crumpled. "My love," she had never used such an endearment before, "what future can we have? If Henry keeps the throne, Hubert will go back to England, and how could I stay here without him? If Edward of York returns, we may lose this estate, and I will have to beg a safe passage to join my mother in her convent. Or else marry some Yorkist knight."

"Do you want to do that?" Gwyneth choked on the question.

"About as much as you'd want to come with me as my servant, and hand me over to my husband every bedtime."

Their eyes widened, and they clutched each other.

"Oh God," Agnes' voice was faint through her kisses, "let's not talk about it. Hurry, you'll have to do some painting today."

While Gwyneth and Agnes found comfort behind the curtains, Alexander sat in the winter sunshine waiting for Madog or one of his henchmen to call. He had realised that he was still alive when he had woken up with a disgusting taste in his mouth to see Madog peering anxiously at him.

"Ya wee bastard," he had croaked, "wha' the fuck happened?"

"You nearly died," Madog hadn't expected gratitude. "My friends rescued you, then I gave you too much medicine."

"Your friends?"

Madog had waved to two shapes behind him, and Alexander had squealed like a girl. He had seen most things, but never such mutilated beings. Madog had seemed impatient.

"It's only what they do. Look, they've given me a pattern." He rolled up his sleeve, and Alexander managed to focus on the fresh black lines.

"Does it hurt?"

"A bit," the young man admitted, "but not as much as a whipping. How're your cuts?"

Alexander squinted down, and saw the bandages round his body. "I cannae feel much. Who was that fat shite?"

Madog smiled. "Sir Giles. I used to work for him. It was his horse I sold you. The big one."

Alexander marshalled his thoughts. "You were afraid I'd talk?"

"Not me. My brother was, though. He was going to shoot you."

"Family's a gey wonderful thing. Where's my ship?"

Madog raised an eyebrow, "I was hoping you would tell me. So we can get you back to it."

"Och Christ, this is nae a rescue, it's a bloody shambles. Help me up, I need a piss."

That had been yesterday, and today he could walk unaided, his head was clearer, and if he sat still, the pain all over his body almost disappeared. The little Welshman didn't understand a word he said, but still brought him food and some vile herbal concoction, and showed him the cleverly concealed hiding place under the floor at the far end of his hut, where a few sheep were partitioned in as shelter for them and warmth for the humans. Alexander grasped from his gestures that he was to lie in this odourous hole if any English were spotted, and he prayed that none would appear. He had been through enough recently, and if his crew had sailed back to Scotland, as he guessed they would have done if they had any sense, he could be stuck here for months with a host he couldn't talk to.

The man limped round the side of the hut, and sat next to him.

"Madog," he said, and pointed to the hillside opposite them.

Alexander's sailor eyes were sharp, yet he hadn't seen the tiny movement in the distance.

The man gave a bark of laughter, nudged Alexander with his shoulder, and started pulling off his clumsy boot.

"Madog," he repeated, and showed Alexander the old scar above his ankle. He mimed drawing a bow and the whistling of an arrow, and clutched his leg in mock agony.

"Why aren't I surprised?" Alexander said out loud, smiling agreeably. "You're all bloody touched, shooting each other left, right and centre."

"Doesn't he mind that you shot him?" he asked Madog after he had trotted up to the hut and embraced his former enemy.

"Not any more, he thinks it's a privilege." Madog wasn't going to explain his long search for the poachers after he had ceased to be Sir Giles' servant, the awkward apologies, the recompense in gold and the useful sharing of knowledge. "Don't worry, he still hates Sir Giles more than he hated me, and with any luck, you won't be here much longer. I've a plan to find you a passage for Scotland."

"I'm nae going with Gwilym. He'd wreck us before we hit open water."

"That would be too obvious. Even Hubert's ninny of a harbour-master would have his ship searched if he left now. No, I think the Salt Fair is your best opportunity. Here's a razor, start shaving off that horrible beard."

Chapter 12

The origins of the Abertroddi Salt Fair were lost in the mists of antiquity, and nowadays salt was not even traded, apart from a symbolic exchange at the start of the day. The timing of the fair was decided every preceding spring by a cabal of older inhabitants, who were fully conversant with phases of the moon, tides and dubious Saints' anniversaries, and since it always fell some time in Advent, successive priests had wisely concluded that it was essentially a Christian event. It would have been a foolhardy English overlord who tried to interfere with this one day of relief from the onset of winter, and Sir Hubert carried on the custom of sending down waggon loads of free beer and bread for the populace. The local children looked forward to the one night of the year they would go to sleep free from the nagging of never quite satisfied hunger, and everyone with anything to trade turned up to haggle, look for husbands and wives, and settle old scores. If the weather had been kind, the fair attracted travelling craftsmen and pickpockets, and sometimes even a few larger vessels anxious to off-load the tail-end of cargoes no-one else wanted. This year, such a battered English cog rolled into the harbour two days before the fair, and immediately rumours started that it carried pepper, saffron, cloves and fine wine, all being sold for an exiled Yorkist at a knock down price. The sight of a messenger leaving the ship, borrowing a pony from the smithy and riding off to the castle only heightened speculation, while the master, shooing premature customers away from his gangplank, did nothing to dispel these rumours, and looked forward to finally disposing of the water-damaged spices he had acquired earlier in the year. On the next day, traders and farmers from outlying districts straggled into Abertroddi, the ale-house girls began to get busier, and, in keeping with the general indulgence in bad habits, Owain was listening at a door in the castle. He knew that it would be painful for him if he was caught, but the sight of Bartlett and Sir Hubert slipping into Hubert's private chamber had been too tempting to resist, especially for a man who resented having to hear of his younger brother's exploits at second hand. No-one from the family had seen fit to inform him personally of whether or not Madog had been involved in the Scotchman's escape, and he wanted to regain his position as Llewelyn's source of reliable information. In his own way, he could be as quiet as Madog, he never sneezed at crucial moments, and he could adjust his hearing to the low rumble of voices beyond the thick oak as skilfully as Madog could isolate a deer's footfall in the forest. He listened, and forgot his petty annoyances.

"Do you think that Somerset is unaware that you have never supported the king in the field?" Bartlett's voice managed to be both silky and threatening.

"I still don't see why it has to be me who does this," Hubert sounded mulish. "Somerset knows I will come out if he asks me directly as a kinsman."

"He is asking you. Do you want those estates back? You have to do more than turn up and wave your sword about in the background." The voice became more unpleasant, "Or is it too much for you, to ride through Wales and remind everyone of their duty should York return? Somerset will need to know who he can count on, and you are the man we have chosen to do this for him. This is a great opportunity for you."

"Surely there are others more able than me." Hubert seemed less than enthusiastic about his great opportunity.

Bartlett snorted. "That is undeniable. Nevertheless, you are available. You can set out after Christmas if the roads are passable, and take your following and that villain Llewelyn with you. That'll keep him and his sons from mischief."

Hubert was silent for a while, no doubt contemplating the discomfort and inconvenience of leading a cumbersome armed party through Wales in the winter. Owain was considering Bartlett's casual bandying about of Somerset's name. He spoke of the king's powerful magnate, who was abroad as far as anyone knew, as if he were his equal, and he spoke with him every day.

"And if I don't?" Hubert said finally. "If I don't force my men to leave their homes in the winter? If I wait until Somerset himself orders me?"

Bartlett laughed, and Owain's heart knocked. "Don't be a fool. I have that marriage certificate, remember, and the priest's statement, which prove that Sir Hugh married my grandmother long before he was forced into a bigamous alliance with Simon's mother. My father was his legitimate heir, not that waster Simon, and I was born in wedlock, which means that I, not you, should be master in this place."

Hubert, perhaps wounded by the reference to his father, was more coherent than Owain had ever heard him.

"You have two worthless pieces of paper that anyone could have forged. Your grandmother was some kitchen girl who seduced Sir Hugh and every other man in his household. My grandmother was a lady. God knows why Sir Hugh acknowledged your father as his bastard, and then let you leech off his fortune. I am half-minded to turn you out, so you can take your little papers to any grasping lawyer you choose, and see how far you get in the courts with them."

Owain's mouth fell open. He and his father had speculated for many enjoyable hours over why Hubert tolerated Bartlett, and now he had the answer. He would find an excuse to ride over and tell him the good news as soon as the two men had finished their argument.

Bartlett laughed again. "I can see you doing that. What would it do to your wife, in her delicate condition, to know that her husband's father was the product of bigamy? She is at the time when many woman go into labour and give birth to tiny mannikins not yet fully formed. You forget," his voice was silkier still, "Somerset trusts me. He is more powerful than you can imagine. He can tell the courts what to think if he decides he would be better served by me as Sir Hugh's heir, than by a coward who would rather sit with his wife than fight for his king."

Owain expected to hear blows, and the violent explosion of Hubert's rage. Instead, he heard Hubert's voice, low and clear, and full of unexpected dignity.

"I will overlook your insults, since you are a low-bred dog. I will leave this castle only when my wife has come to term, and she and the baby are safe. If I find you have spoken to her of this, or caused her any distress, I will whip you myself, and drive you from here without a penny in your pocket. I'll fight for the king, and find out what I can for Somerset, but I'll do it because it is right, not because I am afraid of a fusty errand-boy with ideas above his station. Good day, sir."

Rapid footsteps approached the door, and Owain fled down the passage.

He stood in the courtyard, breathing in the cold air, forgetting to be entertained by the sight of Fitzjohn giving his acolytes another deportment lesson. Disliking Sir Hubert was second nature to him. The Englishman was arrogant and stupid, and it required constant vigilance to prevent him from crushing the few liberties left to the Welsh. It had never occurred before to Owain that he might be concerned with anything but his own skin, that he had a care for those beneath him, or even have any feeling, beyond cursory duty, towards his wife. The realisation that he had a worthy streak dimmed Owain's triumph at discovering Bartlett's secret, and although he would tell Llewelyn, it would not be with the relish he had anticipated. He made to return inside, when there was movement at the gatehouse, and into the courtyard rode his elder brother, followed by a retinue of four stout farm-hands armed with cudgels. Cynan did not usually travel in such state, and Owain also noticed that he seemed unusually well-groomed, and that his chin was set at a determined angle. Owain went to take his bridle.

"Is the whole family moving in here?" He hadn't been

told properly either why Gwyneth was spending so much time at the castle, and what lay behind this absurd portrait painting. She exchanged meaningless pleasantries with him if she saw him on her visits, and he could only think that Llewelyn had let her in on some little plot he was hatching, and was using her as another spy in Hubert's household.

Cynan looked down his nose. "I have a message for Lady Agnes."

"How grand. You won't have time to talk to me then."

Owain saw Cynan hesitate, and lose some of his air of dignified superiority, and relented. "I'll find some wine for us, if you can stop after you've delivered it. I haven't had a decent conversation for weeks."

Cynan dismounted. "Yes, thanks." He looked around a little desperately. "How does one go about . . . ?"

Owain obliged. "I'll find a steward to send a girl to her woman." He looped the bridle round a post, "Into the hall here."

Cynan straightened his clothes and followed him inside. He didn't think he wanted to stay chatting if his mission was unsuccessful, and he still couldn't believe that he had confided in Gwyneth the previous evening. True, in the matter of Madog's pirate, she had shown herself to be more than an efficient housewife, but that had been an emergency, and he had been a little unnerved by her readiness to adopt an unnatural costume and behave in ways he was sure his mother would never have sanctioned. He was sure, too, that Heledd would never have approved of the way Gwyneth had coached him in what to say. A door at the end of the hall opened, his heart beat faster and he forgot his opening line.

"Sir?" Mona was curtseying in front of him, and she was as lovely as he remembered.

"Mistress Mona," he wrenched off his hat, and tried to bow as he had been taught.

Owain coughed by his side. "I'll see to your men," he said, and went out, smiling unnecessarily.

Cynan gathered his wits. "Mistress Mona, please forgive my boldness. I am aware that it is not for a person of my rank to offer an invitation to you, let alone to your noble lady, and I am prepared to be refused. However," this was the part he didn't understand, "Gwyneth would like to convey to her ladyship that today would be a suitable opportunity to have her wall hangings taken down, with all that means for her accommodations." He dared to look into her eyes, and thought he saw a gleam of comprehension. He pressed on before he forgot the rest. "My father will be Gwilym's guest on his ship for the next two nights." Ostensibly this was so Llewelyn could keep an eye on the Salt Fair, and make sure that none of his workers got into trouble, although Cynan suspected he wanted to be led astray by Gwilym away from his household's beady gaze. "Do not take his absence as a sign that protection will be lacking. I have a suitable escort with me, and of course Fitzjohn and any other attendants are welcome."

He thought this whole speech was unbearably obscure, and that unless Mona could read his mind, she could not possibly see it as an invitation. She was giving him a cool look, and he worried that he had left out some vital phrase, and had sounded like a village idiot.

"I see." Her voice didn't convey that she thought he was simple. "Then forgive me if I am equally bold. You have a woman in Abertroddi."

Cynan swallowed. She had grasped his intentions, and wasn't afraid to come to the point. His heart lifted.

"Not any more." This was partly true. An owner of two fishing boats, whose wife had recently died, was giving every sign of wanting to marry the mother of his girls, and the two of them had discussed the benefits of such an arrangement.

"And you are betrothed."

He bowed his head. This was the hardest part, and he wasn't convinced by his answer.

"It would be unusual for a man of my age and position to be without such a tie. I'm not married yet."

"Hm," Mona sounded unimpressed, "I beg you not to presume anything. I may be a servant, but I'm not a daft dairymaid."

"Of course not, you are far from . . . Mistress Mona, how could you think . . ." Amid his stutters, Cynan saw his hopes of a minute ago drain away.

Mon curtsied again. "Never mind. I'll take your message to Lady Agnes.If I were you, I'd talk with your brother for about an hour."

She left the hall, and Cynan didn't see her dance to Agnes' door.

He spent an hour with Owain at the low end of the hall, drinking indifferent wine and trying to look amazed at his news, aware of unexplained comings and goings. First Fitzjohn and the boys were summoned, then two servants who were dozing on a bench, then there was a distant outburst of male shouting, and the steward ran past, holding his ear. Puzzling all the time over whether Mona had said yes or no, he told Owain as much as he dared about Madog.

"Where is Alexander now?" Owain asked. They were speaking quietly in Welsh.

"None of us want to know. We pray he is out of the country." He was cut off by a high-pitched screaming coming towards the hall.

"It's a rats' nest I tell you, a rats' nest. By God, you expect a lady to sleep in such a verminous pit. I swear I'll not spend another night under this roof."

The door flew open, and Lady Agnes appeared, trailed by the miserable steward and Mona, who flickered one eyelid at Cynan. Agnes saw him as if by accident, and clutched her bosom.

"Sir, I throw myself on your mercy. Please, from the kindness of your heart, grant me the hospitality of your excellent house once more until these appalling scoundrels have cleaned the rats and poisonous snakes from my apartments. Mona, put the boys to packing. I can't bear to set foot in that room again."

It was a happy party which crossed the ford, and turned up the track to Llewelyn's house. A group of threadbare thieves, skulking towards Abertroddi, saw the lady in her finery, the pony laden with baggage, the squire and pages in their good coats, and thought about ambushing these carefree gentry and putting an end to their cheerful noise. Then they noticed the heavy cudgels, the squire's sword, and the broad shoulders of their leader, and slipped back into the undergrowth. No-one wanted a broken head, and there would be easier pickings at the fair.

By mid morning the next day, Abertroddi was heaving. Braziers burned on corners, the free beer flowed like water, there had already been several fights, and everyone agreed that it looked as if this was to be the most successful fair for years. The roads were just as lawless, and no-one believed that the restoration of King Henry would bring order and stability, yet a respectable number of tradespeople had travelled to the town, in defiance of the miserable condition of the countryside. The more prosperous sort had set up stalls to display their goods, while the poorer kind made do with pieces of canvas spread on the muddy ground. Among these were a small basket-maker and his much larger wife, sitting cosily together on bale of straw near the alehouse behind their piled-up wares. Madog stopped on his way from buying a bag of pepper from the English ship, and fingered a pannier. He supposed he'd better think about equipping himself for when he was called out to follow Sir Hubert, which, according to Cynan, who had made a brief call on him the previous evening and who seemed to have exclusive information, would be before the end of winter.

"How much for this, good woman?" he asked.

The good woman glared at him. Not much of her was visible, apart from her eyes, since her head was swathed in layer upon layer of cloth, and even her hands were wrapped in bits of rags. Her husband answered for her.

"She's been afflicted for many years and can't speak. How much do you want to pay? Name a price, sir."

Madog named an astronomical sum, and, far from being pleased, the woman growled through her head-gear.

Madog spoke quickly. "It's going up by the hour. He's already carrying spies from both sides. You'll have to owe me." He raised his voice, "If you take the baskets to the ship, you'll have a better chance of selling them. He doesn't want to leave his cargo."

The woman nodded, and stretched out a hand made even more enormous by its primitive glove. Madog placed a bag in her palm, picked up the pannier, and began to retrace his steps to the ship.

"Is that for your clean shirts?" The familiar voice from above and behind him stopped him in his tracks. It was Cynan on their father's horse, his clean-shaven face wreathed in a benevolent smile. Madog looked to see who was with him and quailed. Only Lady Agnes, her woman, her squire and her new pages, Gwyneth and a surrounding phalanx of servants, carrying staves and trying to look businesslike. He attempted to edge between his brother's line of sight and the basket-makers.

"You're right, as always. I'm sorry, I have to go, I'm in a bit of a hurry."

"Where are your manners? I must present you to Lady Agnes, since she has honoured us by being our guest. She wouldn't want to miss this chance of meeting you."

Lady Agnes, somewhat sleepy and drunk with pleasure, acknowledged this unremarkable-seeming young man with an equally benevolent smile. He didn't look like a dangerous thief, he looked rather charmingly domestic with his basket and bag of shopping.

"I'm so pleased to meet you," she purred. "Now I can count all your family as my friends. Oh, look, Gwyneth, baskets. Mona, do we need baskets? May I see yours, Madog? There is nothing so useful as a finely made basket."

Madog had the leaden sensation that his luck had finally run out. He couldn't catch Gwyneth's eye because she was giggling like Glynis, and Fitzjohn was giving him a filthy look. A group of men boiled out of the alehouse.

"Bastard. She's my woman."

"Not any more, you sodomite. She wants a man, not someone who fucks his farm-boys and his sheep . . ."

The fighting started, and Madog snatched his basket back.

"Cynan, the ladies. We must move along." He took Agnes' bridle, and urged the little mare forward. Agnes was looking back with unladylike interest.

"Dear me, isn't anyone going to stop them? Or is it the custom for everyone to join in? Should Cynan's men hit them with their sticks?"

Madog flashed a smile at her. "Only if they come too close, my lady. It'll end when someone falls into the water, that's the tradition."

"How reassuring. It reminds me of Carnival in Venice."

"Well, we might be a bit rough in Abertroddi, but we know how to enjoy ourselves. Let's stop here, I don't think they'll come this far."

He left them watching a troop of singing tumblers, and nearly ran to the ship.

No-one thought it was unusual when the basket-maker's wife stood up, let her husband load a choice of baskets on her back, and started to walk along the quay-side towards the English cog. A less harrassed man than the harbour-master might have noticed that she felled a drunk who accosted her for a kiss with rather more facility than was usual for even the toughest fishwife, and that she went on board with uncommon agility for a woman with feet that size. By the time the ship set sail on the evening tide, the master being keen to avoid disgruntled customers who might return their goods when they had sobered up, only Madog realised that she had not come back on shore. He slipped down from the cold roof where he had been watching, and went unseen to the smithy. The smith had been drinking steadily all day, and it only showed in the faint sheen on his face.

"Are you sure you'll be safe, riding home with that lot?" he asked, following Madog from his hidden room. "There's some disreputable buggers hanging around. You could wait a few days."

Madog stowed the heavy bags under his shirt. "I'll manage, I've an escort waiting, and I can gallop out of trouble."

Climbs Trees swung down from an oak at the edge of the town.

"Men up there," he pointed in the direction of the ford.

"Let's not go that way," Madog said, and struck out across the fields, his mind lighter than it had been for days.

"I wish we could be like this every night," Agnes stretched out on top of Gwyneth, and buried her nose in her hair.

Gwyneth had never felt so comfortable. "If only you could have inherited from Sir Simon. You would never have to marry, and I could move into the castle and satisfy your every whim."

"And who would look after Llewelyn and Cynan?"

"I think Mona would be quite happy to take my place."

Agnes giggled. Neither of them had mentioned openly that they had heard Mona leave the other mattress, where an oblivious Nyrees snored, and go through into Cynan's room.

"She knows what she is doing. God knows, she hasn't had much fun this past year," Agnes slipped her hand between Gwyneth's legs. "It's not only this. When Edmund died, I thought I would never laugh properly again, or find someone I was happy with. I don't want it to end, I don't want to leave you here if we go to England."

Gwyneth held her breath. Lust was one thing. It could happen between kings and commoners, a great lord and his lowliest servant, and even between men and beasts, if the sniggering farm-hands were to be believed. Wanting to be with someone because you liked their company above anyone else's and because you couldn't bear it if they came to harm, was something much rarer, and she hadn't been sure until these two nights that Agnes loved her.

"I would come with you as your servant if you wanted. I'm not so proud."

"I couldn't ask you to leave your home and family."

"You left your home to come here."

"I was with my mother until we reached England, and it's different when you have money and connections. My family might be out of favour, but I was never turned away from any great house or convent." This was the gap between them. Agnes carried on, "You are mistress in this house, how could you endure being entirely dependant on me? And it all comes back to what happens with the king. If our party is successful, I might be freer to choose who I marry, but if we fail, I can hardly do this with you in a convent."

"I thought you were fond of nuns. I could take my vows with you, and sneak into your cell every night." It was difficult to be serious when Agnes thought she was too grand to be a servant, and was kissing her ears in a way Ceinwen never had.

Agnes paused, "I could found my own nunnery, I suppose, if I can wring more money out of my lawyers in Venice. You could be the prioress, or abbess, or whatever you wanted. I'd call the order the Poor Virgins of Abstinence."

Gwyneth rolled her over. "The Little Sisters of Relief would be better. Don't laugh so much, you'll wake everyone."

Chapter 13

Life was quieter after the Salt Fair, although not as quiet as everyone would have liked. Snow fell in the New Year, blanketing the hills and discouraging travel, and no ships ventured along the coast to the harbour, bringing unwelcome news from the outside world. Llewelyn spent the short days going over estate business with Cynan, and more than one dusk saw him riding up the valley to Madog's house, where the two men sat into the night, laying plans for the coming expedition, to which they had been formally summoned by Sir Hubert. The smith in Abertroddi measured Madog, fetched a rusty set of battle-harness from one of the rooms in his yard, and began repairing broken rings and oiling joints. The castle smith too was busier than usual, and the servants found themselves shaken out of their indolence by the Lady Agnes who, having had her room restored to her liking and her portrait painted to adorn it, took it upon herself to interfere in her brother's sketchy preparations for riding forth before the spring. It had started when she had made an innocent enquiry at the dinner table about the state of his tents, and on seeing his blank look, had thrown up her hands and declared that no brother of hers was going to sleep under the stars in this abominable climate. For a while, Hubert thought that this was no business for a lady, before realising that she and her mother had organised themselves all the way from Venice to England. It had also not escaped his notice that his steward moved faster when she was around, the cooking seemed to have improved since the autumn, and that even the hall fire appeared to be smoking less. From the day when she persuaded him to give her a list of what was needed to maintain his following in the minimum of comfort, no-one had any rest. Storerooms were re-organised, supplies piled neatly on swept floors, and a group of sailors turned up to sew canvas and make sucking noises through their teeth at the state of what they had to work with. If anyone tried to sit down, he was hounded by that tyrant Fitzjohn, who had grown a foot taller and broader, and who had obviously forgotten that this was the season for dozing in front of any available fire. The women didn't escape either. They were goaded by Lady Agnes' morbid fear of death by cold and damp into a frenzy of sewing padded clothes for Sir Hubert and his captains, using every scrap of cloth which could be found, and some days Lady Agnes sent for Gwyneth to bring her own work over and make sure that they didn't stop if she had to leave the room to shout at the steward. Lady Margery took very little part in the proceedings. After Christmas, she rarely emerged from under the bed-covers, and took up her maids' valuable sewing time in dispatching them to the kitchens for a taste of what she thought she might be able to nibble. After a week of false alarms, she went into labour on a night in late January, when the temperature had fallen, freezing the afternoon's snowfall into an iron whiteness and turning the puddled courtyard into a death-trap.

"Oh Christ," Agnes pulled the pillow tighter around her ears, "surely she can't carry on much longer. If this is normal, I'm amazed any woman lets her husband touch her. You must be sorry now that the weather stopped you going home."

Gwyneth winced at another shriek, audible through several thick stone walls and intervening passages. "She's certainly suffering. Perhaps we should be grateful that what we do doesn't have such consequences."

"Lord, yes. If it did, I might even have been able to resist you."

"I doubt it."

"What do you mean? I can control my passions . . ." She stopped at a tap on the door. "That can't be Fitzjohn at this hour."

"I'll see." Gwyneth pulled on her under-gown and a

cloak, and picked up a taper. This was probably the warmest room in the castle, and the chill still went through to her bones.

"Who is it?" She couldn't think of anyone, except for Sir Hubert, who would dare to disturb Agnes' slumbers.

"Mistress Gwyneth, please, we need help . . ."

It was one of Margery's English maids, shivering with cold and fright. She babbled through lips which were turning blue. "There's something not right with the child, perhaps it is the wrong way round, none of us know what to do, the Welsh girls say your woman, Nyrees, is the best midwife in Wales." She must have heard from the girls that Heledd had given birth to three fine sons without a squeak.

Gwyneth pulled her cloak tighter. "I can't send for an old woman on a night like this. She would be dead before she arrived." She cursed her own ignorance, and Margery's stupidity for surrounding herself with women as brainless as herself.

The girl dropped her voice. "Mistress Mona? Everyone knows she has a box full of foreign medicines, and she cured the cook's burn."

Gwyneth lied. "Mistress Mona went to see a sick peasant woman, and she hasn't returned."

Another scream made the girl whimper, and Gwyneth felt her fear, and an unwelcome compassion.

"All right." Gwyneth shooed the girl away, "I'll try to send for her, but I can't promise anything. Keep with your mistress."

"What is it?" Agnes saw her face in the light of the taper.

"It's going badly. I'll have to fetch Mona, she's the only one who might be any use."

"You can't. Alone, it's not safe, it's too cold for a dog to be out there, you could be set upon and killed. I won't have it."

"It's your brother's child. And I know what you think of Margery, but wouldn't you want someone to do the same for you? Anyway, we can't lie here listening to this noise all night."

"There's a limit to charity, why don't we send Fitzjohn?

You could give him directions."

Only Agnes and Gwyneth knew that Cynan and Mona used a dilapidated hut just inside the boundaries of Llewelyn's estate, about a mile from the castle. At harvest time, it was sometimes used by Llewelyn's labourers when they worked until sunset, and didn't want to walk home and back before dawn, but in winter it lay empty, and no-one had a reason to visit it.

Gwyneth sat on the bed. "Agnes, how will it look for Mona if anyone else finds out where she is and who she is with? Once gossip starts, she will have no peace or respect." She looked round the room, "I think I can make it safer for me."

"Can't you at least take a horse? Luddy would help."

Gwyneth shook her head. "I'll go the way Mona uses. Then no-one else is involved."

"Jesus you're stubborn. Don't blame me if you're attacked and raped. What are you doing?"

Mona had taken pity on Fitzjohn, whose clothes were now too short in the sleeve and too tight around the chest, and only that day had put the finishing touches to a new warm outfit for him. It lay on a bench, and Gwyneth stood by the fire to strip off what she was wearing, and put on the shirt, the jacket, the hose and the short gown. Mona had even rescued from Clegge's clutches a pair of hardly worn boots which Hubert had discarded, and they stood ready, together with a fur-trimmed hat, to surprise the squire in the morning. Gwyneth bundled her hair into the hat, and turned round.

"There. If I can have your knife, any wicked man abroad will think twice about raping me."

"Unless he is partial to handsome young men." Agnes' eyes were open and surprised. "I believe I'm twisted. If it wasn't so cold, I'd leap out of this bed and drag you back."

"There's no time for that. When I've brought Mona, and she's busy."

Agnes pulled the covers up to her chin. "I wish I'd gone into the convent with my mother. I wouldn't be a prisoner in this ruin, being tormented by a woman who dresses against God's laws. Go, if you must. I warn you, though, if you're not back within the hour, I'll wake the guard and send them to search for you. You'll have to explain why you're wearing Fitzjohn's clothes because I can't. I've lost my wits."

Gwyneth leaned across and kissed her forehead. "I think we may have broken several of God's laws already. I'll be as quick as I can."

She picked up the cloak, slipped behind a wall-hanging and disappeared.

Taking down the wall-hangings before the Salt Fair had revealed a forgotten door. It led into what had probably been a watchtower on the old curtain wall at the rear of the castle, and there was a crumbling opening on to the walkway, where guards had once paced and perhaps fired on recalcitrant Welshmen. The wall itself had started to collapse, and a nimble person could climb down to the remains of the moat, now choked with generations of rubbish and a healthy growth of thorn trees. This was where Cynan waited for Mona, and in the clear sky, Gwyneth could see her footprints along the walkway and down the masonry, and how they changed into the prints of one solid horse, leading across the snow. She followed the trail, her knife in her hand, with the crunching of her feet the only sound. The moon was up, icy stars filled the bowl of the sky, she had the beauty of the unearthly night to herself, and she was free and strong and suddenly wanted to sing. Her exhilaration lasted through the business of rousing Cynan and Mona, and while she rode behind Mona on Cynan's horse as he walked alongside, carrying her above the lovers' silent embarrassment. Mona only spoke once.

"Margery would have done better to let me see her earlier, and not to have lain on her back for a month. There are ways to tell if a child is lying wrong, and to move it."

"Will you be able to help her now?" Gwyneth whispered. Cynan was good at delivering lambs, but no man, unless he was a doctor, wanted to hear about this.

"Perhaps. I can give her something for the pain, though I can't say for the child."

In the moat, Gwyneth dismounted like Luddy, and Cynan caught her arm.

"Does anyone else . . . ?" He must have hated being caught out like this.

Gwyneth shook her head. "No-one knows except Lady Agnes."

He looked up and down at her, and frowned. Gwyneth expected some sort of reprimand, to hide his own shame.

"If you were a man," he said, "you'd be better than any of us. Get inside out of the cold now, you won't be able to sew Madog's trappings if your fingers fall off with being frozen."

Gwyneth took this as a compliment, and scurried up the tumbledown wall.

At dawn, Mona came back into Agnes' room, grey and exhausted. The terrible cries had ended soon after she had run, her box of medicine under her arm, to Margery, but neither Agnes nor Gwyneth had possessed the courage to venture along the passage to see how the labour was progressing. Agnes stuck her head though the bed curtains.

"Well? Am I an aunt?"

Mona slumped by the fire, and started poking at the ashes, dropping kindling on to the embers.

"You're an aunt. It's a boy. He's feeding off his wet-nurse which is a good sign."

Only Gwyneth saw Agnes' shoulders relax. "And Margery? Do I have to go into mourning?"

Mona forced a smile. "With any luck, she'll sleep for two days and wake up having forgotten all about it. If she falls pregnant again, please let's move away from here."

Mona was right. The infant Hugh, having been so reluctant to enter the world, took a firm grip on life, while Margery woke up and pronounced that she couldn't see why women made such a fuss about childbirth, and that it would only take a week or so for her to be back on her feet. Her maid, who had seen her mother give birth in the morning and milk a cow in the evening, kept quiet, and thought it would be best not to mention Mona. Agnes professed to have no interest in the child, although Mona did catch her coming from the wet-nurse's room when she had said that she was going to see the steward about bandages, and Hubert, a new decisiveness in his step, practised galloping in his armour. The thaw came quickly, and he set the day for his departure. Before it was light on that February morning, Madog stood with Climbs Trees and Sleeps At Noon in front of his house, a hollow feeling in his chest. He was sure he wasn't afraid, since he had grave doubts over Sir Hubert's ability to find the fighting, if there was to be any, but he wished he wasn't leaving his friends. Sadly, there was no way on earth he could disguise them as Welsh archers. Climbs Trees had a final laugh and shake of his head at the battle-harness and equipment piled on a pony, and took Madog's arm.

"You're coming back. We wait here till then. Look after Lady Gwyneth and Ellis."

For no logical reason, Madog felt better. "You must go with Gwilym if he sails. I could be away for a long time."

Climbs Trees seemed certain, "You back before then."

Sleeps At Noon nodded in agreement. "You good hunter and fast man. Not get caught."

"I don't think you've quite understood our notion of warfare," Madog gave up. If they thought he was going to be running away from trouble, he didn't have time to dissuade them. It had been hard enough trying to explain why he was going away, and he suspected that they believed they were all off to steal women and sheep, and that the noble ideas behind the expedition meant nothing to them. He said goodbye quickly, and trotted off to his father's house without looking back.

Between them, he and Llewelyn had scraped together the thirty able-bodied men Sir Hubert thought was the number they should bring to his force. The only relatively good time to drag workers away from their homes and fields was after the harvest, and neither of them wanted to leave Cynan with just old men and boys to do all the spring labour. They had had to reject unsuitable volunteers like the ancient bodies who burned to kill an Englishman before it was too late, the very young and the strong family men who fancied a few months away from their wives, and they still had more than one youth escaping a pregnant girl as well as several shady characters recruited by Madog.

"Sir Hubert won't know they're not from your estate," he had said to Llewelyn. "He doesn't recognise half his own tenants. They can shoot, that's the main thing, and they won't complain if the living is rough."

"That's because they should have been hung several times over before now. Every day alive is a blessing to them. I'll hold you responsible if they desert."

Llewelyn hid his satisfaction that he had managed to avoid taking his best workers. Sir Hubert wasn't going to get them killed, no by God, nor his son if he could help it. In any confrontation, Madog was going to be with the archers, where he stood less chance of being hacked down by some fool of a knight, and Hubert was about to think it was his own idea. It dawned on Llewelyn that the months ahead should provide a wealth of entertainment, and he was livelier than his family had seen him since Heledd died.

"I don't know why you think you have to trail with us to the castle," he grumbled to Cynan and Gwyneth. "Do you want to make sure I'm going?" The sun had risen, and his company was assembled in front of his house.

"We want to view the spectacle. It's not every day you see a knight and his army ride out to war." Cynan refused to take offence.

"You might have to wait until evening. They won't be ready."

Llewelyn was too pessimistic. At midday, Sir Hubert came down from the private apartments, Lady Margery and the baby being too fragile to wait in the fresh air with the rest of his household, and strode towards his horse. Fitzjohn straightened his back in his new clothes, and hurried from the waggons to his station. If the wheels fell off and they lost their baggage because the waggoners hadn't bothered to check the bolts as he'd ordered, he wouldn't be the one to blame. It had been his worst dread that Sir Hubert would make him stay behind to guard the women, and he wanted to be out of the gates before the thought occurred to him. As much as he enjoyed being Lady Agnes' right hand man, his proper function was to fight with his lord, and he would die of shame if he couldn't fulfil it. Almost before he had mounted, one of the huntsmen blew on his horn, Sir Hubert's horse whinnied, and Sir Hubert was on the move. There was a last minute panic around the waggons and pack animals, and a man-at-arms ran from behind a wall where a kitchen girl sobbed dramatically, her wails rising above the stamping of hooves and bad-tempered shouting. Llewelyn embraced Gwyneth and his older sons.

"Keep cultivating Lady Agnes," he said to Gwyneth's surprise, "a connection like that could be useful." He paused, and looked away slightly. "You're the daughter I never had. I wish I could leave you better provided for. My share in Gwilym's ship will go to Owain, and you must ask him if you need anything. You're not going to cry, are you? I'm an old man, don't deny me my one chance to be a hero." He jumped on his horse like a man half his age, and smiled down at his men.

"Come on, gentlemen. It's a nice day for marching."

A murmur of appreciation went around the household servants as the muddle of men and animals fell into some kind of order. They had done Sir Hubert proud. It was mild, and Sir Hubert saw the ridiculous side to riding through his own estate in armour, so he and his captains were dressed as if for a special hunt, and all the bright colours and polished spurs flashed in the sunshine. Fitzjohn, swelling with pride, carried Sir Hugh's banner, which had been touched up by a team of embroiderers working through the night, and he acknowledged Lady Agnes' wave with a dip of the flag and a brave smile. A pannier fell off one of the pack ponies, and the overloaded waggons struggled to get started, but the king's enemies would scatter when they saw such a noble force, and even that haughty Lady Agnes was wiping her eye, while Mistress Gwyneth was weeping openly.

Owain blew his nose, as Llewelyn and Madog vanished through the gateway. "Come and sit with me for a while," he said to Cynan and Gwyneth. "If you leave now, you'll overtake them in minutes, and it'll look rude."

Gwyneth saw Agnes and Mona go into the hall, and knew she could not follow them without an invitation. For a moment, her heart hardened. Agnes' brother was leading Llewelyn and Madog away, perhaps to their deaths, and for all the love she professed to have for Gwyneth, Agnes would not give the merest hint of it in public, nor could anyone be allowed to know that it was only through Gwyneth that Margery had been successfully delivered of an heir. I should never have gone for Mona that night, Gwyneth started thinking, I should have let that silly woman suffer and die like the peasants she despises.

"Lady Gwyneth?" Luddy's piping disturbed her peevish maunderings. "Lady Agnes asks if you and your relatives would care to join her in the hall before you ride home, to drink to the party's safe return."

Agnes knew she had to be careful, with servants hanging around unwilling to settle back to mundane tasks.

"I know you'll be busy in the coming weeks," she spoke directly to Cynan, "but I must ask you one great favour. My brother has only been able to spare a few men to protect the castle," she didn't need to say that they were the most decrepit sort, "and his son's safety must be my greatest concern. If it ever looks like this will not be the best place for him, can I call on you to help me take him and his mother to the convent in Llancaegy?"

Cynan realised that she wasn't ordering him, or using her knowledge of him and Mona, and that her fear for the baby, if the king was defeated and Hubert never returned, was genuine.

"You can count on me, my lady," he said. "I'll let you know if I hear of danger heading our way, and we'll do our best to keep the roads safe." A few months ago, it would have been unimaginable for him to want to preserve any offspring of Hubert's, and now it seemed natural.

Agnes smiled. "Then I will take the liberty of visiting you at least once a week to exchange news and see how we can help each other. We must stick together and not stand on ceremony while Sir Hubert and your father are away."

Gwyneth and Cynan understood her perfectly, and the servants believed that her courtesy and good neighbourliness meant that they were in for an easier ride. They were disabused the next morning, when Agnes discovered that her pages were missing. Her temper didn't improve when Mona showed her the slate on which Luddy had tried to write a farewell note.

"I think they've gone to join Sir Hubert," Mona said, peering at the misshapen letters.

"Then someone must go and bring them back, they can't have gone far, where's that damn steward? I'll ride after them myself, the ungrateful little sons of devils, and they can go back to the stables and kitchens."

Mona stopped her shouting for the steward. "Agnes, they're boys. Of course they want to go to war. They think it's an adventure. Wait a day or two, Fitzjohn might box their ears and send them home."

"Fitzjohn will keep them to clean his boots and polish his iron hat and steal eggs for him," Agnes said, showing a neat appreciation of Fitzjohn's character. She stamped her foot, "They'll get themselves killed, and all that training will be for nothing."

"Even the king's enemies don't kill base-born children for sport. They'll be made to stay with the servants and camp-women, where they'll pick up rude habits, then they'll come home and tell everyone they fought in the front rank. Leave it, let's call on Margery, and see if she's dared to stand up yet."

Agnes put the slate carefully to one side. "I'll have to tell his poor mother. Maybe Gwyneth will come with me to translate. Forget Margery, I need to find out if there are any men left who are capable of riding round with us, and defending us from wandering thieves. Master Owain might not be as scholarly as he seems, let's see if he can advise us. He might like a ride out himself."

She intended to make good use of this time, when there was no man equal to her in rank in the castle to restrict her.

Chapter 14

Madog and Fitzjohn rode down the track. Neither of them particularly wanted to be with the other, and they were arguing intermittently about where they were going, and how they should be getting there.

"Sir Hubert said to scout down to the Wye River, and report back on the state of the road to England," Fitzjohn said. "That's what we're doing. If you want to crawl through the bushes, go on. I'm not afraid of a few cattle thieves. Or are you scared of going into England?" It was towards the end of March, and uncommonly warm. New buds unfurled on either side of the track, celandine and violets delighted the eye, and he had enjoyed this past month. Sir Hubert, who had somehow found a mind of his own, had not led them on a gruelling march through the cold mountains of central Wales to test the king's support and compile intelligence for his commanders. Instead, with London in his sights, he had headed east for the Marches, and then they had had an easy time moving slowly southwards, descending on friendly gentry, and avoiding the lands of Yorkists who still remained on their estates. Away from his wife, Sir Hubert was more even-tempered, and happy to leave minor decisions to his squire, who watched the captains and every day learned something more about herding men and cumbersome waggons through the countryside.

"Fear and discretion are two separate things," Madog said, his eyes flicking around as if he was trying to see ahead where the track descended into a wooded gully. "A few cattle thieves are different from an armed Yorkist party guarding the way into England."

"We've heard that rumour for two weeks, and not seen

any evidence. Everyone here is loyal to the king, and we would have noticed any force which wanted to stop us."

"Not everyone makes as much noise as us." Madog wished he had been sent with a couple of his poaching archers, not this upright booby whose idea of spying was to ride along with his head bare because his helmet was making him sweat. Good God, now he was whistling, and any minute would probably break into song. A branch cracked in the gully.

"For Christ's sake be quiet," Madog stopped, and reached for Fitzjohn's bridle, "we must get off this track, there are men down there."

Fitzjohn pushed at Madog's hand, "Don't be an old maid, it's sheep." He kicked his horse, and reached for his helmet. If there were any lawless robbers in the gully, they would think twice about tackling two well-equipped soldiers, even if one was a nervy Welshman. He trotted on for a few yards down a steep slope, and glanced over his shoulder to make sure Madog was following. There was nothing, the bastard had disappeared, horse and all. He opened his mouth to shout for him, his horse stumbled, and an overhanging bough clanged on his beautifully shined helmet. He ducked, and saw a man, a drawn sword in his hand, at the bottom of the dip. For some reason, his poor horse was finding it difficult to stay on its feet, and he began to dismount, tugging at his own sword, and keeping his gaze on the man, as he had been taught. Something jarred his left arm, and he swayed as the man ran lightly up the slope, followed by two others.

"Drop your sword, youngster," the man said, smiling through several days' growth of beard. "We've winged you, and if you're not sensible, we'll gut you and leave you for the crows."

"Fuck off," Fitzjohn said, and raised his weapon. Typical, Madog had left him to deal with these brigands, he wouldn't be surprised if they were friend of his, the treacherous shit. He forgot finesse, and slashed at the man, who grunted and stopped smiling as the blow caught his shoulder.

Fitzjohn laughed. "You didn't like that. Have another, arse-breath." He swung again, tripped over a root, and was on the ground. He pushed himself up and screamed. His left arm was on fire, and now the sword was raised above his head, and he'd forgotten to tell Luddy where he'd put the dignified and heroic letter to his mother. The man fell down beside him, and the dropping sword missed his neck by a hair's breadth.

"Arse-breath indeed," Madog's voice came from somewhere above him. "I hope you don't use that kind of language in front of Lady Agnes."

"The others . . ." Fitzjohn tried to get his legs to move, so he could stand up. Madog was kneeling next to him, panting as if he'd been running.

"I'm afraid I shot them. One of them's still alive, we could take him prisoner, except that your horse is dead, you're wounded, and I think we should get out of here before their friends turn up."

"Wounded?"

Madog pointed to his arm, and Fitzjohn saw the arrow sticking out of his sleeve above his elbow. The trees started to dance in circles, and he felt the cold sweat trickling from his eyebrows. Madog had hold of his hand.

"I don't think it's serious, I've got some drugs back at the camp, and I'd pull it out now except I don't want to make it bleed more and mess your new coat." He half-turned. Both of them could hear crashing further down in the gully, and dogs baying.

Madog put his hands under Fitzjohn's shoulders. "My horse isn't far. I think it's time to retreat, unless you want to practise your sword play some more."

Fitzjohn couldn't speak. He let himself be helped round boulders to where Madog's horse was tied to a tree, and had to accept a leg up on to its back.

"You saved my life," he managed to say when they were cantering away up the track, Madog's hard arm around his waist.

Madog sounded relaxed, "You'd do the same for me."

Fitzjohn's head hung lower, and the arm tightened. "We're meant to be on the same side, remember. It's not your fault you're deaf as a post and blind as a bat, and have spent so long pouring wine for ladies that you can't tell when you've been shot."

"I wasn't brought up as a poacher, I've got a lot to learn. Where's that other noise coming from?"

"Damn." Madog heard the answering cry of hounds ahead of them. He had suspected someone was trailing them all morning, and it seemed that their pursuers meant business.

"I should've listened to you," Fitzjohn tried to wriggle out of his grasp. "Leave me, you can get back to the others easier on your own."

Madog turned his horse from the track. "Don't be bloody stupid. I'm not telling Sir Hubert his most useful squire is a corpse. Try not to fall off, this won't be very comfortable."

Later, Madog sat outside the gateway of the small monastery, watching the evening shadows creep along the grass. He had no doubt that whoever was after them knew they were there, and had someone in that clump of trees, watching him as he was watching. There was nowhere else they could have gone, and Madog wondered for how long their hunters would respect its sanctuary. The monks hadn't hesitated in taking Fitzjohn to their tiny infirmary, but he had sensed their reluctance to let him in further than the gatehouse, so he had chatted inconsequentially with the Welsh gatekeeper, eaten the food sent from the kitchen, and come out here to decide his next move. The sun's last rays melted away, a tinny bell rang over the deceptively peaceful fields, and he shivered. In his mind, he saw a grave, and a deep grief at being shut away from the living world whispered in his heart. He shook himself. He wasn't going to die here, and neither was Fitzjohn, unless his wound went bad faster than any other wound he had seen. The gatekeeper came out.

"You can come in and see your friend if you like."

Fitzjohn was lying in a neat bed, his eyes bright in his white face.

"They cut off my sleeve," he said, his voice shocked. "Have they kept it?" Madog couldn't help smiling.

"I don't know. Can you ask? One of the women could sew it back on, when we . . . if we . . ." His mouth twisted. "You'd better try to get back to the others. I think the monks know who attacked us. They said they'd do their best not to give us up, but . . ."

Madog sat on the end of the bed. "I'll take you if you want."

You idiot, he said to himself, you will die if you have to nursemaid this clodhopper back to Sir Hubert. He could outwit anyone in the dark, but with Fitzjohn, he would be caught in a trice.

Fitzjohn kicked him. "If I was bad as a spy before this, I'd be worse now. You can spend the night sneaking back, I'm tired. I think I'll have a sleep, and hope they don't come for me before morning."

Madog stood up. "We won't abandon you."

"Steal a horse for me while you're out there," Fitzjohn shut his eyes, "and some wine. They're a very strict order."

He was still there when Madog returned the following afternoon with an impressive half of Sir Hubert's force, which their elusive enemy had let pass unmolested, and, laughing from Madog's medicine, he didn't mind riding on a horse of unknown origin alongside the Welshman into England.

"Let me be certain I understand you," Agnes treated Owain to a piercing look. "Master Hooper has spent hours assuring me that my brother intended to have a new mill built this year, and that it would bring immeasurable benefits to the estate. He says he is only asking for my consent out of courtesy, but Sir Hubert did not sign some paper before he left, and my signature would quicken the process, since Lady Margery is reluctant to involve herself in business. He has a site ear-marked, and can order the workmen to start tomorrow. Now you're trying to tell me that a new mill would be an expensive mistake, and, correct me if I'm wrong, that Master Hooper intends to line his own pockets from this enterprise?"

Owain squirmed. He was suffering a crisis of conscience, and the experience was new to him. Last year, he would have been delighted for Hubert to waste money on this unnecessary mill, and wouldn't have objected to the bribes which would find their way into Hooper's purse, or the inaccurate bills for materials presented by the carpenters, the masons, the mill-wrights and everyone else involved. Unfortunately, he had spent a month riding backward and forwards with Lady Agnes, and knew that she was sharper than a needle in business and softer than a peach in her regard for his family, and that his former preoccupation with ruining Sir Hubert now seemed horribly shabby.

He studied his nails, "I don't think I was quite so blunt, my lady, and I wouldn't dream of slandering Master Hooper. I only put it forward as a possibility, that this might not be the best time to embark on such a costly construction, and that people might be tempted, in Sir Hubert's absence, to be less than scrupulous, or, indeed, might be targets for the kind of dubious business practice that would not be attempted if Sir Hubert were here to . . ."

"Oh shut up!" Agnes slammed her fist on to a pile of papers. "You don't have to act the lawyer with me. The mill isn't a good idea, I shall instruct Master Hooper not to go ahead without Sir Hubert's signature, and if he decides to send someone with the paper to find my brother, then that's up to him." She picked up a household bill which had fallen to the floor. "Still, I'm glad I asked you to bring me these accounts, and that you said what you said. You didn't have to warn me, and I'm grateful." She gave him another look, and his insides writhed. "You're wasted here, you need to go to Oxford, and read for a degree in law, otherwise you'll never get on in the world. My mother's cousin teaches law in one of the colleges. I'll write you a recommendation to him, and if the roads are safe, you can leave this summer. I'm sure a modest sum for your keep would be an investment for me. Who knows what will happen here, and if you study and stay out of politics and the alehouses, you shouldn't be troubled by any reverses of fortune in Wales. Please, an open mouth like that won't help you become Lord Chancellor."

Owain shut his mouth. All he had to do was to bow

and be suitably thankful, and his dreams would be realised. Escape from this place, the freedom to study properly and to mix with people who used their minds instead of brute force, the possibility of position and riches. His conscience murmured, and he couldn't stamp on it. He bowed anyway.

"My lady, I don't deserve such kindness. Please, don't think me ungrateful, but I am unwilling to leave." He abandoned lawyerly obfuscation. "How many men are there left here who you can rely on? Hardly anyone can lift a sword, Master Hooper is not the best of lawyers, and I don't want to see you cheated, let alone exposed to danger. I should stay until Sir Hubert returns, or sends word that he has been successful in England." Farewell, law degree and fat living, he thought, I'll either die defending her from a highway robber, or she'll throw me out for insulting her brother's man.

Agnes' smile made him wonder why he had never thought her attractive. "Now I'm sure I've made the right decision. By the summer, you'll have taught me all I need to know to keep Master Hooper in his place, and I'll have found some other bodyguard. Your brother will help . . . for God's sake, doesn't anyone knock these days?"

The door had swung open, and the steward tumbled in, followed by the harbour-master, his clothes dishevelled and his eyes deranged.

"Oh my lady," the steward said, "the French are here, the dogs, and are sacking Abertroddi. We must flee, the castle will be next."

The harbour-master shoved him aside, "No, no, you ass, it's a ship they want, and they are all for taking Gwilym's and he's paid his dues so how can we stop them or I'll have to pay him back, and they're armed and in my office . . ."

The French bishop huddled miserably in an upstairs room of the alehouse. What had started so agreeably as a fraternal visit to the Church in Scotland had descended, through an unseaworthy ship, to this farce, wrecked in a smelly foreign port, with him seeking refuge in a place which was probably a brothel, judging from the way those girls were giggling with the armed guard outside his door. The master of his unfortunate ship and the soldiers' captain, having frightened the one official who might have been able to help them, were still trying to reason with the owner of the only other decent ship in the harbour, which was difficult since they couldn't find a language in common, and he wouldn't be surprised if an English army arrived before nightfall to kill them all. He fingered his rosary, and thought of the lavender fields of home. For his part, Gwilym stood on his deck, wilfully not understanding the Frenchmen shouting at him from the quay. As soon as he had seen the pennants on the crippled hulk listing into the harbour, he had pulled up his gangway and called for the few sailors who were good shots, and they crouched behind the bulwark, ready to let fly if those handy-looking soldiers tried to climb aboard.

The French master spat. "We're going to pay you. I'm not a pirate," he said for the tenth time in a combination of French, English and Latin.

"You will be soon," his companion, who was getting colder and hungrier, spat as well. "We can take this ship, even if a few of us get shot. With your sailors, we'll outnumber them easily."

"Mother of God, get that money-box off the bishop. If we show this idiot gold, he might start speaking some civilised tongue. I want to move all those damn ceremonial robes off my ship before it sinks completely. They're worth a fortune."

"Let's rush him now, before it gets dark and before a bloodthirsty English milord turns up. I should have stopped that squeaky man, he'll have gone for help."

"We're travelling with a man of peace. We should try reason."

"Reason be damned. See, I told you, we're in for a fight." He could hear hooves, and one of the guards he had posted at the edge of this collection of hovels was running towards him. "Is it an army?"

The guard shook his head, and bent double. His legs were not as they should have been, after days on that hideous boat. "No sir," his chest heaved, "it's ladies."

"Ladies?" The captain automatically rubbed his boots

with a corner of his cloak, and watched with interest as a small procession advanced towards him. Two, no three, ladies, one of them quite grand, a clerk of some kind, a small group of soldiers, most of them on the old side, and, more dangerously, a dozen hard-bitten peasants carrying staves and billhooks, and led by someone who might be a gentleman. Following the English fashion, the captain took off his hat. He would be polite while he decided when to attack.

Agnes knew she had wasted time in sending for Gwyneth to meet her at the ford, but she didn't want to face abduction by the French without her. Slightly less selfishly, she hoped that more women present would mean less violence, and that Cynan and his workers would look more frightening than her men-at-arms. She was relieved to find that Abertroddi wasn't burning, and that no-one was fighting yet, but a growl went up, even from her mature soldiers, at the sight of their hereditary enemy standing free as you please on their soil, drinking a barrel of beer from the alehouse.

"Stop that," Cynan snarled. His men were already flicking two fingers at the Frenchmen.

Agnes bowed in her saddle, and spoke clearly in French.

"Good afternoon. I am the Countess of Peruzza. I see your ship has run into difficulties." It was lying lower in the water by the minute, and sacks and bundles were flying through the air and thudding on the quayside. "Welcome to my brother's estates. How can we be of service to you?"

The mellifluous French phrases floated back and forth, Mona translated for Cynan, Owain and Gwilym, who conducted their own wrangling conversation, English men-at-arms and Welsh peasants made vulgar gestures at the French soldiers, and dusk filled the alleys between the houses. Gwilym's sailors lit their lamps. The French master smiled at their neat movements and the comfortable light telling of familiar things, and it was decided. Gwilym would carry the whole French party to Dumfries, leaving on the afternoon tide the next day, in return for an entirely reasonable sum, most of which would be deposited with

Owain as the representative of the ship's co-owner.

"That might stop them cutting my throat and seizing my ship," Gwilym said, "especially if the soldiers are sea-sick."

Through Agnes, the master asked him some intelligent questions about loads and weight distribution, and Gwilym signalled for him to come aboard. "He can stay with me. We'll see what we can salvage from his poor wreck, he can't help being a Frenchman."

Agnes, expressing shock that a bishop no less was marooned in the alehouse, invited everyone else back to the castle, where they could be given the hospitality they deserved after their ordeal.

"Cynan says they cannot be left here," Mona murmured behind Agnes' back. "There will be bloodshed within the hour, bishop or no bishop. Cynan and his men will stay with us at the castle, and he wants Gwyneth there too. If everyone is under one roof, he thinks it'll be easier to keep order. Bartlett can entertain the bishop."

"I can't wait," Agnes said, and sent Owain on ahead to warn the steward. They would have to fill these men with greasy food until they were too heavy to fight, and the captain lost the amorous twinkle in his eye. She waited for the bishop to be produced and placed on a pony from the smithy, and told herself that Hubert would not have handled this better.

"Cynan," Gwilym leaned over the rail, "my cargo, I'd nearly forgotten. You'll have to send it to me tonight."

Cynan swore at this extra burden. "I can't leave the castle. Someone has to stop these animals murdering each other."

"Owain can find them."

"They might not want to go with you, they're waiting for Madog to come back. You'll have to pick them up when you return from Dumfries."

Gwilym lifted his eyes to the sky. "Haven't you listened to anything I said? This ship needs caulking. I might make it to Dumfries, but I certainly won't make it back without ending up like that sieve. I'll be in Dumfries for months while the work's done, and I want to sail for you know where before Lammas at the latest."

Cynan saw the French captain order his men from the beer barrel, and heard the obscene song beginning in the English ranks. His own bodyguard was starting to hum along.

"Gwilym, it's too bad. Madog will have to take them to Dumfries. Wait for him there."

"But . . ." His words were lost in the hubbub. Cynan roared his men into submission, and made them sing a hymn in honour of the bishop, who appeared looking more like a wretched shop-keeper than a great prelate, and the cavalcade moved off, the singing masking hawking, taunts, and universally-understood gestures.

Chapter 15

If Cynan hadn't been so vigilant, and if the bishop hadn't remembered his manners and been graciously generous with the contents of his money-box, the night would surely have ended in bloodshed, and in the destruction of the order Agnes had nurtured since Hubert's departure. As it was, the French party embarked the next day with little more than aching heads and indigestion to show for their sojourn in hostile territory, and only after the cables had been untied did the English and Welsh give vent to their frustrated indignation by hurling insults and the odd stone after them. More powerful leaders were less inclined to keep the peace. While Hubert was ambling through the Marches, Edward of York had returned to England, and as Fitzjohn nursed his arm in a hospitable manor owned by one of Margery's relatives, Edward entered London and went on to defeat Henry's supporters outside the city. Hubert and Llewelyn, ensconced in the countryside at the time, knew nothing of this, nor that Henry's indefatigable queen had landed in Dorset, and that they were moving closer to the fighting they had so far avoided. On a sunny day in very early May, Agnes and Gwyneth, equally ignorant, sat in Gwyneth's herb garden, sewing and watching Nyrees potter through the beds, pulling out weeds and murmuring to herself.

"She's talking to the plants," Agnes said, biting off a thread.

"Naturally. Otherwise, how would you expect them to grow? It's the reason my garden is so beautiful, and yours is a sea of mud with a few stalks in it."

Agnes pointed her needle at her, "It's not that bad, considering the hens found their way in, which, incidentally, is not a problem I had in Venice, where my garden was famous for its taste and elegance."

"I'm sorry, you're going too fast." Today was an Italian day, when they tried to speak to each other only in Agnes' favourite language, and the previous day had been Welsh. Gwyneth had put her foot down at having a French day as well, but was secretly proud of how much she had learned. It helped to have a distraction from worrying about Llewelyn and Madog, and from dwelling on the feeling that underneath their busying about, everyone was anxiously waiting. One messenger had arrived from the expedition, carrying a note Llewelyn had written to Cynan about ploughing, and a letter for Margery, which she had not thought to let Agnes read, and which Agnes and Mona hadn't been able to steal from her room. These missives proved that Hubert and Llewelyn were still alive, yet by now they were several weeks old, and Agnes had not been sure if she was joking when she had asked Gwyneth earlier that morning if Nyrees had second sight, and if she could tell what was happening in England.

"Maybe it's better not to know," Gwyneth had said, "and not to spoil the day."

Agnes looked around at the sun dancing on new leaves, the birds flitting in and out of the eaves, and the little flowers bursting out of every crevice in the garden walls. She spoke more slowly, and explained a few words. "I didn't think it could be so lovely here," she added.

"It's all the lovelier for your presence," Gwyneth replied, so she could see Agnes' face crease with laughter. She thought the day was like one of those gold cups in the castle, filled to the brim with wine. It was perfect, and so delicately poised that the slightest jolt could ruin it. She saw Glynis walking slowly from the dairy, and Agnes followed her eyes.

"I don't know if I should tell you this, but Mona thinks that girl's pregnant."

Gwyneth's needle went into her finger, and she abandoned Italian. "Hell and damnation. I knew Nyrees was keeping something from me, how stupid can one girl be? How can I marry her off to some reliable shepherd now?"

She sucked her finger and frowned at Agnes, "It's no laughing matter. I wanted to have her settled before . . . in case anything happened to the estate."

Agnes bent her head to her stiff embroidered leaves. Gwyneth knew she was sewing a cap for little Hugh, and was purposefully not mentioning it. "Can't she marry the father? Isn't that the usual arrangement?"

Gwyneth puffed in exasperation. "Hardly. I'd bet anything it's Sleeps At Noon, the vile foreign seducer. I wish they'd gone with Gwilym, for all they shadow us around and would frighten off any stranger."

Agnes tried to seem serious. "It'll be an interesting looking baby. Will it come out with those marks on its face, do you think? Perhaps Sleeps At Noon will want to take her back with him."

"I doubt it. From what Madog says, he has at least one wife at home. Anyway, Glynis would hate it, even if she survived the voyage. They don't have proper clothes, just skins, and they eat raw meat."

"They've adapted quite well then, I must say. How strange to think there might be many other places and people in the world we don't know about, and to whom our concerns are nothing."

They considered this for a while. It had been inevitable that Agnes would finally come across Climbs Trees and Sleeps At Noon, who moved more openly about Llewelyn's house, and who had taken to following Agnes backwards and forwards from the ford when she came to visit. Although she hadn't fainted when she first met them face to face in the hall one evening, she had been contemptuous of Gwyneth's explanation that they were Turkish sailors.

"I've seen plenty of Turks in Venice, and none of them looked so nasty. God, Mona's father was a Turk, and I'm certain his face wasn't mutilated. Where are they really from?"

Gwyneth had told her, and she had taken it in her stride. "Don't let Bartlett know, whatever you do. He'll have them captured like animals, and sent to London to be displayed in a menagerie. I don't trust that man, I wish he had gone with Hubert, instead of roosting like a crow in his tower. I don't know why my brother puts up with him."

Gwyneth knew, and didn't tell Agnes. It was the only big secret she still kept from her after Agnes had clutched her that night and whispered, "I can see why Sir Giles' men thought they were being attacked by devils. The matter's over, but when Madog comes back, he's going to pay me for that saddle. Ssh, it's finished, we've more important things to worry about now, and if Madog hadn't stolen those horses, we most likely wouldn't be together, and that would be a terrible waste." Then they had fallen to recounting the day of the hunt, and when exactly they first wanted to do the things they had just done and were about to do again, and Agnes never mentioned horse-stealing again.

In the familiarity of her garden, Gwyneth watched Agnes' deft fingers and half-smiling mouth, and decided not to be too hard on Glynis. She wasn't the first girl, and wouldn't be the last, to succumb to temptation, and it wasn't as if her mistress was a model of chastity. She would be upset enough when the time came for the Vinlanders to leave, and in a way, it was oddly comforting that human desire had triumphed over their differences. At least Glynis would have something of her lover to remember him by . . .

"An island," Agnes was saying, "an island where it only rains at night, and it's never cold. It's ruled by a queen, and a few men are kept just to do the heavy work. We can live together in a sumptuous palace, and Gwilym will call every year to bring us news, and we'll laugh to think of a place where men are in charge and spend their time fighting to make life miserable. There, do you think such a place could exist?"

Gwyneth smiled back at her, "I wish it did, and we could find it. I suppose we have to remember that if the men hadn't gone away, we wouldn't be so free as we are now."

"That's true, although it's a shameful state of affairs when only their trouble can make us happy . . . what's wrong with Nyrees?"

The old woman had stopped weeding, and was staring at the sky, her withered face empty of its former contentment. Gwyneth looked upwards, and a strange quiver ran up her spine.

"It's a buzzard. Oh God, please don't let it land." She saw the pattern on the underside of its wings, and heard its mewing cry, and fancied she could feel its yellow eye gazing intently upon them. It circled, swooped, and came to rest on the wall. Nyrees sank to her knees, and the bird cried out again before flying off, the beat of its strong wings disturbing the air.

"It's a bird, for heaven's sake," Agnes said, her voice loud in the stillness, "we see dozens like it every day. What's the matter with you?"

Gwyneth's needle shook in her hand. "It's not just a bird. Everyone knows, the day Llewelyn's grandfather was killed fighting the English fifty miles away, such a bird came to Anchoret, his wife. They say it was his spirit, telling her good-bye. And when my own father, Gwilym's brother, died in France, a great bird sat for a day and a night on Gwilym's masthead. Something terrible has happened and we're sitting here gossiping. We must send someone to find out."

Agnes grabbed her wrist, "That's superstition, and you know it. How can you believe such rubbish?"

"What do you know?" Gwyneth tore her arm away, "Nyrees speaks one language, and has more wisdom in her little finger than you have in your entire body. Oh go back to your castle, and laugh at us, then when the news comes, you'll know we were right. What are you doing? We can be seen . . ."

Agnes had stood up, and was holding Gwyneth in a grip she couldn't break. "I'm not laughing, and I'm not going back to the castle. I won't leave you like this. We'll hear soon enough if anything has happened. Let them see us, we're together until someone forces us apart."

Gwyneth leaned into her, then went to help Nyrees. The cup had been toppled over, and there was nothing she could do.

His arm aching, his head pounding and his mouth dry, Fitzjohn led his horse onwards in the trudging sea of men. I have never been so tired in all my life, he said to himself, and the words went round and round in his head like a tune he couldn't shake off. He could scarcely remember how they had come to be here in Somerset's forces, supposedly marching into Wales to join up with Jasper Tudor and the rest of the queen's supporters, but in fact being chased by Edward of York who was probably getting closer by the minute. Somewhere in this grim column were the great lords, the queen and her young son, yet this desperate struggle to reach the crossings over the Severn had nothing of the stirring glory he had imagined would accompany the progress of a royal army. Men and animals, helped by no-one, were lying by the road, overcome by the unseasonal heat and the lack of water, they had lost their waggons days ago, and only some obscure feeling that he had to mind the collapsed foot soldier from the castle whom he had lifted on to his horse stopped him from leaving the track and lying down in the stink with the other wretches. The days their little band had spent inching their way towards London were now like an impossible dream of comfort and regularity, from which they had been woken to this reality of forced and frightened movement by the news that Somerset and the queen were in the West Country. At the time, it had seemed a happy miracle that in their doubling back and heading south they had found Somerset, and that the duke himself had received Sir Hubert with effusive thanks and promises which had even Llewelyn smiling and talking about English estates for his second and third sons. Today, Fitzjohn knew that there was barely a man on this road who would not exchange these promises for a bucket of water and a bed.

"Good afternoon, Fitzjohn," Madog had materialised beside him in his uncanny way, "would you care for a drink?"

Fitzjohn made himself match his everyday tone, and not knock him from his horse. Apart from the dust on his face and clothes, the bloody man showed no sign of strain or weariness.

"I dare say I could force one down. Have you enough for this poor fellow here?" He nodded to the soldier on his horse.

"You're a shining example to us all. Here, I'm afraid it's only water." He passed down the flask, and Fitzjohn used up the last of his pride in letting his passenger drink before he gulped at the muddy sludge.

"Quite delicious. Where did you find this nectar?"

"There was a little stream over the fields. Luckily I got there before the horses, though not before that shoddy bunch of Devon farmers."

Fitzjohn wiped his mouth. It was odd that such a small thing could make him feel so much better.

"Have you any idea where we are? I've lost my sense of direction."

Madog smiled. "Don't you recognise the countryside? Nearly back at Tewkesbury. I expect Somerset's idea is to cross the Severn tonight, and then Edward will have a job catching us."

"But we were here a few weeks ago on our way into England. We could have waited here with our waggons if we'd known, and not missed anything."

"I know. Marching in circles loses its charm after a while. Never mind, I expect there'll be more of it to come. I'd better get back to my father, and help him shout at the stragglers." He touched his hat and trotted off, as composed as if he was back in the Troddi valley.

Fitzjohn wasn't surprised, and he regretted later that he had been relieved, when Somerset decided not to cross the Severn that day. The column ground to a halt outside Tewkesbury, and after a few hours of being ordered to take up a position first in one place, then another, then back in their original spot, Sir Hubert's men almost wished they had been able to carry on walking. By evening, Fitzjohn was hoarse and had passed beyond exhaustion to a state where everything swam when he looked beyond the nearest object, yet he sensed that the chaos had, against all the odds, resolved into an order of sorts. They were on a slight rise, not far from Somerset's banner, the horses had been watered and were tethered in a line, someone had stolen a tent for Sir Hubert and Llewelyn, and the men were lighting fires and sharing out the last provisions from the few pack ponies they had managed to hold on to. He would collect his blankets from his horse, and then go to attend Sir Hubert, who might allow him to sleep inside the tent door. On the other hand, he could lie down here by this fire, and let his master look after himself for once. The man who had ridden his horse had recovered, and was smiling at him, and holding out a loaf of bread. Fitzjohn stretched out his arm, and a queer noise, almost like a groan, came from the front of the rise. The man stopped smiling, and his pupils dilated.

"Jesus Christ, sir, it's York. There they are, the whole fucking lot of them."

Fitzjohn turned, and screwed up his eyes. Men, men and horses and banners in the dusk, streaming along the tracks they themselves had made earlier, and something else, too many wicked shapes on wheels, pulled by straining beasts.

"Guns," he licked his lips, "by God, we'll be . . ." He saw the man's face. "Everyone knows they can't aim for shit. They're more likely to shoot themselves. Have your supper, they won't attack tonight."

He walked towards the tent. He wasn't going to think of it, how the hot iron from Gwilym's gun had crashed smoking through the wrecked boat they had used as a target, and how flimsy his body was compared with that weathered oak. Llewelyn was standing at the tent door.

"Ah Fitzjohn," he was polite as always, and had managed to wash his face, "you've missed Sir Hubert. He is to sup with Somerset. You see we have company?"

Fitzjohn nodded. He was afraid his voice would revert to a squeak like Luddy's if he spoke.

Llewelyn grinned. "I doubt they'll be so rude as to disrupt the Duke while he eats. Get some rest, dear boy. Sir Hubert will send for you if he needs you. The men are settled?"

Fitzjohn cleared his throat. "Yes. Are you sure I can't do anything for you?"

Llewelyn gave a half-bow. "I have Dafydd here to sharpen my sword, and Madog and the boys are by that fire over there. Do join them, I believe they have some chickens."

The boys? Fitzjohn had told them only that morning,

on pain of a thumping, to stay with a friendly Welsh carter in what remained of the baggage train. He staggered to the fire, trying to rouse up the energy to shout.

Madog stared into the blaze, blocking out the boys' shrill voices as they baked the chickens in a round helmet they had taken from some fainting soldier, and all the other grating sounds of a scared and weary army. When he had made his promise to Cynan, he hadn't realised how hard it would be, to be deprived of freedom and solitude, the calm of the forest and the sweet smell of his stables. He watched the flames lick at a branch, and saw how it had been alive, drawing in water and sunlight, before its power went, and it turned into red heat and grey smoke, streaming like a spirit into the sky. It's not nothing, he thought dully, it's something, even though it's dead. He felt the wolf's tooth pressing against his skin. and wondered whether Climbs Trees would know if he died tomorrow, and would stop waiting for him to return so that they could hunt together in forests which went on for days, and which were innocent of armour and guns and brutish shouting . . . Fitzjohn slumped down beside him like a felled tree, and he had to come back to the crowded ridge, and the clutching fear of the night before a battle.

The battle was not as Fitzjohn had imagined. There was no glorious charge in which he could gallop along with Sir Hugh's banner held high, cutting through the enemy like a knife through butter. A night spent drifting in and out of consciousness on the hard ground merged with a scene worse than the depictions of hell on the chapel walls, filled with the crump of explosions, the whistle of arrows, and the screams of men turned into shredded butcher's carcasses by flying metal. He cursed their commanders, who had marched them until they were too spent to throw up proper defences, he cursed every shot which landed near him, and every son of a whore firing those guns, and every minute which had brought him here, and the monotonous refrain kept him from running off like that fancy squire a few yards away, his face contorted above an expensive breastplate splashed with someone else's brains. He cursed the numbed men into carrying their equipment and weapons when a bawling Sir Hubert ordered them to withdraw to a natural hollow, and he cursed while they built a barricade of dropped shields, rocks and two dead horses, and crouched down behind it.

Sir Hubert pushed up his visor and scowled at Llewelyn. "What the hell are you singing, man?" They were sitting shoulder to shoulder with their backs against a horse's spine.

Llewelyn stopped the droning he thought no-one would hear. "It's a psalm my grandfather is meant to have sung when he went into battle with Glendyr against the English."

"A psalm? Christ, I think my grandfather would have sung that rude song about the miller's daughter. I wish he was here, and yours as well. They wouldn't have us pinned down like sheep waiting to be slaughtered. You could go, you know, you've got that ridiculous old helmet with no protection at the front. Let me give you a little cut, and you can pretend you've been hit."

Llewelyn stared at him. "I can't do that. I have to stay with you."

Hubert banged his mailed fists together. "A piece of paper. It shouldn't mean you have to be turned into a bloody pulp for a cause that isn't yours. Do you care who's king?"

Llewelyn saw his life turned inside out. "Do you?"

Hubert flinched as something thudded into the horse. "All these men killed and ammunition spent. If we had used them against the French instead of each other, we would be sitting in Paris, my friend. Now I'll be lucky to see my son grow as fine as yours." He pointed to Madog, who was zig-zagging towards them from where the archers were stationed.

Llewelyn smiled at his old enemy. "I think I'll stick with you. We'll have to move off here and attack soon. At least I can see in this helmet, I'll tell you where we're going."

"Might as well have a drink then." Hubert pulled a leather bottle from under his shield, "It's wine, and it's not bad."

"Where on earth did you get that?" If there was any wine left in the army, even Madog hadn't been able to sniff it out.

Hubert winked. "Stole it from Somerset's tent last night. Don't see why he should keep his luxuries to himself."

Madog, carrying a message that they were to get ready to advance, saw his father laughing, his hand resting on Sir Hubert's shoulder, and his eyes full of astonished delight. Then he saw the almost spent ball carve a singeing plough mark across the horse and on to that ancient helmet, crumpling it like a shell.

Chapter 16

The monks at the small monastery were uneasy. It was hard at the best of times to follow a life of prayer and work, when all around the sinful peasantry and rapacious landowners distracted them with demands for food and medicine, and with lawsuits over grazing rights and fishponds. The wars had made it worse, especially since Henry had been restored, and Sir Ralph had turned outlaw, rampaging up and down the Marches, firing houses and stealing cattle, and they had had to use all their moral authority to protect the wounded boy who had been brought to them in the early spring. It was fortunate that a rumour of a poorly-protected waggon load of weapons and silver had sent Sir Ralph haring off to the south, and the monks had breathed a sigh of relief when the boy's friends had picked him up. In all conscience, they could not turn such wounded men away, but what would happen if there was serious fighting in the neighbourhood, and they had to deal with the stricken from both sides? Their discussions about moving away to a remoter spot, where politics and its violent practitioners would not intrude upon their contemplation, became more frequent, and in turn, the gatekeeper became more morose. He was comfortable here, with the small benefits he received from his position, and he didn't want to go to some bare mountain valley, where supplicants would be too few and too poor to provide him with the luxuries he kept from the monks, to shield them from temptation. On the other hand, he didn't want to be turned loose to try his luck with the likes of Sir Ralph, and end up like the poor devil he could see struggling towards the gatehouse on a misty evening, his clothes tattered and his worldly possessions tied on the back of a lame pony. He screwed up his eyes. The poor devil looked vaguely familiar, and the bundle on his pony was an odd shape, long, and with what seemed to be feet and . . . Jesus Lord, it was a body. Either that, or someone who was so badly wounded he could not sit up. He crossed himself, and started calculating. That young man couldn't make a habit of bringing cases for the infirmary without being advised, ever so courteously, that it was the custom to pay for the gatekeeper's good offices, although he was Welsh, which wasn't as expensive as being English, and, from the way he had vanished into the night on his first visit, he might be a slippery customer. He was obviously a gentlemen, though, and could afford at least one piece of silver, and he had been polite, if distant, so he was unlikely to grab him by the throat and kick him, which had happened before when he had made the wrong judgement. The gatekeeper put down his beer and rose from his bench by the wall, the price fluctuating in his head.

The young man came closer, and the gatekeeper decided not to call out a cheerful good evening. He was changed, and not only because he was filthy dirty, hadn't shaved for days, and had a nasty mess on his thigh where an untreated wound had bled repeatedly over his hose. His face was grey under tangled hair, his eyes were feverish and haunted, he looked ten years older, and his companion was definitely dead. He saw the gatekeeper, and parted his cracked lips.

"I'm in Wales, now, aren't I?"

"Where else would you be? Who've you got there?" The gatekeeper saw his price falling, this scarecrow wouldn't be able to find his purse if he still had it.

The man ignored him. "There, father," he said to the corpse on his pony, "you're home. We can bury you now." He unclenched his hand from the pony's bridle and fainted, landing at the gatekeeper's feet like a sack of flour. The gatekeeper swore briefly, and called for help. It would be too untidy to leave him there until he turned into another body, and the monks were quite particular about neatness.

It was another warm afternoon, and the monks had opened the shutters of the unglazed infirmary window, letting in fresh air and a beam of sunlight, which travelled across the floor, angled up the bed, and finally eased on to Madog's face, waking him up with a start. What was he doing, lying in the sun, when he had to carry his father to Wales, and keep his body safe from those who would hack it to pieces and stick his head on a spike as a warning to others? Then he saw the cross on the wall opposite him, the pain in his leg hit him, and he remembered.

"I expect it hurts?" A voice beside him made him turn his head and focus through the water in his eyes on the austere monk watching him.

"Yes." He found himself pawing at his covers. "My father, can you . . . ?"

There was no change in the monk's expression. "We buried him yesterday."

Madog frowned. "But I only came last night, you can't have, unless you tipped him in a ditch. He is Llewelyn ap Gruffydd ap Llewelyn, not some vagrant, take me to whoever's in charge . . ." He was conscious of his voice rising. A cool hand pressed on his forehead.

"I am the Father Superior. You came here the day before yesterday, and we buried your father in a proper grave. Lie still, you're lucky we haven't taken your leg off."

"Did you say prayers?"

The monk didn't smile, but his nose twitched. "We usually do. Do you want to tell me what happened? Should we expect more visitors like you?"

"I don't know." It was difficult to explain anything, when he was so inexplicably confused. "There was a battle, at Tewkesbury. I was running to speak to Sir Hubert, and my father was hit. So Fitzjohn and I . . . we carried him to the waggons, and I think we went back to find Sir Hubert again, but there'd been an attack, and there was some fighting, and I lost sight of everyone . . ." He couldn't describe the scrambled memories of shouting, distorted faces and chaotic rushing around, or recall when he'd been wounded, or how he'd found his way back to the waggons,lifted Llewelyn on to a pony and slipped away, consumed beyond care for the living with the desire to take his father to Wales.

"What side were you on?" Did this monk really believe that was important?

"King Henry's."

"And who won?"

Madog frowned again. "I think we might have lost."

The monk sighed. "I hope your enemies don't come looking for you. I suppose Tewkesbury's a fair way from here. You did well to bring your father so far. Tomorrow you should be able to pray at his grave, if you rest and drink your medicine."

The cool hand returned to his forehead, and Madog reached up to the bony wrist. "I ran away, I left the others, I'm a coward."

This time, the monk smiled slightly. "I don't think so. And neither do your friends, from the way they've been hounding me to let them see you." He disengaged Madog's fingers, "They came earlier today. That boy who had an arrow in his arm and some others. I didn't tell you until I'd heard your side of the story."

Madog's head suddenly began to clear. Fitzjohn, Fitzjohn had shouted to him as they ran to find Sir Hubert, "If it goes against us, we should make for that monastery where I was." He looked more directly at the monk.

"You were testing me."

The other man shrugged. "If you had lied and told me you were Edward's man to save your skin, I would be less inclined to keep you. As it is, you'll have to move as soon as you're able. Our neighbour, Sir Ralph, is for King Edward, and he could return at any time. We've given your friends food, and they can find shelter in the gatehouse and barn, but I'll not have fighting in my monastery." He paused. "I saw what you have round your neck. I've left you your pagan charm, will you respect my wishes?"

Madog met his hard grey eyes, locked in a purpose of their own. "Yes, father. Thank you."

The monk rose. "It's time for my prayers. Don't try to get up today. I don't want your wound re-opening, and leaving you here for weeks. I'll see you tomorrow."

He left the room, and the infirmarer fussed in, bringing more potions which Madog swallowed without complaint. The swirling disorder of his dreams was better than the reality of the last few days.

A gentle May shower swept over the woods and fields the next morning, and Madog, leaning on a stick, stood by Llewelyn's grave, his senses coming to life in the clean rain. All that time, leading the pony on his hideous journey, he had felt his father's spirit hovering close, not yet ready to abandon his stiffening body completely. This morning, however, there was nothing but a peaceful emptiness, a moment of calm before the next tide of grief rolled in, and there was no point talking to this mound of earth as he had talked to his father all the way from Tewkesbury. He muttered a prayer out of duty, and limped to where Fitzjohn and Stamford were standing at a tactful distance. He found it hard to believe that his leg was so painful, when he had barely noticed it before, or that his body was so weak and sluggish, forcing him to think about every step.

Fitzjohn put his hand unobtrusively under his elbow. "It's good you can walk. We were saying that we should leave today if we can. We've more chance of getting these fellows home if we keep on the move."

Madog stared at him. All traces of boyishness had gone from his face, and a rigid mask covered whatever he was feeling. He looked like any one of the tens of captains they had seen on their march with Somerset's army, sharp with responsibility through their fatigue, and unsparing of weakness.

"Shouldn't we wait another day?" Madog was conscious that he was talking to him as an equal, "The others might arrive."

Fitzjohn stared back. "What others? This is all we are."

"Christ Almighty." Madog had seen Luddy, but not Morgan, huddled against the gatehouse wall, and had counted ten of his father's men and about a dozen of Sir Hubert's force. There was no sign of his archers, or of Sir Hubert himself, and Fitzjohn had so far said nothing about him.

Fitzjohn put his hand over his face. "We were broken. We ran like hares. Sir Hubert was wounded, and he went with Somerset to the abbey for sanctuary. He wanted me to join him, but I thought we should cross the Severn. We heard that Edward's men entered the abbey and slaughtered them all. The rules have changed, Madog, we cannot rely on anyone to save us."

"And Morgan?" Madog didn't know why he was asking this now. A small boy was of no significance compared with his father and Sir Hubert.

Fitzjohn's voice cracked. "The bloody silly little fools. They wouldn't stay with that carter, and he got an arrow in his neck. At least it was quick."

Madog flexed his leg. "Would you and Stamford be better off making for Bristol? You could disappear, take ship for France, not be there when some Yorkist bastard comes to take over the castle."

"Don't think I haven't considered it. Either that or throwing away my sword and joining the monks here. It might be a better way of living than working out how best to kill people."

Madog was staring at him again, "Are you serious?"

Fitzjohn grinned, like a break in the clouds. "Of course not. Poverty, chastity and obedience come naturally to me, but I do need a cup of wine every now and then. Besides, someone has to tell Lady Margery she's a widow, and mind out for Lady Agnes." He gestured around, "This is a cruel day, yet we're still alive. Sir Hubert wouldn't thank me if I moped around, and I reckon that since I was spared on that damned hill, the devil isn't ready for me yet. Nor for you. Let's pack up and leave while we can."

Madog had one more thing to do. In the privacy of the infirmary, he struggled out of his doublet and took his knife to one of the inside seams. He weighed the bag in his hand, got dressed properly again, and set off to find the Father Superior. He found him in his plain room, no fire in the hearth in spite of the cool wind, reading a book on a lectern, and seemingly oblivious to the draughts licking at his unstockinged feet in their sandals. Madog bowed.

"Father, I apologise for disturbing you." He held out the bag. "This isn't a payment for what you've done for us, and it's not to pray for my father's soul. The priest at home will do that. It's a gift, and I hope you will accept it, to use as you please."

The monk took the bag and glanced inside. His eyebrows rose, but he didn't hand it back straight away.

"You know where this came from? Is it stolen?"

"Only if a mountain can be stolen. No-one was robbed or killed because of it, and what the mint officials don't know won't hurt them."

The monk sighed. "We have taken presents of more dubious origin. It's not so easy to live simply here nowadays, and we are not an order of hermits." He looked Madog up and down. "You could be a rich man if you chose, yet you keep no state."

"I'm rich enough, and I have a mind to travel where this kind of wealth means nothing." He had told his unresponding father his plans on the way to the monastery, and now he wanted to tell someone living.

The monk touched his shoulder, "God calls men in different ways, and who am I to question him. Go carefully, my son, it is harder to find peace on this earth than you might think." He stowed the bag in a pouch hanging from his belt, and moved back to his book. "The cook will have some bread for you to take, and if your men have any spare coins, the gatekeeper would appreciate them. He is a good servant, if a trifle more worldly than us, although not as cunning as he thinks."

Madog took the hint, and when he rode from the monastery on Fitzjohn's horse, the gatekeeper smiled as he waved, glad that he had acted like a true Christian.

Bad news travelled fast, and, coming down from the hills into the Troddi valley, a sob of relief in his throat, Madog wasn't surprised to see a reception waiting in front of his house. He was surprised, however, to see Gwyneth and Lady Agnes gazing towards their tattered band, and Climbs Trees and Sleeps At Noon standing openly on either side of Cynan and Lady Agnes' woman, with Owain, silent for once, behind them, at the head of a throng of workers from Llewelyn's estate and the castle. Gwyneth sat straight as an arrow on her pony, holding hands with Lady Agnes, her eyes searching and counting. Madog reined in the horse he had taken from an unguarded field, and there was a deadly silence. Those who had stayed at home to fret stared in misery at those who had gone away to suffer unknown horrors, and returned bringing with them defeat and loss. Then Cynan threw his reins to Climbs Trees, and ran to Madog, lifting him down like a child and folding him in his arms.

"I'm sorry," the tears Madog hadn't shed until that moment coursed down his face, "I'm so sorry, I didn't look after him."

"Don't let me hear you talk such rubbish again. What's wrong with your leg?"

The dam was broken, and the two groups turned into one. Agnes cuffed Luddy around the ear before hugging him fiercely, and, seeing the look on her face, Fitzjohn knew that all his old illusions had been swept away, to be replaced with a strange conviction. He would protect her, because otherwise he would be no better than the men who had broken into the abbey and butchered her brother, and if they came after him, he wouldn't submit easily. They had brought the survivors home, everyone knew the worst, and surely he could now eat off a plate, take off his boots and sleep in the bed he had longed for. Whatever happened next, they must be owed a few days' grace.

As it happened, the few days stretched to over a week. Madog limped through the woods with Climbs Trees and stopped seeing the ball hit Llewelyn every time he shut his eyes, Cynan and Fitzjohn escorted a red-eyed Margery and her plump son to the convent in Llancaegy, and Bartlett vanished. No-one saw him and his man leave the castle, and no-one, not even Owain, bothered to climb to his room to check for signs that he planned to return. Master Hooper was disintegrating rapidly, having taken to drinking all day with the harbour-master, so it fell to Owain to help Agnes sort through the mass of papers left by Sir Hubert. They were sitting in the hall one morning, and it wasn't thought odd that Gwyneth was with them, while Mona was at what was now Cynan's house. The war and the death of the castle's master had shaken all their certainties, and it was no secret that families on Llewelyn's estate, whose fathers and sons had not returned, were offering places to the castle men-at-arms who feared being turned off or worse by a new lord.

Owain trimmed his quill with his little knife, "My lady, it is worth doing this." He thought Agnes seemed sad and distracted. "Yes, it is likely that this estate will be subject to an attainder, and Hugh and his descendants will be disinherited for ever. But you know that attainders are reversed with changes in politics, and if that ever happens, we must record Sir Hubert's holdings exactly, so that Hugh doesn't lose an acre or a barn.

Agnes smiled wanly. She had sent Luddy to his mother, at least until his screaming nightmares stopped, and she was wondering whether Nyrees or Mona would have any concoction to make him sleep better. She would never have thought that she could miss him, or her blockhead brother, or even the prattling Margery so much, or that she would be plagued by her last sight of Hugh, his round blue eyes popping above his fat cheeks. Thank goodness Gwyneth was here, and they were getting used to bursting into tears at odd moments.

"Shouldn't you be doing this for your brother? His estate is at risk as much as Hugh's."

Owain inspected his nib. "I don't mean to be rude, but my father was a trifle more . . . organised than Sir Hubert. Cynan knows what is his, down to the last nail."

"Is he going to marry that Angharad?"

Owain didn't know what Agnes wanted to hear. She might want Mona back, in which case it would upset her more to be told that Cynan had openly discussed breaking his engagement. If she wanted Cynan to make Mona an honest woman, though, she would not be pleased to hear that Cynan had done precisely nothing to contact Angharad's father. He sought for a diplomatic answer.

"It may not be in his hands. He is waiting for . . ."

They all looked up at the sound of hooves outside, and Agnes reached for Gwyneth's hand. For a warped instant she thought that Fitzjohn had been wrong, and Hubert would come in, tired and hungry and cross from riding all the way from Tewkesbury on his own. Instead, it was only Fitzjohn who walked through the door, leading a small man in a new gown and a hat that was just a bit too big.

"Bartlett," Agnes dropped Gwyneth's hand. "You've come back from your travels."

Bartlett gave a pretence of a bow, strode to the table, and swept away Owain's carefully ordered papers.

"Don't worry your head with this, Contessa," he said, his mouth set in a sneer, "the future of the estate is decided. I am old Sir Hugh's grandson, and now the traitor Hubert is dead, it belongs to me." He produced a package from inside his gown. "I have been to see my neighbour, Sir Giles, who is in favour with King Edward, and he supports my claim. You are my ward, and when Sir Giles has finished some pressing business, he will do you the favour of marrying you, to save you from disgrace and being forced into a nunnery like the luckless Margery. Fetch me some wine, boy." He handed his gloves to Fitzjohn, put the package on the table, and sat down in Sir Hubert's chair.

Chapter 17

Owain laughed into the shocked pause. He didn't care any more. His father was dead, his brother had nearly been crippled, and he would throw away his chance of escape to Oxford and become a shepherd with Cynan before he was polite to the man who had caused all this grief. He reached for the package.

"You still believe that Sir Hugh married your grandmother, and was a bigamist when he married Sir Simon's mother? I'm amazed Sir Giles let you through his gates, especially since you've been corresponding with Somerset for months, and you were the one who sent Sir Hubert to his death. Let me see." He started unwrapping the oiled cloth, and tipped out a handful of papers. "Here we are, a warrant from Sir Giles which any court of law would throw out, and, oh dear, a badly forged marriage certificate and a statement supposedly signed by a priest. Here, my lady, this is what the poor man has been clinging to for years."

Agnes stopped mouthing, "Bartlett's ward? Marry Sir Giles?" and took the yellowing scraps. She laughed as well, seemingly jolted out of her sadness.

"So it's true. My mother warned me about Bartlett's peculiar beliefs, and how he misread Sir Hugh's charity in taking him in when he was orphaned and having him educated, then granting him a pension. You could have told me that you knew, Owain, I hoped that it was a family matter, and not gossiped about in the kitchens."

Owain took the insult calmly. "It wasn't common knowledge. I found out by chance, and kept it to myself."

"Apart from telling your family I expect." She had seen Gwyneth's guilty blush. "Oh Bartlett, what a disappointment for you. I'm afraid I don't quite see myself as ward to the grandson of a scullery maid. I think you'd better ride back to Sir Giles and inform him that I can't agree to a marriage arranged by a madman." She screwed up the brittle papers, and threw them neatly into the fire.

Bartlett's face twisted in disbelief, and he sprang up towards the blaze. The flames took hold, and his papers blackened then disappeared.

"You silly little cow," he rounded on Agnes, "don't you understand? I'm the lord here, and neither you nor that Welsh boy you've probably been fucking can speak to me like that. I'll take a stick to you, and so will Sir Giles, until you learn some manners." He drew back his hand and hit her on the cheek, sending her back in her chair. Gwyneth cried out, and Fitzjohn leapt on him like a wild animal.

"You turd, how dare you, I'll cut your fucking hand off . . ."

"Sir? Sir?" Drawn by the noise, three men-at-arms blundered into the hall, and goggled at the sight of their betters brawling like common soldiers and the ladies in tears.

Bartlett dodged Fitzjohn's flailing arms, and ran behind them. "Get that man, and put him in chains. I'm your master now and he attacked me. When Sir Giles comes next week, he'll deal with him and anyone else who disobeys me. I mean it!"

The three men looked from one to the other. Fitzjohn had led them across the Severn, and cajoled and bullied them to safety, when he could have abandoned them to be ridden down by Edward's men and left for the rats and crows. Bartlett's hat had fallen down over his eyes, and he'd always been an arrogant shit, considering he was a bastard's son.

"Now sir," the eldest addressed Fitzjohn, "what's going on here?"

Fitzjohn steadied his breathing. "This son of a whore claims the castle is his, and he struck Lady Agnes. I think we should put him on his horse and drive him away."

The man-at-arms looked at his companions. They all had bolt-holes arranged if retribution came.

"Yes sir," he said, and seized Bartlett in an iron grip.

"Fool!" Bartlett spat in his face, "I'll remember you when I come into my own."

"Your own is a brothel," the man said, chuckling at his wit. "Come on, your sort isn't wanted here with the gentry."

They dragged Bartlett out of the hall, and those inside heard his curses drowned by the noise of men slapping his horse and chasing it across the courtyard and out of the gate.

Agnes blew her nose. "I'm all right," she said, forestalling any sympathy. "Thank you, Fitzjohn, my brother would have been so proud." She sat upright, her cheek flaming and her eyes dignified. "It still doesn't change anything. He will be back, bringing Sir Giles and his soldiers with him. We must make plans to send you somewhere safe, and Owain too. I won't have you suffer because of me."

Owain saw that Gwyneth had gone whiter than her best sheets on wash day. He pretended to sort through the papers Bartlett had scattered.

"Well, we are here to obey you of course, my lady," he said in his lawyer's voice, "and if you are determined to marry Sir Giles, then we cannot question your wishes. However," he started fiddling with his quill and knife again, "if you are open to persuasion, I'm certain we can arrange things differently."

"Are you sure you'll be up to it? Why don't you find a ship to take you to Dumfries? What are you looking for?" Cynan followed Madog into the storerooms at the back of the hall. "Oh Jesus, what did father expect to do with all these furs?"

"Make himself a set of winter underwear?" Madog poked his stick at an unidentified bale. "There aren't any boats in Abertroddi which would last the trip, and I don't want to spend time hanging around in ports in Wales. If we cut through the hills, we should catch Chester John and once we're at Chester, we might hear of a ship. My leg's fine, even though I can't move as fast as I'd like, so I'm looking for something to make us less obvious." He pulled a length of cloth from a bundle, "Something like this."

Cynan watched him. His face was still moulded by pain, and his clothes hung loose on his scrawnier frame.

"You're determined to go with Gwilym?" He tried to make the question casual.

Madog didn't look at him. "Yes." He ran the cloth through his hands, "It's not to do with being afraid of getting caught for Tewkesbury, or because I want to be rid of you all. It's difficult to explain."

Cynan leaned against the wall, "You always were a strange one, although it's not going to be very enjoyable when a new English lord turns up."

Madog started wrapping the cloth round his head, "Have you decided what to do?" He found it incomprehensible that his staid brother was so struck with this foreign woman, and that he wasn't running to his betrothed's father for help.

It was Cynan's turn to look away. "Ride to Glyn tomorrow, and tell him I can't marry Angharad. After that, I don't know. Be ready to take to a cottage in the hills if I have to, I suppose."

Madog stopped rummaging among the bales, "He'll be cross."

"Maybe not. If the English take the trouble of confiscating this estate because father was at Tewkesbury, he might be relieved."

Madog grinned at him, "Not if he knows the family secret."

"What family secret? What are those?" Madog was lifting some small bags from beneath a heap of old fleeces. "I didn't know they were there."

Madog tossed a bag to him, "Catch, it's heavy. This wasn't the best hiding place."

Cynan opened the bag, and had to sit down on the fleeces. "Good God, boy, where did you get this? Whose is it?"

Madog dropped the rest of the bags on his lap. "It's yours now. Naturally, it would only be fair if you gave Owain some, and Gwyneth if she needs it, and didn't spend it all on sheep. Which reminds me . . ."

Cynan listened to his request, and banged his forehead with his hand.

"That's crazy. Don't they understand? The poor beasts will be dead before you reach Chester, let alone Dumfries. As for the sea voyage to Vinland, you might not survive, never mind a bunch of sheep."

Madog was laughing, and for a moment was his old self again. "Come on, Cynan, it's not much to ask. They've set their hearts on this, I can't persuade them otherwise. Pick out one of your toughest rams, one of those buggers that you can never catch in the autumn, and three good ewes. If the worst come to the worst, we can always eat them. Hello, Owain, I didn't hear you come in. What's the matter?"

Owain stood at the storeroom door, looking as if he had ridden hard. He spoke without his usual elegant locutions.

"Brother, we need your help. Bartlett has switched sides, and is bringing Sir Giles to take over the castle. Can you take a few more people with you to Dumfries?"

Sir Giles' squire sat outside the alehouse on the main road into Chester. It was a poor place, and the beer was vile, but it wasn't raining, and he was better off here than back in Wales with Sir Giles in his present mood. His rage when he had arrived with a small army at Sir Hubert's castle and found no contessa, no useful men-at-arms and no-one of any standing except for an impossibly drunk lawyer and a whimpering steward had not been pleasant to behold. They had ransacked the empty Welsh house in the next valley and fired the barns, and banged on the doors of the convent in Llancaegy, yet the bravely obstinate nuns had denied all knowledge of Lady Agnes, and the soldiers, remembering the attack by devils in this very area, could not be persuaded to spread out into the hills to look for her. The harbour-master had sobered up and sworn blind that she hadn't been in Abertroddi, and the Welsh fishermen, who couldn't be expected to have any love for a grand English lady, had agreed. Sir Giles had sent a captain to make his way south to Bristol, in case she was fleeing there to take ship to France, and his favourite squire to Chester, in case she was heading for Scotland, while he stormed backwards and forwards along the coast of North Wales. A lady and her entourage could not disappear into thin air, and he would find and have the arrogant bitch before the summer was out. The squire looked at the traffic on the rutted track. Peasants, a cartload of firewood which she would hardly be hiding under, and, more promisingly, a covered waggon pulled by oxen and accompanied by a few soldiers and a couple of servants, one of whom was a woman. He whistled to his men-at-arms, and stepped into the road to stop the driver. Half an hour later, he was still being shouted at by the fat merchant's wife who had been dozing in the back, and one of his men had been knocked out cold by the driver after he had groped the woman servant. He called off his men and waved the waggon on, ignoring the driver's insults and complaints at having to set off in the middle of a packhorse train which had been steadily catching up with the waggon. People liked to travel in company, especially in these lawless times, and it seemed that the world and his wife and his livestock had joined the train, creating a chaos of lowing cows, bleating sheep, barking dogs and motley travellers, none of whom paid any attention to his orders for them to stop. He seized a boy leading one of the ponies.

"Who are all these people?"

The boy stared insolently back at him. His eyebrows were full of dust, and he smelt to high heaven.

"What people?"

The squire hit him round the head,and wished he hadn't. His hand felt sticky and grimy, and he thought he could see the vermin jumping on to his sleeve.

"Those people," he said, pointing at random to a tall young man in a garish outfit, riding alongside a dowdy, possibly pregnant, woman on a mule. She had a great mole on her cheek, and looked as if she was having a fit of the sulks. A grubby servant tugged at another laden mule in their wake. The boy put his finger to one nostril, and expelled the contents of the other at the squire's feet.

"Signor Piero and his wife, and Tom, their man. He's a foreign painter, they don't speak no Christian language.

Nor them," he gestured to two exotic figures swathed in robes and turbans, walking with a friar with a greying tonsure. "Moors. Converts, they're on a pilgrimage." He started on his other nostril. "Cows belong to Master Gerald, then there's them soldiers looking for a new place, that family with the carpenter, them weavers, them stone-masons . . ."

The squire gave up. They were all travel-stained and dingy, and he didn't want to have to speak with any of them. He stepped back, and threw a coin to the boy. Soon it would be dusk, and he could return to the comfort of the alderman's house where he was staying. Out of the corner of his eye, he saw a sheep run under the laden mule's feet, and the grubby servant swore. His ears pricked. There was something familiar about that voice under its rustic accent . . . no, he couldn't place it, and the man's rough, dirty face under his straw hat was unknown to him. He went back to his seat, and called for a bucket of water to throw over his unconscious man. If he didn't recover, he'd leave him here, since he certainly wasn't going to spend money on a doctor.

Although John of Chester was of lowly station, he had a multitude of contacts in the city, and a wealthy wool merchant of his acquaintance was more than willing to offer hospitality to the distinguished Italian painter and his wife, who had travelled many weary miles with the packhorses. The merchant recognised that the couple needed rest and privacy, and sent servants with hot water and carefully-prepared dishes up to their well-appointed chamber, rather than making them eat with him for that first evening. He would be a model host, and maybe the painter would be persuaded to stay and make some alterations to the unflattering likeness of himself on the altarpiece he and other dignitaries had commissioned last year. He was sure his nose wasn't so crooked or his face so jowly. The young man didn't speak much English, but his servant seemed a bright fellow, and he would put paid to the sniggers of his colleagues every time they entered the church. He sat drinking happily in the room below his guests' chamber, hearing nothing above their footsteps and indistinguishable words.

"Don't do that," Gwyneth finished drying herself with her shirt and grabbed Agnes' hand. "You'll never get it back in the same place."

Agnes pushed her away, and carried on picking at the patch on her face. "Yes I will, it'll have left a terrible mark. I just can't bear it any more, or this stupid thing." She kicked at the padding she wore under her gown. "I'm completely exhausted, I'm fed up with play-acting, I'm sore from that damned mule and you're a useless husband to me."

"Why's that?" Gwyneth smiled at her. Agnes hadn't complained once through the hardship of hurrying over the hills with Madog, sleeping in shepherds' huts or out in the open, and she hadn't shown she was afraid that their flimsy disguises would be penetrated, and she would be exposed and dragged back to Sir Giles. Neither had she expressed any regrets about discarding all status and ease and releasing Mona to stay with Cynan, and her courage had reduced the aching void in Gwyneth's heart at the loss of her entire former life to a mere splinter of grief.

"You haven't touched me since we left the castle. Am I so unattractive now I'm pregnant, or are you eyeing up that carpenter's wife? I've seen her simpering at you. A hair cut and a wodge of cloth down your hose doesn't make you a proper man, you know."

Gwyneth picked up Signor Piero's hose and draped them over a chest. "We haven't had much opportunity, and anyway, I wasn't sure if you wanted . . ."

"Why else would I put myself through this suffering? Come here."

The merchant did hear the soft cries and the bed creaking through his new floorboards, and he smiled to himself. What it was to be young and healthy. That should put a sparkle into the sulky girl's eyes, she had a stallion there from the length of time he was taking. If he was as good with a paintbrush, he'd end up painting kings. He had another cup of wine, and thought about the charms of the new maid in the kitchens.

Having lived as a child outside Chester, Fitzjohn knew the city well. With some reluctance, he left the merchant's cheerful kitchen and the pretty maid who kept giving him beer and encouraging smiles, explaining that he had to run one more errand for his master. It was hard work being a servant, yet he had to admit there were compensations. He had never realised that so much good food and drink never made it out of wealthy mens' kitchens, or that there was no such thing as discretion among those who served.

"That poncy young gent who's been hanging around at Bertha's?" The groom had said before supper in reply to his question. "Oh, he's staying with Alderman Richard. Looking for some runaway heiress who's worth more than the queen of France and has breasts like peaches. Upped and went with her squire, so they say. We should be so lucky, eh Tom? He won't be sleeping in a stable with only rats for company. You look worn out, I'll do your other mule if you fetch me a beer."

Fitzjohn slipped through the alleys to the back of Chester John's house, his straw hat pulled down to his eyebrows. He didn't think that any old family friends who might be out and about on this fine summer's night would recognise him, but caution came more easily to him now, and he climbed over a wall and slid quietly down a roof to land in John's stable yard. Rapping on the gate would only attract attention. One of Madog's strange foreign friends, whom he had learned all about on their journey home from Tewkesbury, came out of the shadows.

"In here," he said in his Welsh which was almost as bad as Fitzjohn's, and showed him into a windowless outbuilding. By the light of a dip, the other foreigner was shaving Madog's tonsure, his lips tight with effort. Fitzjohn had no idea what Madog was using to dye his hair and the beard he was cultivating, and although it was convincing enough to add twenty years to his age, it was ineffective against the new black stubble already springing up on his scalp.

"Problems?" Madog asked, his voice muffled with the strain of keeping his head still.

Fitzjohn sat down on a bale of wool. "Sir Giles' squire. I'm afraid he'll work out who I am if he sees me again. He looked a bit puzzled when we passed him. He's staying at Alderman Richard's, I know where it is."

"Do you think we should kill him? A street brawl? An assassin sneaking into his bedroom?"

Fitzjohn thought. "It's tempting, but it would cause more trouble in the end. There'll be a hue and cry when his body's found, and if we heave it in the river, he'll be missed and it'll be just as bad."

Climbs Trees finished his work, and Madog smiled his thanks. "You're right. A false trail, maybe? Would he recognise me? I don't want to involve anyone else."

Fitzjohn yawned. "He might have noticed you at that Mass and dinner last year. God, it seems like a lifetime ago. He probably won't remember you, even if you went as yourself. You've changed."

Madog gave him a surprisingly kind grin, "So have you, Tom. You'd better go and get some sleep. This is what I'll tell him."

Fitzjohn listened, made a few suggestions, and went back to the merchant's by a different route. The house was abed, and he made himself comfortable in the stable with some blankets and a pile of straw. It was better than a hedgerow, snug and dry, and if it wasn't for those rats rustling, it would be perfect. Christ, that wasn't a rat. He tried to sit up, and a body, all warmth and curves, flowed over him.

"Oh Tom," a voice tickled in his ear, "you speak so nicely, and you're such a fine young man." A hand, roughened by work and yet curiously gentle, went where no woman's hand had yet been. "Oh my, a very fine young man."

Fitzjohn gulped, and thought he should struggle. What if Lady Agnes wanted him, what if this girl was a spy for Sir Giles, what if this was a trap? The hand moved slowly and he surrendered. Pleasure was taking away all those pictures of guns which fired at him in his dreams, and he might as well play the part of servant to the full. He rolled over and forgot everything.

Chapter 18

The squire scowled at the friar who had interrupted his breakfast. He hoped that this was not a request for alms, or a message from the parents of one of those girls in Wales. None of them had exactly pushed him away, so it wasn't his fault if they'd got themselves into trouble.

"I saw you yesterday," he said, pointedly not asking the man to sit down, even though he seemed somewhat lame. "What do you want of me?"

The friar fixed him with his intense dark gaze. "I want nothing from you, sir. I am provided for by God, and my work is to save souls for him. I have prayed for guidance, and my conscience tells me to speak to you."

"About what?" The squire wiped his fingers. "Hurry up, I'm a busy man." He detected the gleam of a fanatic in those eyes.

The friar was not put off by his rudeness. "I am travelling to holy shrines of the Blessed Virgin with my charges." The gleam became more pronounced. "How God performs his miracles, even in these blasphemous times. They were Barbary pirates, cruel and lost in sin, when their ship sank in the Middle Sea. A Christian captain lifted them from the waves, and by that example of mercy, they came to know the true religion and renounce their heathen ways. Surely, heaven will be rejoicing at these lost sheep who have been brought into the fold of righteousness and . . ."

"Yes, yes," the squire shifted in his seat, "very commendable. Is this what your conscience wants me to know?"

The friar dropped his voice, "No. As I said, we are on pilgrimage, and four days ago, we prayed at the shrine of St Matilda near the manor of Trewarne in the Marches. The lord of the manor was kind, and gave us shelter for the night." He paused. "I do not concern myself with gossip, yet it is well known that you are looking for a lady, the widow of a foreign count." His mouth signalled his disapproval.

The squire leaned forward, "And?"

The friar lifted his eyes to the ceiling. "Pray God I am following his will. I would not involve myself in such a matter were it not for the sin I saw openly flaunted in that good man's house."

"What sin?" The squire hoped he didn't sound too eager.

The friar's mouth screwed up further. "There was such a . . . lady there. Resting for a week or two on her way to London."

"London?"

"Yes. And she had with her, among her servants, a young squire, God forgive him. What temptations lie in the paths of youths, and how easily they are snared by women who lack a husband's rule."

The squire's mouth fell open, "You mean?"

"I will not defile my lips with repeating what I saw. I'm telling you this only for the sake of her soul and that of the boy. It is not too late for her to repent, and be properly instructed in a convent, or by a forgiving husband."

The squire thought of Sir Giles and grinned. "What did she look like?"

The friar seemed affronted. "I spent no time gazing upon her. Like an idle rich woman who indulges in fashion. Short, not old, and haughty, in spite of her vice. I heard one of her servants call the youth Fitzjohn."

The squire jumped from his seat. The bastard. He would have come home from Tewkesbury, played the stricken hero and wormed his way into Lady Agnes' bed. Well, his goose was cooked and no mistake. Three or four days journey by walking with a packhorse train would take less than two by horse, and if he set off now . . . He scrabbled for some coins for the pious noodle, and sped from the room.

The merchant strolled back from the church, pleased with himself, his guest, and his noble city. Signor Piero had appeared at breakfast, a little tired round the eyes, although that was to be expected, and had excused his wife in broken English. She was still tired from their journey, and was enjoying the comfort of this marvellous house. The merchant winked over his fine bread, and gave the painter a knowing slap on the back. The young man looked alarmed, and even more so when the merchant rushed out his request. Then he seemed to gather himself, and said he would be honoured to perform such a task. The merchant interpreted the way he covered his mouth with his sleeve and bowed his head as Italian manners. Their servant was summoned and slouched behind them, a foolish grin on his face, carrying paints and brushes. It took seconds for the artist to examine the painting in the church, less than an hour for the pigments to be mixed, and minutes for the merchant's transformation into a straight-nosed firm-chinned philanthropist. The merchant showed his gratitude by leading his new friend on a tour of the sights of Chester, and was gratified by the look of bewildered amazement on his face for most of the day. These foreigners weren't as bad as people made out, why he had even given some money to a wandering friar who had stopped to harrass him, and had pocketed the written blessing the friar had forced upon him, instead of tossing it in the nearest ditch, while the servant, Tom, was a jolly chap, whistling to himself as they walked along and tipping his straw hat to every woman they passed. He would be able to boast about his visitor for weeks.

"Madog has found us a ship," Gwyneth said when she was released to the privacy of the guest room. "It leaves tomorrow, though we have to take a boat down the river to reach it. Are ships really so uncomfortable?"

"Terrible. It's a bit of a shame, I'm beginning to like it here." Agnes was reclining under the covers, nibbling a cake. "How was the painting?"

Gwyneth sat on the bed and put her face in her hands. "Oh lord. I don't know how long my improvements will last. The colours might all run off in the first damp spell.

And I'm so tired, this place is so big and noisy and full of people. Is Venice as big as this?"

Agnes smiled and rubbed her back, "It's much bigger, my treasure."

Gwyneth sighed. "I must seem such a peasant to you. Maybe I should have stayed in Wales and opened an alehouse."

Agnes moved her hand round to the front of the padded doublet. "I would never allow it. You suit me far better as a handsome artist than as a brewer. Take this thing off, I want to be your wife again."

"I think wives are meant to be more docile." Gwyneth kicked off her boots. If the ship was going to be a nightmare, they might as well enjoy their time on dry land.

By evening, Sir Giles' squire and his men had reached another squalid alehouse, this one in a small village. They bought what food they could, and let the horses rest. The summer nights were short, and they could set off again at dawn and be at Trewarne before noon. Even if Lady Agnes and Fitzjohn had already left the manor, they wouldn't have travelled far, and it wouldn't be hard to track them down. The squire laughed into his cup. He couldn't wait to see the look on Fitzjohn's face when he rode up and ruined his elopement. Sir Giles would have his balls and more. He looked around for someone to serve him. The slatternly woman who ran this place was having a shouting match with some withered crone who had come in to fill a filthy leather bucket with beer.

"Wasn't him, you addled old bat," the alehouse owner slopped her barely drinkable brew into the bucket. "When young Fitzjohn comes home it'll be as a knight or in a coffin. He wouldn't be dressed as a servant walking with a load of packhorses. Why would he do that? You're going blind."

The crone cackled, "He'll be in some scrape. Here fill it up, you miser, I've got the money."

The squire's hand tightened round his cup. Of course, Fitzjohn's family lived somewhere around here. An awful feeling crept into his stomach. He stood up, and took hold of the ancient's shoulder.

"Who are you talking about? Have you seen Fitzjohn, the Fitzjohn who's Sir Roger Fitzjohn's second son? Where? Here? Recently?"

The crone yelped, and nearly dropped her bucket. "Oh sir, don't startle an old woman so. Yes, I saw him here a few days ago, even though this miserable penny-pinching daughter of mine denies it. I nursed his father, God bless him, and I'd recognise little Fitzjohn anywhere, even though he's grown so tall and his pretty face was under that straw hat." She leered, revealing two stumps of tooth, "I would've run to him, but then I thought," she tapped her nose, "he'll be up to something naughty and won't want me interfering. I'll tell his brother mind, when he comes back from visiting his mother-in-law. He'll want to know he's safe. Hey, give my girl her money before you go."

The squire ran out. He thought he was going to be sick. That servant in the straw hat, no wonder his voice had sounded familiar, and come to think of it, that could have been Fitzjohn's face under the dirt and whiskers. The sulky woman on the mule . . . He thought back to the times he'd seen Lady Agnes at her brother's castle, and yes, if you took away that blemish, she was the right height and colouring, and any woman could stuff a cushion up her gown, unless she truly was pregnant. The friar must have been in on it with them. He had seen that beaked nose before too, on the face of that Welshman and all his bloody relatives, God, any one of them could have been the painter. He retched, and it wasn't only the sour beer. He had left his post, and been fooled by a troop of natives. Sir Giles would kill him. He had seen how he was when his blood was up and he had a whip in his hand. He rushed back inside, and roused his men with kicks and blows. They were riding back to Chester tonight, and he would pray that these charlatans were still in the city.

"You forget yourself sir," Alderman Richard looked coldly at the wild young man standing in his hall. "I cannot call out the watch when no crime has been committed, and we are not in danger. I don't see any army at our gates. There are proper procedures." He wasn't taking kindly to being ordered around by someone who was a lot less elegant than he had been two days before.

"Proper procedures, proper procedures," the squire added an obscenity which made even the servant standing behind the alderman jump. "These are traitors, Welshmen, the King's enemies, who have kidnapped Sir Giles' betrothed."

The alderman shrugged. "So you say. I have only your word for it. I think you had better curb your tongue and leave. We are respectable people here, we mind the law, and will not let ourselves be sucked into private quarrels. We'll have no mob rule in our city."

For a horrible second, the squire thought he was going to throw himself at this pompous sod's feet and beg for his help. He bit his lip, and tried to speak calmly.

"I'm sorry. Forgive me for my intemperate language. My master is in great distress at the thought of what his lady might be suffering. At least, can you find out if a foreign painter, his wife, a servant called Tom and a friar travelling with two Moors have left the city?"

The alderman raised his eyebrows at this list of unlikely companions. "I suppose I could try. You may wait in the yard. It might take some time."

The squire galloped along the riverbank towards the deep-water inlet, sweating as much as the horse he had taken from the alderman's stable. His own was nearly spent, and this fat beast hadn't had so much exercise for years. It had been purgatory, hanging around in the yard while messengers came and went and refused to tell him anything. At last the alderman had called him back into the hall, and had sniffed at him, as if he were a bad smell.

"There is a ship down river, the Chester Rose, due to leave for Scotland on today's tide. She has all the licenses in order. A river boatman took a group of passengers matching your descriptions to her this morning. There's no point rushing off, she will probably have set sail by now . . ."

The squire ignored him, snatched the horse, and set off, scattering street hawkers and children in his path. There was always a chance that something would have delayed the ship, and the master would give up his passengers, especially if he was told they were defeated rebels. He would deal with the so-called friar himself, and save Fitzjohn for Sir Giles, or he could break a few of Fitzjohn's bones to be going on with, and since it was clear that Lady Agnes wasn't fussy, he would have a go with her himself, and no-one would believe her if she complained, the whore. The inlet came into view and, praise the lord, a substantial ship lay in the water, her sails still furled and cables still over her sides, despite the activity on her deck and up in the rigging. He threw himself off the horse, and shouted to a boatman sitting on a little jetty, fishing while his moored craft bobbed up and down beside him.

"Row me out to that ship. Now. In the name of the king."

The boatman looked up. "No."

The squire lifted his whip. "Didn't you hear me? Take me to that ship."

The boatman concentrated on his line. "Can't. She's setting sail. I'll never catch her on this ebb."

He flicked his rod at a swirling eddy in the brown water, and the squire saw the patched sails flopping from the yards.

"You can reach her," he screamed, and made to strike the man. Two burly figures came out of a shed at the side of the jetty.

"Trouble, Michael?" one of them asked.

The squire flung down his whip and pulled out his knife. He pounded down the jetty, jumped into the boat and slashed at the ropes keeping it tied to the wooden piles. The three men made no effort to stop him as he fought with the oars and, after a couple of false starts, put his back into rowing as hard as he could.

"Looks like you've lost your boat, Michael," he heard someone say, and then he was rocking sideways down the river, faster than that lazy horse had galloped, but far too close to the bank and yards of racing water from the ship. The last cable went up her side, the sails filled, and she was moving, her bow lifting as if catching the scent of the sea. A faint bleating floated towards him, and through despairing eyes, he saw a figure in a straw hat, standing on the deck and staring in his direction. The figure lifted his hat and bowed, and even from this distance, the squire could make out the gloating smile on Fitzjohn's face.

Alexander and Gwilym sat on the wall of the harbour which served Dumfries. The sunlight making diamonds on the water, the purposeful bustle of activity, the lack of pain in his body, the sympathetic chatter of the Welshman, all these could not raise Alexander's spirits. After a difficult and convoluted voyage back to his home port, he had found that his incompetent landlubber of a mate had managed to drive his ship on to the rocks and drown half his crew not two miles along the coast. Moreover, the news that he had dressed as a woman to escape had somehow reached the ears of Dumfries' inhabitants, who usually regarded him with a superstitious awe, and he was plagued by wolf-whistles and saucy invitations whenever he left his house. Even the fact that Murray, his patron at court, had secured him yet another pardon from the king and was putting up some of the money for a new ship could not shift his malaise. The summer was half gone, he would miss the whole raiding season, and he had had to dig deep into his own reserves to pay for what was still a shell on the stocks in the shipyard. If there was a nice little war with England now, he would be tempted to knock Gwilym on the head and steal his newly-caulked vessel which was bouncing smugly in the harbour, a daily reminder of his ill fortune.

"She's an English ship," Gwilym said. They had been criticising the master of a cog which was trying to come into the harbour.

"The bugger wants sinking," Alexander replied. "Och, you're no' going to make it doing that." The loose sails shivered and cracked, and the ship went beam on to the waves. "Give them a wee shot from your gun, Gwilym, put an end to their suffering."

"I think she's the Chester Rose from the look of her," Gwilym shielded his eyes from the sun's glare. "I've come across her master before. He wanted a copy of my rutter for sailing to the Middle Sea."

"I hope you didna' give it to the bastard. He's no' fit to be in charge of a wee fish boat."

"He'll make it this time. Here she comes."

The ship turned round the right way and rolled through the harbour approaches, with men in the rigging pulling frantically at the sails.

"Too quick," Alexander and Gwilym said together and covered their ears, waiting for the crash. There was a rending of timber, a lot of hoarse shouting, then relative peace as ropes hissed through the air and men hopped on shore to tie them fast.

"Looks like she's carrying passengers," Alexander observed, noticing the bowed figures clustering round the gangway. "They've no' enjoyed the trip."

A friar of some kind and a younger man, supporting a woman between them, staggered down the planks and lay on the wharf.

"My God," Gwilym said, and jumped up to run to them. He knelt beside the young man, whose once bright outfit was stained with salt and grime, "Madog, Madog, is that you?"

The man raised his head, and Gwilym saw the tears in eyes which weren't Madog's after all.

"Good afternoon, uncle," Gwyneth's voice was frail as an old grandmother's, "Madog's over there. He's the religious one." She flapped weakly at the woman weeping helplessly next to her, "You remember the Lady Agnes?"

A peculiar sound rose above the cries of gulls and the normal ship noises. Gwilym turned and saw Alexander, who hadn't smiled for months, standing over the friar and laughing until his beard was wet.

High tide came just after dawn, and the rising sun, hidden behind a bank of cloud, could only put the merest pink touches to the pearl grey sea. Madog and Gwyneth stood on the wharf, unable to speak now that the moment had come. Gwilym's ship, laden with stores and four apprehensive sheep in a pen on the deck, was ready to leave, and Climbs Trees and Sleeps At Noon were wafting the smoke from burning herbs up the masts and down the hull, their lips moving in prayer. Madog looked into Gwyneth's face. She was beautiful. She had bid farewell to Signor Piero in the privacy of Alexander's house, and greeted Lady Gwyneth, a Welsh heiress who had escaped King Edward's wrath with her fortune intact, and the means to buy the best cloth Dumfries could offer for her gowns.

"You have enough money?" Madog asked for the second time.

Gwyneth smiled at him. Their expenses so far had hardly made a dent in the precious bags Cynan had given her. "Yes. You and Cynan have been very generous. When we go to Edinburgh, Murray will advise us on some suitable investments."

"Don't give it all to Alexander," Madog said, trying to smile back. "Gold cannot compensate you for all that you've had to leave behind, but . . ."

"It makes it easier to bear, Madog. We would have been lost without all that you've done. You know that, and you must know how grateful we are . . ."

Her voice trailed away as he met her eyes. He hadn't expected to feel this. Since he'd been a man, in some secret recess of his heart he'd seen her as a prize which would one day be his, and now he was undone by the end in this world of his hope for her.

He gestured to the ship, "It's not too late. You could . . ."

She knew, and was crying. "I cannot. This can never be, my sweeting. You must go."

She and his mother used to call him that when he was tiny, and he saw the part of her which could have received him as he desired disappear. He hugged her once and ran on board, and Agnes left Gwyneth alone until the last link to her old life had dwindled to a white speck on the horizon.

Chapter 19

Their servants in Edinburgh agreed that the Countess of Peruzza and Lady Gwyneth kept an interesting household. True, they were not the easiest of mistresses to work for, since the countess had not stopped complaining about the cold since they arrived last summer, and Lady Gwyneth, who found it difficult to understand their honest Scots tongue, was a stickler for cleanliness and was given, every now and then, to brooding like one of those highland women with the second sight. They both indulged the English captain of their armed retinue, who was an appalling womaniser, and refused to dismiss him when he was detected in one of the court ladies' bedrooms, and had to run barefoot in the snow back to their rented house in the High Street. However, they paid wages and tradesmen's bills on time, which was more than could be said for many of the other English exiles clinging to the fringes of the court, and they appeared to have the protection of Murray, who balanced skilfully between rival factions at the centre of power, and who had never looked in danger of losing his head. They liked to entertain in a quiet way, and painters, musicians, architects and scholars all passed through the house, filling it with pleasant sound and intellectual debate, which was far more stimulating than the dreary rants about land and politics which most serving men had to put up with when they waited on table. If neither of them were conventionally beautiful, their teeth and complexions were passable, and they had enough admirers for bets to be laid in the kitchen on which Scots lord or foreign gentleman would be successful in his suit. So far, no-one had collected.

"They're invited out for dinner tomorrow," a maid

announced to the cook one afternoon in May. "They willnae be wanting you to save those leftovers for them." She had a horde of hungry brothers and sisters back at home, and this was the best position she'd ever had.

The cook, who had a kind heart somewhere under her massive bosom, pinched her cheek. "Leave the salmon pies for us, hen, rich food is nae good for weans. Where're they going?" She settled down on her stool with a cake that was too singed on the top to serve up to her delicate employers.

"Murray's. He's entertaining yon English loons who've come to ask the king to be friends."

They both spat into the fire. Ecky on the door had seen the English ride down the High Street, pricing up everything with their piggy eyes.

"I suppose it's natural. The countess is a kind of English after all," the maid ventured.

The cook sprayed out crumbs. "It disnae count. She'll no' be wanting to trample us down and burn the roof over our heads. And it was a wicked English lord who drove her and Lady Gwyneth from their homes in the dead of night, with only the gowns they stood up in."

"And the gold they'd hidden in their stockings and you know where." They had gleaned all sorts of information about their ladies.

"Aye, good luck to them. Draw us a beer, hen, we'll drink to their health, and hope the English keep their hands off them. I wouldnae trust them, not even in Murray's house, God protect him."

"Murray's probably bored and wants a little amusement," Gwyneth said from her seat in the window where she could watch the comings and goings on the High Street. "It's conceivable that in law you are still Bartlett's ward, but I can't see Murray handing you over to the English delegation, unless he's being even more devious than usual. Are you such a great prize? What would the Scots want in return? The border to be moved ten miles south?"

Agnes fussed over a new headdress, "Twenty miles at least, you hussy. Of course I'm valuable. A Beaufort, the sister of a prominent rebel, rich and beautiful. They could marry me off to one of Edward's brothers, and it must really hurt their pride that I'm out of their reach. I think we should take Fitzjohn, in case there's any unpleasantness."

"The only unpleasantness will be caused by him. Murray's wife won't be safe, nor any of her maids. I don't know what's come over him."

Agnes smiled at her censorious expression. "I keep telling you, it's only natural. Do you think a few more pearls on here would be too ostentatious?"

"Yes, but you're going to sew them on anyway. If you're worried about being snatched, maybe you should look poorer and less desirable."

"That would be impossible," Agnes threaded a needle, "as you can testify."

Gwyneth had to smile back. On days like this, it was difficult to remember her fits of gloom, when she was unutterably homesick and in an agony of worry over what had happened to Cynan and Mona, Nyrees and even Glynis. In the noisy and cramped High Street, she missed the peace of the Troddi valley, and the comfort of her old routines, and grew weary with the struggle to communicate with their incomprehensible servants. Yet this new existence had different compensations, and nearly every day brought the opportunity to see artists painting or buildings rising from the ground, and to hear stories and ideas which would never have reached her if she had stayed in Wales. Neither would she have had Agnes in her arms every night, and she knew that her moments of suffering were nothing compared with what she would have had to endure if Agnes had been forced to marry Sir Giles. In their present circumstances, they had unimaginable freedom, and she would have been a fool to wish for more change. She moved from the window, took the needle from Agnes' hand, and made her squeal with laughter and desire.

Of the Englishmen gathered in Murray's hall, only Dr Vasey looked truly comfortable. One of King Edward's lawyers, he was far outranked by the other members of the delegation, yet they all suspected that, with his long meetings with other men in dark gowns, he alone knew what was going on. The noblemen had to bear being entertained by their Scottish counterparts and take part in a singular form of torture involving sticks and balls and holes in the ground, all the time praying that nothing went wrong and they didn't end up detained in that ferocious castle for unfeasibly high ransoms. Sir Giles was in the most pain. He had accepted that the awfulness of a trip to Scotland was the price he had to pay for increasing his influence at court, which had become more necessary since his plans in Wales had gone awry, and he had been prepared to risk his health in these fine clothes which were still damp because they had not been packed properly for the journey. He had even been prepared to be polite to Murray, and gallant to his sour-faced wife and her lady guests. Nothing, however, had prepared him for the shock when he found out who these lady guests were, and he was finding it hard not to drive his knife into the table, and throw this dish of scraggy mutton at his host's face. He was sure that everyone present was laughing up their sleeves at his humiliation, and bitter plans for revenge almost prevented him from speaking.

"Sir Giles," Agnes' face was untroubled, "how pleasant it is to see an old neighbour. I am so sorry we were unable to call on you before we left Wales, but alas, it was not the happiest of times. If your squire is attending you in Scotland, I am sure Fitzjohn would be pleased to see him."

Sir Giles' cheeks darkened even further. He had got rid of the young fool, and the last he'd heard, he was with the English garrison in Calais, where he hoped he'd die of the fever. Agnes sailed on.

"Sir Giles used to come hunting on my brother's estate," she explained to Murray, as if, Sir Giles thought savagely, he didn't know the whole story, "and we enjoyed many a day in the chase. He is rightly proud of his stables. I daresay few can match his judgement when it comes to horses."

She laid the slightest emphasis on the last word, and Murray's wife, whose appearance belied her wit, raised a napkin to her mouth. Dr Vasey smiled blandly at a fellow delegate who'd raised a questioning eyebrow at him. Sir Giles had worked hard to give the impression that his relations with his rebel neighbour had not been cordial. Murray, who liked to amuse his wife, joined in.

"I gather you are a widower, Sir Giles. Perhaps we can find you a Scottish bride, to strengthen the goodwill between our countries. I am sure that the ladies can come up with some suitable names between them. It is a sadness when a man has no heir to follow him." Even some of the Englishmen winced. Sir Giles' wife had born her first husband two sons in two years of marriage before his untimely death, but in ten years with Sir Giles had produced nothing, and the inference had not been lost at court, with its love of gossip and scandalous rumourmongering. Dr Vasey feared his colleague was about to ruin months of diplomacy, and stepped graciously in.

"Far be it from me to criticise matrimony in front of such a happily established man," he bowed his head at Murray, "but I suspect match-making to be a pernicious art. It would be far more profitable for men to be urged to enter the Church, where they may strive for the common good without being distracted by the petty concerns of wives and female relatives."

As he expected, the ladies objected hotly to his line of reasoning, and the argument continued until the dinner ended and Sir Giles was led out by a steward to visit the stables. Giddy with relief, Agnes and Gwyneth were on their way out, when Dr Vasey stopped them, and ushered them politely but definitely to a private room off the hall. It was dim and quiet, and Gwyneth wished Agnes had won, and been allowed to bring Fitzjohn.

Dr Vasey seemed taller and less affable than at the table, as he closed the door and checked that no servants were listening outside. Gwyneth saw Agnes' back straighten, and she let her hand stray to the knife hidden under her outer gown. The Englishman surveyed them without hurry, and then spoke.

"Contessa, Lady Gwyneth, forgive me for detaining you, but I must have a few private words with you." His Italian was fluent, and Gwyneth sensed Agnes' surprise. "If I may say so, Contessa, you are bold, which is not always to be recommended. A semblance of meekness can often help one avoid life's pitfalls."

Agnes' chin went up. "Is this going to be one of life's pitfalls? If I've fallen into it already, it's a fraction late to pretend to be humble."

Dr Vasey smiled, and Gwyneth saw how Owain might be in twenty years' time if he lived. Subtle, confident, and with a humour that had survived years of politicking.

"Not necessarily. I will do you a kindness, and tell you that Sir Giles has less influence at court than he would like." He twitched his shoulder, as if shrugging off a fly. "You may, or may not, have heard that Bartlett, the claimant to your brother's estate, died last winter, and Lady Margery and her son returned to her father's house, where the boy will be provided for. Your brother's estate and your wardship reverted to the crown." He looked even more unconcerned at Agnes' involuntary gasp. "The king has many more substantial matters to trouble him than local feuds in Wales, and he has an admirable grasp of practicalities. Neither is he vindictive towards his former enemies. Because of negotiations in foreign affairs, it suited him far better for your wardship to go to your late husband's brother in Venice, rather than to have the bother of arranging your marriage." He coughed, "I will not be indelicate, but the financial settlement was favourable to him."

"I beg your pardon?" Agnes' eyebrows came together. Her late husband's brother was in his dotage, and she doubted whether he remembered her existence.

Dr Vasey tutted, as if she was being peculiarly stupid. "Legally, you are beyond Sir Giles' reach. Naturally, it would be wise for you if you returned to Venice, though you cannot be forced to do so, since you are admirably protected here in Scotland, for the moment at least. Nevertheless," he reached to a table beside him and picked up a bag, "I have a collection of documents and letters for you from your mother, your lawyers in Venice and your young lawyer in England which might induce you to remove once more. I believe there is a letter for Lady Gwyneth as well." He became less forbidding. "Your smart student friend will go far. He was persuasive enough to convince me to act as your courier, and I emphasise that my involvement ends here. Your mother approves of his part in these arrangements, and I hope you understand that if you disapprove, the responsibility lies with him." He handed Agnes the bag, "And now I must beg you to excuse me. I wish I could spend more time with you but . . ."

Agnes and Gwyneth remembered to curtsey, and shifted from the room as fast as courtesy allowed.

"He sold me!" Agnes hissed once they were out of earshot. "That Owain of yours has sold me to my brother-in-law. If it was enough to buy me from King Edward, it'll have taken everything I have. Why did I say he could manage my accounts instead of those lawyers in London? I must have been deranged, we'll be penniless in a month."

Gwyneth, overcome with gratitude that Owain was apparently alive and very busy, was not over-sympathetic. "What are you complaining for? You can never be made to marry Sir Giles or anyone else in England."

Agnes jumped up and down with pique. "That's not the point. Now my husband's addled brother can marry me off. We'll be stuck in Scotland for ever, your money won't last long at the rate we're spending it and I'll have to beg and I'll die of cold."

Gwyneth took her cloak from a maid, "If your brother-in-law is addled, he won't be able to choose you a husband."

"The lawyers will do it, I can't escape."

Gwyneth wondered why she was being so obtuse. Perhaps the meeting with Sir Giles had caused her more anxiety than she would admit.

"Well, your lawyer would have to agree. And who is your lawyer?"

Agnes stopped shouting in Italian, and gave the maid a loose pearl from her headdress. "Of course. Put this towards your marriage chest, my dear." She slipped her arm through Gwyneth's, "I always knew he was a clever boy. I wonder what words of advice my mother has for me."

The household knew something was afoot. The ladies had returned in one piece from Murray's, and closeted themselves away with candles and no servants allowed in the room to conduct business. The maid, who was the lightest on her feet, crept up and down the stairs, listened at the door and reported back to the kitchen, although her audience made little sense of what she said.

"I cannae understand them when they talk so fast," she apologised. "They're gey worked up, laughing and crying over someone who's bought a castle and what lawyers in Venice have done. I cannae tell if it's good news or bad, or whether they're for flitting or no'. And don't tell me knock and go in, I dinnae want another candlestick thrown at me."

"Ah, the countess is that way out, is she?" The cook heaved herself to her feet, "I'll make her a wee bit of her favourite supper. She'll no' fling that at you hen. Call Ecky to do their fire, his hearing's good enough when he's in the same room, and you get up there and have another listen. Jamie," she pulled out a wine flask from beneath a cooking pot and gave it to the boy who ran errands, "take this round to my sister at Murray's. See what she's heard." She winked at the maid, "Could be one o' them's had a proposal and I'll be in the money. Murray's nephew, I said he was a sound bet." She started breaking eggs into a bowl, and no-one dared to contradict her.

Gwyneth read Owain's letter again, in case she'd been mistaken, and this terrible rift was unnecessary. The even letters marched across the page, and she could hear Owain's voice with a smile behind it, pretending not to be exultantly proud. "I'm not convinced that Cynan has spent his fortune wisely. When he heard that Bartlett had sadly passed away and Sir Giles was gone to court, he came down from his cot in the hills, repaired the damage which Sir Giles inflicted on the hall, and wrote to me with certain enquiries and instructions. The king had desired to grant Sir Hubert's castle and estate to some relative of the queen, but upon hearing that a certain Welshman was willing to pay for it in gold, was minded to disappoint the relative and take the money. Cynan and his wife, Mona, are therefore installed in the castle, and none may dispossess them, since they have titles and warrants from King Edward himself, whose loyal servants they have always been. I detect a woman's cunning behind this." He hadn't needed to spell out what this meant for Gwyneth. She could go home. She could leave this fascinating yet undoubtedly foreign city with its feuds and undercurrents of violence, and go back to a wonderful peace, where she and Agnes could probably live in either Llewelyn's hall or the castle and do as they pleased, watching the seasons come and go unmolested by Sir Giles. She saw Llewelyn laughing with his grandfather in a heaven that was not unlike the valley in summer, because his sons had returned his family to their rightful place after seventy years of disappointment. Then her dream had been shattered by Agnes putting down her mother's letter and saying, her voice cold and certain,

"You can go back to Wales if you must. I'm going to Venice."

They were still arguing. They had stopped while someone came in to see to the fire, and when a maid brought a tray of food which lay untouched, and now the windows were dark, and they were hoarse with tears and obstinacy.

"Can't you see?" Agnes wouldn't look at Gwyneth, "Edmund had a child, she must be three by now. She is my niece, so what if her mother was a servant. I'm going to find her and bring her up properly, so she never has to go through what Mona endured. The lawyers have come to a settlement, and I can have my husband's palace. Do you think I will let Edmund's daughter, my own defenceless flesh and blood, be put into service where men can do what they want with her? I must be in Venice, to protect her."

Gwyneth saw the pool of golden candlelight on the page which carried this shock.

"How do you know it's true? It might just be some gossip your mother has heard . . ."

The plate hit her above her ear.

"How dare you? My mother is not a common gossip.

I told you, she has known all along, and is telling me now because she's a sick woman and her conscience is troubling her. Go to Wales, you peasant, leave tomorrow, take Fitzjohn if you're scared. I have all these safe conducts Owain organised for me, I'll ride alone to Dover if I have to . . ."

"Very well." Gwyneth picked up a candlestick and walked towards the door, "I'm going to the guest room. I'll send to Murray in the morning, and see if he can find me an escort for Dumfries. I'll sail to Wales, and I'll leave Fitzjohn for you. I've had enough of the English, I was stupid to run from home in the first place with a woman as grasping as you. You only want your palace and your rich Venetian friends. Don't worry, I'll pay my share of the bills before I go, although I'm not giving you anything for your jeweller. You can buy your own damned pearls from now on."

She went to the guest room, and cried like an abandoned child. She had promised Agnes those pearls weeks ago, when the jeweller had said a consignment was due. She didn't care, she would return to her former life, and maybe Madog would come back from his great adventure, and she would marry him after all, and not see Agnes' ghost riding up the track to the hall and smiling in her bed . . . The door flew open.

"No!" Agnes stood there, her candle making wild shapes on her face. "You're not spending the night in here. You can leave in the morning, but I'll have you before you go. Then you'll see what my palace means to me."

She was stronger in her fury than Gwyneth thought, and they were in an exhausted sleep when the maid tiptoed in to wake them up and to goggle at the gowns on the floor and the bedclothes in such a tumble.

The port officials in Dover took their responsibilities seriously. It might be well over a year since the king's enemies had been routed at Tewkesbury, but that didn't mean that there weren't wanted men still trying to sneak out of the country on any one of the ships which sailed in and out of the port. Why, only last week they had apprehended a disgraced noble with jewels sewn into the lining of the clerk's gown he was using as a disguise, and, their eyes hard, they scrutinised the passengers waiting to board the Swift Passage. Unfortunately for those who wanted to gain promotion through zeal, it seemed as if this party had everything in order. The small countess had letters from every functionary between here and the Scottish border commanding safe passage for her and her entourage, which in any case consisted merely of a useful-looking captain at the head of a few men-at-arms, and a nervous maid, whose unintelligible speech betrayed her Scottish origins. The countess wasn't in a good mood, but her black looks and sighs as she handed over her papers and submitted her baggage to be searched could easily be explained as justifiable dread of a channel crossing even on a fine day. An official saw her look at the activity on the ship, and heard her imperious voice interrogating the maid.

"Are you sure she wasn't in the kitchen? Can't you remember her saying anything to you about going out?"

The official had once served in Berwick-upon-Tweed, and he understood the girl to reply that "she" had only said something about stretching her legs and getting a breath of fresh air before they embarked, and that perhaps she had gone to a church to pray they weren't shipwrecked.

"A church my . . . foot," the countess said. "Another alehouse more like. She'll get plenty of fresh air if she arrives in time, and if she doesn't, she can stretch her legs walking back to Edinburgh. If I'd known you were both going to be such trouble, I'd never have taken you on. Being able to sing doesn't make up for being the worst servants anyone has ever hired." She ranted on, and the maid began to cry. The countess stuck her nose in the air, until the captain, who was watching the approaches to the quay, bowed and said a few low words, at which her sharp features relaxed into something which could almost be called a smile. A tall woman in a plain gown, accompanied by two more men-at-arms, joined the party, and behind her staggered a well-endowed servant, held up by a laughing shore porter.

"My companion," the countess said to the official, flapping her papers under his nose again, "and my cook. Now can we get on board?"

He had no choice but to wave them on.

"You can change your mind," Agnes said as Gwyneth shuddered at the movement of the deck beneath her feet. "Quick, leap ashore before they untie those ropes."

Gwyneth clutched at the rail. "Your cook is a drunk, your captain chases every girl who gives him a second look, and your maid jumps at her own shadow. How can I trust you to reach Calais without me, let alone Venice? If I went home, leaving you in this company, Mona would never forgive me and would make my life a torment. That's the only reason I'm here." They both knew she wasn't telling the truth.

The official noticed the countess smiling at her companion, and wondered why she now looked happier than anyone setting out on a sea passage had a right to be. He shrugged and went about his business, the ship slipped out of the harbour, and he had forgotten about her by nightfall.

If you like Historical adventures,
Onlywomen Press recommends reading
Rebellion by Jay Taverner, ISBN 0-906500-58-3.
A lesbian coming-of-age tale, this one is set
in the early part of the 18th century.